SHADOW WARRIOR

D1502843

SHADOW WARRIOR

A NOVEL OF THE OLD WEST

J. C. GOTCHER

TWODOT®

GUILFORD, CONNECTICUT
HELENA, MONTANA

A · TWODOT® · BOOK

An imprint and registered trademark of The Rowman & Littlefield Publishing Group, Inc.
4501 Forbes Blvd., Ste. 200
Lanham, MD 20706
www.rowman.com

Distributed by NATIONAL BOOK NETWORK

British Library Cataloguing in Publication Information available

Library of Congress Cataloging-in-Publication Data available

ISBN 978-1-4930-3927-2 (paperback)
ISBN 978-1-4930-3928-9 (e-book)

∞™ The paper used in this publication meets the minimum requirements of American National Standard for Information Sciences—Permanence of Paper for Printed Library Materials, ANSI/NISO Z39.48-1992.

Printed in the United States of America

DEDICATION

For all of your patience,
belief, and encouragement—thank you, Carla.
Truly, the possibilities are endless!

Acknowledgments

I gratefully acknowledge my Father, for a desire to write born of a love to read; Wayne, for his dependable advice and honest critiques; and George, for this opportunity.

CHAPTER ONE

A MAN OUGHT TO HANG ON TO HIS HAT, he thought tiredly, feeling the fiery New Mexico sun sear into his scalp. Breathing hard, he turned his face away, seeking some tiny relief. It did no good; the sun hung straight overhead, fixed in place atop a cloudless sky. The move did free the sweat trapped in his hair to pour down and pool in eyes already stinging from the dust the climb dislodged from the cliff face. Burrowing his face into the upper sleeve of his shirt helped somewhat, though the grinding dust trapped beneath his eyelids brought forth salty rinsing tears.

Lifting his face to blink against the glare, he squinted hard and felt a sudden surge of strength. The rim of the canyon was almost in reach! He glanced at the fingers of his left hand, willing them to release the cliff and reach for another, higher, hold. He demanded his exhausted mind and limbs to concentrate—the worst was over. Curiously detached, as if watching from across the canyon as some fool other than himself attempted the climb, he saw the hand relax then rise to grasp a new hold.

Splintered rock pierced the man's face and both hands lost contact with the cliff. It happened too fast to be afraid; he was already falling when fear seized him. From near the top he plummeted down the rough wall, slamming to a stop on a wide ledge one hundred feet above the canyon floor. There was only one shot; none of the others carried rifles and the quick, startled drop to the ledge denied time to nock and loose arrows.

He lay breathless on the rocky ledge, lungs straining for air and ears straining for any sound of those who pursued him. There was no inclination to roll to the edge and peer over the side—if they could see him they could kill him. The crack of the gunshot echoed away, the sound a fading ricochet down the canyon. The echo carried along the angry whine made by the ball as it smacked off the granite above Doc's head, hurling the shower of stinging shards into his face and hands.

A few more feet, five at the most, he thought. Doc wasn't a man given to swearing but he did so now—bitterly. So close! Another minute would have seen him over the top. Glancing up, he studied the ragged lip of the canyon now twenty feet overhead. He knew it might as well be a thousand. There just wasn't any way to climb that rock face, exposed to his hunters below, and live. Doc took in the angle of the sun and figured there were four more hours of daylight. He shuddered at the thought of attempting that climb in the dark. He shuddered again as he realized he'd never live long enough to try.

With four of them down below, it was only a matter of time before they worked out a plan to get to him. He knew what he would do if he were the hunter and not the prey: leave one or two in place to pin the quarry on the ledge while the others sought a way up and out of the canyon. Once on top, they could walk up to the edge above and shoot straight down. Doc knew he might kill one of them, but he couldn't get more than one—he was down to his last ball. It was a testament to his acceptance of the situation that he could objectively consider himself to be "quarry." Although it didn't much matter if he accepted it or not, for that is what he was.

That the hunters would willingly sacrifice themselves to kill him was no longer a strange notion. He had lived, barely, with their dogged pursuit for the past six days. During that time, his puzzlement over their single-minded obsession shifted first to amazement and then to anger. After a time, he'd stopped feeling anything at all, he just ran on, pausing whenever circumstance provided a chance to kill one. He'd taken advantage of circumstance seven times in the last six days.

"Where ya goin', Doc?" Ferguson had asked.

"Out huntin'."

Squatting by the fire sipping a cup of scalding coffee, it seemed simple enough at the time. Hunting for the company was something he'd done countless times over the past weeks and miles. It was his job. Douglas Otho Croft, "Doc" to those who knew him well, was the best scout and shot in the company and right now the company was running low on meat. He'd signed on in Independence, Missouri, as an ox driver for one of the freight wagons Kendell Eldridge was sending down the Santa Fe Trail. The massive Murphy wagons, named for the builder Joseph Murphy, were the largest Doc had ever seen. But then everybody was clamoring for bigger wagons this season.

The year before, Governor Armijo in Santa Fe levied a per-wagon tax of five hundred dollars on all trade from the states. Joseph Murphy, along with the freighters and traders were quick to offset the impact of the tax on their profits by building bigger wagons. If it's true that necessity is the mother of invention, profit must be the father. Kendell Eldridge began the 1840 season with sixteen of Murphy's new wagons. Each of the wagons, whose rear wheels stood seven feet high and carried a wagon bed with sides capable of hiding a man standing inside, was pulled by a team of eight double-yoked oxen. A low canvas top covered freight weighing as much as three tons. To handle the added cargo weight, the width of the wheel rims increased to eight inches and if a man got careless with his feet—he'd have to learn to walk without them.

One week out of Independence, the company scout broke his leg fording the Marais River. Roland Ferguson, the wagon master, wrapped a splint on the leg and afterward the scout left the group and rode alone toward Topeka, fifty miles to the northeast. Ferguson was a powerful barrel-chested man with thick stubby arms and legs. His hands were the size of wagon hubs and his fingers like wheel spokes. He'd won more than one barroom wager bending horseshoes and he'd even been known to bend a shoe nail using just the fingers of one hand. So it was something of a mystery to see how delicate and careful those hands could be when tending to an injured man.

Doc was the first to draw replacement scout duty, returning to the company at the midday break with an antelope draped across the saddle. Trying four other men, each of whom returned empty-handed, Ferguson again sent Doc to hunt. An antelope for dinner that night earned Doc the permanent position of scout.

Gladdened by the news, the young man struggled to keep a smile from his face. Doc carried one hundred and ninety pounds of solid muscle, but stood only five foot nine, and walking beside the huge, lumbering, and dim-witted oxen was torture for him. Raised on a farm in northwest Missouri, he'd spent his first twenty-three years of life working with mules and horses broken to pull a plow or wagon and he'd fairly hated every dirty, sweaty step he'd taken. Finally going west, the dust-clouded glimpses of the tallgrass prairie through which he walked, seen from behind the rump of an ox, didn't live up to the fanciful dreams he'd had back on the Missouri farm.

From the high back of a horse and freedom to roam away from the wagons, a vast prairie commanded him to explore and he took every occasion to obey. Many travelers despaired over the endless plains of grass, but Doc marveled at them. Topping out on each ridge to scan the horizon, he felt no unease at finding more of the same. For Doc, confronting the prairie was a challenge, and discovery was the adventure of which he'd long dreamed.

The Rocky Mountains would rise into view two weeks before the slow-moving company reached them. The Rockies were the purpose of Doc's travel. The day after Doc's fifteenth birthday his uncle returned from Colorado full of tales of the mountains and their bear, beaver, and Indians. As his family sat around the table that night, warm and safe while listing to his uncle, Doc studied on the differences between his father and his father's brother.

Milo Croft, poor but respected, was a father and husband, a landowner and elder at the church. He was a man who saw night as a hindrance to working. Uncle Reese was a man of restless adventure, with no home and family of his own. He was the second oldest boy of five sons and the only son not to follow in the family business of farming. Milo, the oldest of the five, criticized his brother's wandering with often-voiced disdain, though at times with a bit of envy, Doc thought.

In his own way, Uncle Reese commanded respect. Before going to the far western mountains, he had been the man the community would look to for help in finding a child or animal lost in the prairie. Twice he'd led supply wagons through seemingly impassable snowfields, bringing food and medicine to the remote snowbound colony. When news of his return from the West circulated, several men from neighboring farms crowded into the Croft home to listen as Uncle Reese spoke of the fertile, unsettled land beyond the Mississippi River.

Doc looked about his home. The cabin was well built and snug, but with seven children, it was crowded. The mountains sounded wide and lonesome, just what a young man of limited means and constant companionship would long to find.

If there was one thing Doc understood that day, it was that he did not want to be a farmer. His two older brothers became farmers and were now beginning a life of raising crops and rearing children that would put the stoop in their shoulders by the age of thirty. Having made his decision the young man had but two obstacles to overcome: how to get to the mountains, and how to get past his father. With his mind set, Doc knew he would one day walk the high country and learn her secrets for himself.

At the middle crossings on the Arkansas River, Roland Ferguson made a decision to follow the Mountain Route of the Santa Fe Trail. Doc was the only man pleased at the resolution. The Mountain Route drove straight for the Rockies, and then hugged their eastern shoulder all the way to Santa Fe.

The alternate route was the Cimarron Cutoff, and at one hundred miles and ten days shorter than the Mountain Route was the preferred passage for most of the trade companies. The normal lack of water along the cutoff was always a risk, but an absence of rain turned the dry route into what the Mexicans called *La Jornada del Muerto*—the Dead Man's Journey.

The past dry winter worried Ferguson and he opted for following the wet Mountain Route along the Arkansas River westward into the Colorado Territory. At Bent's Fort, near the junction of the Arkansas and Purgatoire Rivers, the Trail swung southwest for Raton Pass. The difficulty, delay, and danger of Raton Pass were the reasons most companies braved the water-deprived Cimarron Cutoff. After a troublesome climb up the pass, the Trail ran south, eventually rejoining the cutoff at the Mora River in New Mexico twenty miles south of the Wagon Mound.

Six hundred fifty miles of prairie and forty-seven days rolled under their wheels before Doc's company made camp ten miles north of Raton Pass. There the men geared up to face a new foe—the terrain. For weeks, they'd fought the prairie's sudden rainstorms, howling winds and dust, and worst of all swarms of flies and gnats.

The company would arrive at the pass tomorrow evening and spend the following day in preparation for the ascent. The Trail up the pass was steep and rough, requiring the wagons to use double teams to make the haul. Eight pair of oxen pulled each wagon up the climb. At the top, the wagons remained with a guard, and the oxen descended to begin the process with the next load. Moving the entire company up to the pass with the plodding oxen could take two days, and a miserable bit of work it would be.

Roland Ferguson sat by the fire speaking in low tones with another man when Doc awoke. He'd risen early, sunup was two hours away, but as usual, Ferguson sat by the fire. The wagon master was always the first man in camp to rise. Walking over, Doc knelt by the flaming wood and reached his hands toward the warmth. Ferguson poured a cup of coffee and handed it over.

The other man was a stranger, one of many who'd stopped by their campsites on the journey. "Doc, this is Shep Knorr. He's been tellin' of Indian troubles." Ferguson uttered the introduction and warning in a single breath. The mountain man nodded a greeting.

Doc returned the nod and studied the stranger. Shep wasn't much older than Doc, but he had the mountains stamped on him. Dressed in buckskin and fur, Shep wore a beard that hung to his chest. His eyes were bright and intelligent, and ever on the move. A lanky frame hinted at a height taller than average and a lean, pale face with sharp cheekbones and hawk nose stood in sharp contrast to the black hair and beard.

A few days of meager hunting had seen the stores of fresh meat dwindle to a point where Doc needed to hunt, but today he would have hunted even if there were no need. After hearing Doc's intention,

Ferguson offered, "We are runnin' a mite low on meat and I suppose it wouldn't hurt none to scout the country, but," he added with a grin, "I'll say you seem a bit eager. You're as good a shot as I've run across, Doc, but you ain't no hunt-in-the-dark owl."

Doc grinned in reply. He wanted the early start to lengthen his day of exploration—his first in the mountains. The full moon provided ample light for travel across the prairie and the sun would be climbing the eastern sky as he entered the mountains so he didn't anticipate any difficulty.

Ferguson knew all about Doc's hunger to be in the mountains, but then so did every member of the company. Peppering them with questions, Doc had spent hours with any man who'd claimed to have been in, been near, or heard stories of the Rockies. Weeks of the farm boy's interrogations had led one of the men to say, "Doc, you know more about the high country than any man alive—and you ain't never been more 'n three thousand feet above sea level."

He learned a great deal from Ferguson, a veteran of many trips over the Trail. But most of his information came from the Mexican ox drivers. All of them were from Santa Fe, Taos, or one of the other nearby settlements and each knew the mountains. From crude maps drawn in the sand with fingers or sticks, Doc learned the names and locations of peaks, ranges, rivers, and passes. He also became fairly fluent in Spanish; not that hard to do when you had plenty of time and wanted information from a man who didn't speak more than ten words of English.

"Figured I wouldn't shoot anything until I start back to camp this evening. Headin' out now just gives me a little more time up there," Doc replied, inclining his head toward the black outline of the mountains.

"You watch your hair, Doc. Shep's sayin' the Jicarilla are riled up 'bout somethin'."

"Happens ever' so often," the mountain man said. "Some young 'Pache gets buck fever and sets out to make a name for hisself."

Shep wrapped a leathery hand around the handle of the coffeepot and pulled it direct from the fire. Filling his cup, he continued, "This time it's the son of Kos-nos-un-da . . . . chief of the Llanero band. His son's called Gunsi. They's several bands that make up the Jicarilla. The two biggest are the Ollero and the Llanero, and the Llanero are touchiest of all." He stopped to blow steam from the top of his cup then swallowed a few gulps of the black coffee. "You should know they call themselves the Tinde; Jicarilla is the name give 'em by the Spaniards. Fightin' and raidin' set the peckin' order, though these partic'lur 'Paches are hunters, farmers, and traders. Been doin' so as far back as anyone can recall. The Spanish trade for their pelts, pottery, and woven baskets. That's what Jicarilla means . . . little basket."

Draining his cup, Shep rose and gathered his gear. After hanging his kit and powder horn over his shoulders, he gave Doc and Ferguson a hard look.

"You boys keep a sharp watch. Gunsi and some others done kilt a handful of folks and I'm thinkin' they'll kill more a-fore they simmer down."

The mountain man walked from the firelight and vanished in the darkness.

"You still figurin' on huntin'?" Ferguson asked, peering at Doc.

"I am and I intend to look around some. We need the meat." Doc, determined to explore his long-anticipated mountains before the labor of the pass ascent was on him, mounted and rode southwest from camp following Gallinas Creek into the Raton Mountains. The Ratons were part of the Culebra Range, themselves a part of the much larger Sangre de Cristo Range.

The camp sat between five and six thousand feet, and in a short five hours he left behind the green ribbon of cottonwoods and willows growing along the waterway and climbed through scattered pinyons, scrub oaks, ponderosa pines, and finally into Douglas fir.

The land rose rapidly, reaching a height of eight thousand feet as he crested the first mountain. East, the plains stretched endlessly, dotted here and there with a lone peak or mesa. To the north stood the Spanish Peaks, and west, across a wide expanse, he could see the San Juan Range. As he viewed the country, a deep excitement began to build. To think that the Rockies were home to mountains more than fourteen thousand feet high, nearly twice the elevation where he now sat aback his mustang, was more than he could imagine.

"Hoss, I feel like my head's a-bumping the sky now, so I don't know what it'd be like to view God's work from one of them high-up peaks, but I intend to find out." The mustang's ears flicked back at his words and the horse turned his head to nip at Doc's leg. The young man laughed and said, "You behave yourself and I'll take you along."

The land teemed with wildlife and Doc crossed the tracks of mule deer, elk, red fox, and turkey. The trees harbored woodpeckers, flickers, swallows, and jays. Startled by his intrusion, some darted away; others simply craned their necks to stare as he rode silently past. A few of the braver squirrels scampered to a high limb and scolded Doc and the mustang. As Doc was not ready to return to camp, he passed up several easy shots at deer. The early afternoon found him pushing still farther into the mountains, now along a westerly course. Due east was the huge Raton Mesa. Six hundred feet higher than the mountains he explored, the eighty-six-hundred-foot mesa was easily seen through breaks in the trees. Keeping the mesa at his back as a landmark meant he traveled west. When he wanted to return to camp, he would ride toward his landmark, for no matter where he exited the mountains, he would cross the north–south route of the Trail before reaching Raton Mesa.

With regret, Doc reversed direction at midafternoon. He knew it would be dark before he made it back to camp, but the sky was clear and the full moon would return at night. Travel after sundown wouldn't be difficult, but he needed to find game before the light faded. He rode with his eyes sweeping the forest around him, searching for deer or elk.

With his focus so intent upon the woods, it was a surprise to realize he traveled along a faint trail. Suddenly wary, he reined the horse to a stop and twisted in the saddle to look behind. The trail meandered for two hundred feet before disappearing into a thick grove of fir, and Doc wondered how long he'd ridden the path. The horse had found the trail and taken it, for trails offered the easiest passage.

He studied the path, needing an answer to a grave question—was it a game trail, or man-made? Game used the path, the tracks of bighorn sheep were plentiful, and a fresh set of prints indicated a large elk passed by not long before. Though no sign of human use was apparent, Doc knew its origins were from man. A game trail often led through narrow openings in dense brush or under low-hanging limbs. Places where a person couldn't walk upright. A man-made trail routed around such difficulties, and Doc was able to travel horseback without hindrance.

The horse stamped a hoof, restless and ready to be on the move. The animal was a tough little mustang and wise to the ways of man and beast. Before capture, the mustang had lived on the plains west of the Mississippi. Over time, he became Doc's favorite mount. The mustang ran all day on a few bites of grass and a smell of water. Together they'd scouted prairie from the tall grass in the east to the short grass in the west.

Doc had learned to trust the sharp-eyed little horse, and he now checked the mustang's behavior. The horse seemed at ease, and the absence of footprints on the trail provided some comfort against the sudden understanding that he rode alone through a strange land. "Well hoss, since we're by ourselves out here . . . let's hope it stays that a-way." He gave no thought to whether he spoke aloud to comfort himself, or the horse. "We best see if we can't sneak our way through this bit of country."

Of its own, the mustang began moving at the sound of Doc's voice. A quarter mile farther the forest gave way to a bald knob and the trail turned south. The mustang kept right on traveling east, straight for Raton Mesa like it had been his idea all along.

They crossed the knob and descended into a narrow valley, pausing in the bottom to drink from a small creek. Remounting, Doc pointed the mustang up the far side and they scrambled their way to the top, and back into the forest. The scent of pine lingered in the crisp air and a bed of fallen needles muffled their passage. In the dark shade of the forest, the sun's warmth disappeared, giving way to a sharp chill. Doc felt the coolness against his entire body despite the homespun cotton shirt and linsey-woolsey pants.

They wound through a mixed conifer forest of pine and fir. He recognized ponderosa pine and limber pine, white fir and Douglas fir, though the Douglas wasn't a true fir. A true fir bore upright cones, and the Douglas fir grew hanging cones like a pine or spruce. He'd seen a few spruce trees on the shady, northeast slopes of the valleys even though the elevation was below their normal range. Here and there, he spied mountain mahogany and American plum.

And then he saw the buck. A fair-sized mule deer grazing near the trees at the edge of a mountain meadow. Less than five acres in size, the meadow was surrounded by forest, creating a small isolated park. Doc rode forward until he was a dozen feet from the meadow and still hidden among the trees.

He checked the pan on his Lancaster rifle and, satisfied that all was in order, raised the weapon to his shoulder. The buck's head lifted and it stared into the trees to Doc's left. The deep boom of the rifle sounded across the meadow and the deer dropped. Doc rode forward through the smoke and paused on the meadow's edge as his hands began the practiced routine of reloading the weapon. The hands became as motionless as the buck when his eyes noticed blood pouring from the ball's entry—and from an embedded arrow.

His mind flashed, and his head turned even as the thought formed. Left! The deer had stared to his left! Six Indians stood forty feet away, frozen in surprise. Doc yanked the reins over and kicked the mustang. The horse bounded into a run back through the trees. A piercing shout came from the meadow and a buckskin-clad form seemed to materialize from the shadows of the pines. The form rushed forward, tomahawk lifting for a throw. Doc clutched the half-loaded rifle in his right hand and, dropping the reins, tugged a pistol from his waistband and fired left-handed at the Indian. The figure crumpled as the mustang rushed past.

Voicing a shrill yell, a second Indian appeared and loosed an arrow. The mustang staggered and fell, throwing Doc in a tumbling roll that swept the Indian from his feet. Reflex and panic spurred him quickly to one knee and he swung the heavy rifle as the Indian started to rise. With a sickening thud, the butt of the rifle caught the Indian's head and snapped it back.

In an instant, Doc was running. Dodging through the trees and away from the meadow, he ran like a man whose life depended on foot speed. No others came forth, though he could hear their shouts behind him. Clearing the trees at the lip of the small valley where he and the mustang rested earlier, he started down without breaking stride. Angling across the slope to keep from overrunning his feet, he sped toward the creek. In the water, he turned downstream and ran through the shallow flow.

The voices faded, and slowly his frightened mind understood there was no pursuit. Abandoning the creek where it tumbled over exposed rock, Doc sped along the rock and into a grove of pines, halting under their cover. His breath came in deep ragged gasps. The thin mountain air tortured him with its lack of oxygen. His head began to swim, then his knees buckled and he collapsed to the mat of pine needles. Thought was impossible; his mind numbed by the narrowness of escape. His only movement was the involuntary heaving of his chest and the tremor in his arms and legs.

Awakening with a jerked movement, Doc sat splay-legged and stared into the little valley. Under the tree branches, he was unable to get a read on the sun and so couldn't tell for how long he'd lain unconscious. Down below, where he'd left the creek, his wet footprints had almost faded away, and the heaving of his chest and beating of his heart had settled down. At least now, clear thought was possible. Fifteen minutes? No, more like twenty, he decided. Either way, it was long past time to move.

Struggling to rise, Doc sagged against the rough, sticky bark of a pine and waited for his woozy head to clear from the effort. It would take a while to adjust to the altitude, and another all-out flight would kill him. He would move, he told himself, but slow and steady until his lungs adapted to the thin air. How long would that take? he wondered. One day? Two?

Chiding himself, Doc realized it was out of his hands. If they spotted him, he would run. After all, dead is dead. He took a stumbling step and stopped when he remembered the rifle still lay where it had fallen. Careful not to topple over, he bent down and collected it. A quick check of his waistband revealed the pistol was missing. Where he'd lost the pistol was as much a mystery as was his hanging on to the rifle. The rifle! Woodenly, his hands completed recharging the weapon. As ready as he could be, Doc slipped through the trees heading south.

Not one to embrace melancholy, Doc held no thoughts of bad luck. Rather, he marveled at his fortune. He was alive and one, maybe two of the Indians weren't. And though he was in trouble, he had a weapon. His bullet pouch containing balls, flint, and steel hung over his right shoulder, and over his left hung the powder horn. There were even a few pieces of jerked venison remaining. He wished for the mustang, though not for its ability to carry him from danger, but more from regret at the sacrifice of the tough little horse.

CHAPTER TWO

H IS SQUARE FACE A MASK CHISELED FROM STONE, Gunsi's dark eyes glinted with rage as he knelt over the body of Sotli. Gunsi was not an attractive or pleasant man. He led others by sheer force of will, size, and an utter ferocity that stemmed from his total freedom from fear. The one weakness of Gunsi was Sotli, and the adoration the fourteen-year-old boy bestowed upon his older brother. But now, Sotli would not see his fifteenth year because Gunsi made a mistake.

Kos-nos-un-da, Gunsi's father, had protested when Gunsi offered to take Sotli on the raid. But Gunsi held firm, saying the boy had earned the right to go. As is common with young warriors of all colors, they dreamed dreams of victory and of inflicting suffering on their enemies, and never of defeat or suffering themselves.

The Llanero brave reached out and scooped the body into his arms. He would face his father and accept whatever punishment Kos-nos-un-da meted out, but first he must bury Sotli and then kill the white man. Turning to Desan and Goso, Gunsi spoke. "Come, cousins, it is our burden to bury my brother."

Leaving the remainder of the Indians behind, the three men walked quickly and quietly into the forest. Tinde custom required immediate burial of the dead, with only close relations knowing of the site. Gunsi carried Sotli to a high point and lay the body upon the ground. Setting the boy's tomahawk and other possessions on his chest, the three men covered Sotli with rocks and brush.

The order to send Sotli and Kitchi circling through the trees came from Gunsi. Except for the rutting season, bucks often moved in groups of two or three, and as leader of the band, Gunsi wanted two deer to feed his nineteen men. He knew the buck grazing in the open meadow offered no challenge, but maybe if there was another buck in the woods, Sotli would get him. He'd wanted Sotli to make a kill, and rise in the esteem of the warriors. Kitchi was five years older than Sotli and should have kept him from attacking the white man alone. Had the white man not also killed Kitchi, Gunsi would have done so himself.

The three Indians made their way back to the meadow and waited until Toh-Yah returned from burying his brother Kitchi. Toh-Yah and Gunsi were friends, and fierce rivals. Gunsi wanted to grieve for his friend's loss, but was too angry with the dead Kitchi to feel any sorrow now. Toh-Yah's eyes showed his anger at Gunsi for sending Kitchi with the boy instead of with a more capable brave. The two men exchanged a short nod of wordless agreement. Together, they would revenge their brothers and settle their argument afterward.

"Goso, you will carry word of Sotli and Kitchi to the village and tell Kos-nos-un-da that I will return to his lodge only after the white man is dead," ordered Gunsi.

"No!" shouted the warrior. "Send Desan. I am the oldest and I will hunt the killer of my cousin."

Gunsi was tall for an Apache, broad and powerful. Of all the warriors, only Toh-Yah on occasion had been able to defeat Gunsi in games of cunning and skill. It was the reason the two were friends. They presented each other with a challenge, one worthy of complete respect. They both possessed the intelligence, strength, and courage to become the Llanero's next leader, yet leadership could fall to one only. Toh-Yah had once spoken to Gunsi of a belief he held that one of them would die in battle, remembered by the tribe with stories and songs. The other would become leader. Gunsi had not mentioned it, but he held the same belief. Both friends were too powerful and capable to be less than chief. An honorable warrior's death was the only fitting reward for the one who did not become leader of the Llanero.

Taller than Goso, Gunsi stepped to the chest of the refusing warrior and towered over him. Piercing Goso with a withering glare, he spoke in a low voice crackling with energy and impatience. "You may be older than your brother, but Desan is a superior warrior. I will send Desan if I must . . . after he has buried you."

Goso fidgeted and glanced at his younger brother. Desan stood impassive. Goso's answer would determine his status as a warrior. If he accepted the order, then he accepted Gunsi's statement that he was inferior. If he challenged Gunsi and the slur on his name, he would die. Desan pitied his brother, but held no animosity toward Gunsi. Goso refused to see his own shortcomings and so he never worked to overcome them.

Gunsi glared at the warrior, waiting. He knew Desan would have fought him for saying such things, and he knew Goso wouldn't. It was the very reason he wanted Desan with him.

"I will go to the village. When you return, we will speak of this." Goso's statement was hollow bravado and all knew it. Desan thought his brother would have been better served by simply turning away. A toothless dog is no threat, no matter how loudly he growls. Even the loss of Sotli couldn't keep a look of cruel humor from the face of Gunsi. Goso opened his mouth to issue the challenge that would end his life but the words refused to form. Slowly, stupidly, his mouth closed and Goso spun to stalk away. It took him almost a quarter mile of steady cursing to realize what he'd done. He openly challenged Gunsi! When the huge warrior returned, Goso must make good his challenge or become less than a man, refused and spat on by women and mocked by children. The shamed warrior uttered a prayer that Gunsi not return.

Gunsi eyed the fifteen men gathered around him, noting the impatience on the faces of the youngest. Good, he thought. He would use their young energy. He and the older men knew there was no rush. The white man couldn't get away without his horse. They would kill him, but first, Gunsi wanted to capture him. For killing Sotli, the white man would die an ugly death for many days.

The thought of his young brother released a flood of emotion that threatened to drown the Apache warrior in shame and anguish. Without thought, he pulled his knife and drew the sharp blade across his chest. The cut was deep, and the blood came forth and dripped down his torso, shedding the only tears a warrior could cry. He would wear the scar for the remainder of his life as a tribute to his brother and as a mark of repentance for himself. Falling to his knees, Gunsi raised his face toward the sky, saying, "Hear my oath. I will avenge Sotli with the blood of the white man . . . or I will die!"

Desan pulled his knife and sliced his palm. Kneeling down beside Gunsi, he pressed his open hand onto the bloody chest of his cousin. "I make this oath my own."

Toh-Yah's hand went to his knife and he grasped the haft. His brother Kitchi called out for revenge. But Toh-Yah knew the white man was only partly to blame; Gunsi must share the blame as well. The white man would die. Must die. He had taken Llanero lives and Llanero warriors did not forget their fallen family. To take an oath swearing to kill those responsible would include Gunsi, wouldn't it?

He stared at Gunsi, confused by his thoughts. Shaking free of the disturbing feelings, his knuckles whitened on the haft and the blade began to lift. It was then a powerful sense of death froze Toh-Yah. Keen to such feelings, Toh-Yah sought to understand the sensation. Several times his mind resolved that the intense perception came from the energy of Gunsi's oath, and the knife lifted a fraction. Each time his arm moved, his mind arrested the movement, holding the knife in its sheath as the perception turned to apprehension.

While his mind and spirit wrestled, Toh-Yah stared at Gunsi, though he didn't see him. Yielding to spirit, his hand dropped from the knife and he again saw his friend. Gunsi's eyes were now upon Toh-Yah, and they held a look of confusion that slowly gave way to disdain. Toh-Yah couldn't speak. He hadn't the words to explain his hesitation to himself, or his friend, and both men felt the wedge drive between them.

A low snarl rumbled in Gunsi's chest and, leaping to his feet, he raised his arms wide, threw back his head, and roared. "Hear my oath. I will honor Sotli's spirit with the blood of the white man . . . or I will die!"

Three miles away Doc paused and cocked an ear to the north. Had he heard something? A cold wind blew over him and he crossed both arms over his chest to huddle inside their limited warmth. He glanced west at the mountains and watched as the sun burrowed behind the craggy peaks. Would they pursue in the dark, he wondered? He had seen seven Indians, Apaches most likely, as this was their country. Doc was certain the man he'd struck with the heavy rifle was dead. He wasn't sure about the one he'd shot. He had hit him; even left-handed, he couldn't miss from that range. If only injured, would the other five remain to tend his wound? Maybe they would take him to their village.

Reasonable, but not probable, Doc admitted. The man he shot hadn't uttered a sound or made further movement; he simply collapsed. He knew, or rather felt, they were going to come after him. Doc glanced around, looking for shelter. He saw nothing that would suit him and decided to keep moving. The inky blackness under the canopy of trees made for slow travel. Several times, he saved himself from falling after catching his foot on a root or rock. In an hour or so, the full moon would rise and brighten the landscape enough for easier travel.

On a thought, Doc swung east and left the trees for open ground. Before the moon rose, he would be hidden from sight beyond fifty feet or so. He decided to take advantage of the dark. He could travel faster in the open. Later, under the full moon, he could see well enough to skirt along the trees beneath their shadows. It came to him that he had abandoned the thought of shelter. It was better that he keep moving, adding distance between himself and the Indians. Besides, movement meant warmth, and it was going to get cold at this elevation.

Finding himself at the top of a long canyon, he dropped down over the edge and made his way to the bottom. Several pools of water remained from the last rain and he drank until he'd quenched his thirst, then drank some more. Dehydration was a danger at this altitude and though water was plentiful in the mountains, he didn't know when he might get his next drink.

He allowed himself a brief nap, awakening fifteen minutes later. Doc had always been able to grab snatches of rest, a trick he'd learned while farming. During sowing and harvesting, a man's workday meant toiling in the fields from gray dawn to blind-dark night. The hour before and after the workday was used to prepare and then repair. A good night's rest came when you got a full four hours of sleep. Any chance he had during the workday for a breather, he'd used for sleep.

Rising from the ground, he stretched his arms and legs to loosen them from the cold, and again drank his fill of water. He followed the base of the canyon as it descended to the southeast. It was warmer in the canyon and the rocky bottom would help hide his tracks. The canyon lay bathed in the soft light of the moon. No wind stirred the scattered pines and Doc saw no wildlife. The silence shrouded him like a thick blanket. The occasional noise from dislodging a rock or stone as he traversed the canyon seemed unnaturally loud. At each instance, Doc stopped and held his breath while listening for shouts that would signal his discovery.

To his alarm, he found he was sweating in spite of the cold. He told himself to relax. The exertion, or fear, resulting in the sweat would only add to the cold and rob his body of heat. A man had to use care in traveling the high country. There were a hundred ways to die up here and the Apaches were only one of them. Despite the lure of her ample beauties, nature is a capricious mistress.

Maybe he'd lost the Apaches. Hours had passed since his fight with them and even now, with the moon's light, he could but barely see his path. Not even the best tracker could follow him until sunrise, and they had miles of rough ground and twisting trail to unravel before they caught up.

Doc began to feel better. He wasn't just thinking such thoughts in vain. They were true and he found comfort in them. He eased up to set a safer pace. As he walked, he considered the situation. Pulling one of the few remaining pieces of jerky from his pouch, he ate slowly, savoring the taste. He wasn't concerned about finding food; the mountains were full of it. His concern came from spending time to hunt for it. The jerky would need to last until he felt safe enough to stop, or until he found a good place to hide for a few days.

If he could find such a place, he would take it. Even as careful as he'd been in laying his trail, he knew the Indians could follow given enough time. He hadn't seen or heard any horses at the meadow, so he assumed the Apaches were on foot. If they had horses, his only chance would be to hide. Going into hiding left no tracks and they couldn't follow what wasn't there. He decided to sharpen his watch for a suitable spot. The drawback to hiding was the added delay in returning to the company, and the safety of the large group of men. What if he found a place to hide along the Santa Fe Trail? He could remain out of sight and wait for the company to roll by.

Encouraged by the plan, Doc walked on. A short time later, the canyon he traveled emptied into a larger canyon. He had followed an almost due south route in the smaller canyon and the larger canyon headed toward the southeast. An hour later, as the sky began to lighten in the east, Doc was heartened by his good fortune. Still within the large canyon, he could see that it emptied out into a wide north–south valley. A dim line of trees indicated a stream flowed down the valley and he felt certain the stream was Raton Creek. Once it crossed over Raton Pass, the Trail followed Raton Creek south until it neared the Canadian River.

The Canadian flowed south along the eastern flank of the mountains, but its origin was miles back into the Ratons. Until reaching the plains, where it turned and began a southern course, the river flowed mostly east. Since he hadn't crossed the river on his run to the south, Doc knew the Canadian lay somewhere farther south of his position. He figured that he'd found the Trail at a point some ten miles south of the pass. If the company kept to Ferguson's schedule, the wagons should pass down the valley late in the afternoon three days later.

Ferguson sipped his coffee and stared at the dark mountains. Doc's absence had him worried. Worried for Doc and for what it meant to his company. He knew the scout might have suffered an accident; it was a common thing in this country. Well, any country, he admitted. He'd known of a man in Ohio, a lone farmer, who'd tumbled from a barn roof, broke his legs, and died of thirst before any of his neighbors happened by. And that country had been settled up, the nearest neighbor living no more than a mile away. Any number of things could have happened to Doc.

Ferguson rolled his wrist and slung the remnants of his coffee toward the fire—maybe it was too early to worry at all. The wagon master chuckled as he thought of the scout's eagerness to climb the mountains. He understood it well; it had been his feeling thirteen years earlier on his first trip to Santa Fe. Something about Doc was different, though. The wagon master believed the young scout never gave thought to what he would do after arriving in the mountains. Ferguson knew. He knew Doc would not be returning to Independence, or to his parents' farm in Missouri. The mountains had claimed another explorer, a man who lived to learn the secrets of the high country. That is, for as long as he lived, and if he still lived.

The camp began to sir around him. In an hour, the company must scale the pass with the first of the wagons. It was a brutal chore to be undertaken sixteen times over the next two days. The oxen were in good shape for it. They fared better on the prairie grasses and had more stamina than did horses or mules. What the oxen lost in speed, they more than made up for in dependability. Best of all, Indians didn't like the meat and rarely attempted to steal the slow-moving animals.

Ferguson's thoughts returned to the missing man. There was nothing he could do to help Doc. No one in the company possessed the skills to track the scout and Ferguson needed every man working on the ascent. The wagon master refilled his cup and took a deep swallow. He sat and stared at the graying shape of the mountains until the coffee turned cold. Suddenly, he slung the oily black liquid into the fire and stood. He barked a loud order to the cook to roust the company and prepare for the climb. Ferguson glanced up at the mountains, then flung his cup into the wash bucket and turned away.

Phil Tule wiped soapy water from his face with the sleeve of his shirt. The cook had been unlucky enough to be bending low near the wash bucket when Ferguson threw his cup into it. The force behind the heavy tin cup had been sufficient to splash water for several feet. Phil knew better than to rile his boss by saying anything. Ferguson wasn't the type of man to act that way out of hand. No, he had something on his mind, and if Ferguson was troubled, the company itself might be in trouble. Phil Tule did as Ferguson instructed and shouted a wake-up call to the camp. He then grabbed a rag and lifted the lid to the Dutch oven, but his mind wasn't on biscuits.

Fifteen miles southwest of the camp, Doc stumbled on numb legs through the predawn cold. Right then, he would have given a week's wage for the cold coffee Ferguson tossed aside.

Desan trotted toward the silent band of Apaches. Out front, Gunsi halted the group and squatted on his heels when he saw the warrior returning from his scout.

"There is no campfire below the notch where the white men cross with their wagons," the panting Indian reported as he squatted to rest.

"Good," replied Gunsi. "They have not yet crossed the mountain and the white man cannot get to them."

Gunsi looked upon Desan with appreciation. All knew his cousin's reputation for speed and endurance. This night, Desan's fame grew even larger and the admiring looks of the gathered men proved it. When the white man's hair hung on the lance of Kos-nos-un-da, they would sing of the fleet warrior's act. As Desan had run to the northeast to scout the pass, Gunsi led the remaining warriors east. Toh-Yah proposed the strategy and Gunsi saw at once its advantage.

The white man fled to the south, and from that direction his only refuge lay in continuing south toward the scattered settlements below the Cimarroncito River, or turning back to the east for possible help along the wagon road. The trip south would take days and require the crossing of the Canadian, Vermejo, and Cimarroncito Rivers.

He would not go west, for that direction took him deeper into the mountains and away from other whites. To go north, the white man must attempt to pass by or through the Tinde, and Gunsi doubted the running man had such courage. It did not occur to the Llanero brave to credit the quickness and efficiency of the white man's skill at the meadow. He looked upon all whites as inferior. In truth, his prejudice extended to any but the Llanero.

Toh-Yah's plan was simple. To survive, the white man must escape east or south. If Gunsi and the others rushed east into the valley of the wagon road, and the wagon men were not there, then the man they sought must either wait for the wagons or continue south on his own. Once in the valley, the Indians could travel south down the wagon road, scouting for the killer of Sotli and Kitchi. The mountain range ran northeast to southwest, and so, even if he continued south, eventually the white man must leave the mountains and cross the flatland to the settlements. On the flats, it would be easy to spread out and find his trail.

Gunsi rose and, leading the way, ordered the men to move. He wanted to travel at a rapid trot, but intentionally set the pace at a fast walk to allow Desan to regain strength. He took no more than three strides before Desan brushed by him at a trot, taking the lead. The band of warriors whooped and followed the swift brave. Gunsi felt the pride swell within. His cousin should not have a brother like Goso. If Desan carried any shame because of Goso, this night had seen it forever wiped from the hearts of all Llanero.

CHAPTER THREE

The sun bathed the valley in morning warmth as Doc stood looking down on the Trail a thousand yards below. He'd made it. He looked around, searching for a cave or other spot in which to hide. Exhaustion clouded his eyes and he rubbed them hard to wipe away the blur. His vision sharpened, but the rubbing did little to clear his tired mind; only rest would help that. He turned to a large, lone ponderosa pine and sat down, resting his back against the trunk while soaking up the sun's rays.

A mountain cottontail bolted from beneath the sparse cover at the base of the tree and bounded away. Floating over the valley, a red-tailed hawk tucked his wings into a dive for the rabbit. The speed of the attack surprised the rabbit and the hawk spread his four-foot wings and carried his prey aloft.

A quick rest first, thought Doc, and then he'd find food and shelter. A short time later, his eyes opened and he stared down into the valley. The quick nap had helped and he felt refreshed. The ruts dug by countless wagon wheels paralleled Raton Creek. A man-made streambed, running alongside one of nature's own, both carrying elements essential to the settlement of the West.

A flicker of movement turned his head to the left and his breath stopped. Seven Indians walked in a scattered line between him and the creek. He knew at once they were the same Indians he'd surprised in the meadow. They were scanning the ground as they walked and with every few steps, each would lift his head to probe the width and sides of the valley. Movement across the creek drew his attention. He blanched at the sight of nine more Indians searching the far side of the valley.

They hadn't tracked him at all, he realized. They must have known where he would go and circled around to cut him off. The group nearest him walked forward less than a half mile from the tree where he rested. They hadn't seen him yet because he hadn't moved. In a matter of minutes, movement wouldn't matter. They would be close enough to distinguish his shape against the rough bark of the pine. How had they missed his white shirt? He glanced down to find that during the long night of travel the shirt had soiled to a color of light brown.

His thoughts raced in circles as he discarded idea after idea as being too risky. Right now, all seven Indians were below him and to his left, though on their present course, one would pass within fifty feet of the tree. While his mind raced, his sight followed a huge Apache searching near the creek. All thought stopped as the Indian snapped his head around and stared toward the tree.

Instantly, Doc averted his eyes to stare at the ground by his feet. He couldn't explain it, but he'd often felt the urge to turn his head and look elsewhere and more often than not, he'd wound up looking straight into the eyes of someone who stared at him. An extra sense or instinct, he figured. That Indian down there had the same instinct, and that was something Doc would need to remember. A moment passed without shouts of discovery and Doc lifted his eyes to find the large Indian again searching his way along the creek.

He studied the Apache from his peripheral vision, careful not to look directly at him. If Doc were to tickle his attention again, he knew the Indian would make straight for the tree. Like all of the others, the Indian wore a single-feather headdress tied into long black hair, deerskin shirt, and hip leggings. A wide, black leather belt with a large brass buckle circled his waist. From the belt hung a long knife, and shoved under the belt were two tomahawks. On his feet, he wore a pair of low moccasins. He was much larger than the others were, although Doc saw one with a red sash around his waist who might be almost as big.

The Indian with the red sash seemed to be directing the search on the far side of the creek. Other than the size of the two biggest Apaches, they looked to be indistinguishable from each other. Doc's mind then caught the difference—the belts, or sashes. The Indians wore no jewelry that he could see, but most wore a sash, and a few wore a belt, which was unique to the wearer. The sashes were of a variety of colors and patterns.

A whoop from the far side of the creek caught the attention of red men and white man alike. Hok'ee, a sixteen-year-old brave, waved his arms and Toh-Yah walked over to him.

"I have found tracks!" said Hok'ee when Toh-Yah arrived.

Toh-Yah bent down to examine the tracks, for indeed the young man had found several. It took but a glance to see that the prints were days old, maybe older, and could not belong to the white man they hunted. He stood and placed his hand on the boy's shoulder.

"You have sharp eyes, Hok'ee," he encouraged. While he spoke, Toh-Yah looked across the creek at Gunsi and shook his head. "But these tracks are too old. The man we hunt could have come this far only hours ahead of us, most likely after the sunrise."

The young brave nodded his head in uncertain agreement then studied the tracks, his brow furrowed in concentration. Toh-Yah, taking the role of teacher, pointed up and down the short path of prints. "What else do you see?" he asked.

The boy answered, "A bobcat crossed these prints. See there, the print of the bobcat has pushed down the edge of the man's print."

"Good. So what do the two prints tell you?"

Hok'ee was silent for a moment before his eyes dulled, and he spoke in a low tone.

"The bobcat hunts at night," he said with shame. "The man's prints were made before the bobcat's and so could not belong to a man passing through this morning. I am sorry."

Toh-Yah's hand still rested on the boy, so he squeezed his shoulder then removed his hand.

"Do not apologize for being vigilant, Hok'ee. Your eyes have found the only sign so far. I am now confident that nothing will escape your vision during the search."

Toh-Yah moved back to his original position. Hok'ee squared his shoulders and began searching the ground in earnest, intent upon proving himself worthy of Toh-Yah's confidence.

All eyes were upon the two Indians as they talked. Doc cast a furtive glance behind him, judging the distance to the tree line—a hundred feet. He returned his gaze to the two Apaches while he thought about making his escape. How long would he need to belly-crawl a hundred feet? No more than a couple of minutes, he figured. Did he have that long? The question died as he thought it. No. He watched as the Indians separated and the search resumed.

It suddenly stopped again when the large Apache wearing the black belt waded across the creek and began speaking with Red Sash. Doc's earlier guess was correct. The Indian with the red sash was almost as big as the other Apache. After a brief conversation, the two motioned the others to join them. This was his chance. Doc slid down and rolled onto his belly. Cradling his rifle across the crook of his elbows, he began snaking his way through the foot-high grass.

Halfway to the trees his pants snagged on something then ripped loose. Doc stopped, his heart in his throat. The Indians were gathering across the creek several hundred yards away. He knew the sound wouldn't carry that distance, but he twisted his head around and looked to be sure. He scanned the group and found that only one remained on his side of the creek. Then his eyes found the large Apache, who stopped talking and looked right back at him. A dousing with a bucket of Mississippi River water in January wouldn't have chilled Doc more than that Apache's stare.

With a triumphant shout, the Indian raised his arm and pointed. Doc lunged to his knees and lifted his rifle. The Apache on his side of the creek turned to look and Doc shot him. He held low on the target, but the warrior was a hundred feet lower in elevation and the ball took him through the center of his chest.

Then Doc was running, his hands recharging the rifle. He paused in the trees for three long seconds to pour the gunpowder. Pulling the rod, he rammed it into the barrel and ran on. The valley below filled with shouts and a rifle sounded. The ball barked a tree to his right but caused him no harm. Doc had wanted to wound the Indian in the hope that some, if not all, of the others would stop to render aid to their fallen friend. Doc was certain the man was dead. Bad shot with a good result— at least he hadn't missed entirely.

Gunsi was the first to reach the dead man. He lay flat on his back, arms and legs spread wide, thrown out by the force of the ball. Unseeing eyes stared into the sky. The others gathered in silence, waiting for Gunsi's move or command. All except for Desan.

He had been the farthest out on the opposite side of the creek from Doc. When Gunsi and Toh-Yah called the braves to gather, he'd been searching a copse of pine and fir. Taking a few moments to complete the search, he'd just stepped from the trees when Gunsi shouted and the white man fired. When he caught sight of the quarry he began to run toward the creek, slowing as he made his way through the water. He again reached full speed as he flew by the Apaches surrounding the body.

He heard Gunsi call his name but didn't stop. Desan wanted the white man, and the white man was within his grasp. Or so he believed.

Doc broke through the thin line of trees and ran back up the canyon along his original path. A crashing in the undergrowth behind warned of pursuit. Moments later the sound died and he glanced over his shoulder to see a lone Indian charging from the trees. Then more crashing reached his ears. This time the noise sounded loud enough that he knew the others had joined the chase.

Doc gave thought to turning and shooting the lone Apache before deciding against it. His heart was beating fast and would affect his aim. To compensate for it, he would have to let the running man get close. He would kill the Apache, but the delay would allow the others to close the gap, and he couldn't shoot them all.

Running while holding the long rifle was cumbersome so Doc slung the weapon across his back. His balance increased and so did his speed. He wasn't a tall man because he had his father's compact torso. From his mother he'd received long legs and he put them to work.

Doc loved to run, and he was relieved to find that his lungs now pumped the thin air without difficulty. He gave thanks for his years of running footraces at fairs and on holidays. At the age of ten, he'd entered his first race on a dare from his friends. Footraces were big entertainment, bigger than horse racing in any farm community. Farm horses weren't bred for speed and watching them race wasn't very stirring.

Children's games had proven him the fastest by far of his companions, and they hoped to see him taken down a notch. They figured that by goading Doc into entering the Fourth of July footrace in town, they would finally see him beaten. To their surprise and the embarrassment of the twenty-three grown men in the race, Doc had won by a stride.

After that, he'd entered every race within a day's travel of the farm, be they sprint or distance. Over the years, he'd run in, and won, several match races. The prize money from racing had been a help to the meager income his family earned from farming. Doc trained by running everywhere he went. He ran to school, church, town, and even to the barn for his chores.

One day his mother had sent him to fetch his father from a field he was plowing and Doc discovered the best training tool a runner could want—acres of freshly turned furrows. The soft dirt and uneven surface made for strenuous running. His father liked to brag that he had the fastest son and ugliest fields in the county.

Doc's muscles warmed and he ran smoothly. He allowed his mind to continue with the musing; he always ran best when he raced with thoughts of his family. At a half mile, he passed by the smaller canyon he'd come down the night before. Its ground was covered in loose rock and he couldn't risk a fall. The large canyon continued to the northwest and he pushed ahead.

The ground rose higher as he ran toward the farthest reach of the canyon. The long grass pulled at his feet with every stride. He wasn't tired yet, but the uphill run, the grass, and his newness to the mountain air would take a toll. The trailing whoops had ceased so Doc threw a quick glance over his shoulder. The lone Indian remained on his trail as though glued there. He'd neither gained nor lost ground. The remaining Apaches were falling back. Another five minutes should place enough distance between him and the bulk of the Indians to allow him time to stop and shoot the lone pursuer.

Doc scanned the canyon ahead, judging speed and distance as he searched for a good site to stop.

Desan was amazed. At first, he thought the white man ran with the speed of fear, but his stride hadn't faltered and only twice had he bothered to check on Desan's progress. The white man possessed great confidence in his running, and it was deserved. He looked now over his own shoulder and saw Gunsi and the rest beginning to lag behind. Good. He wanted to run down the white man, to be the one to capture him. It was not in his mind to doubt the outcome, he was not yet at his top speed, but perhaps it was time.

Desan wanted the braves to see the capture. If they ran much farther, the others might be lost. The warrior leaned forward and drove his toes into the ground. He felt the wind whip past his face and he voiced a wild, joyful whoop. He closed rapidly on the white man, who at the sound of the whoop turned and looked—and smiled? Desan's heart sank as the quarry bolted forward, regaining the space between them, and adding more!

Propelled by rage and humility, Desan's feet hammered the ground. Never before had he run this fast, and yet his best effort could only maintain the separation. With sickening discovery, he knew the white man again paced himself. He had more speed—why didn't he use it?

Desan looked behind and saw the distant warriors, several of whom had stopped and fallen to the ground. He would lose face this day, more so if the others saw his failure. Determined, he kept the brutal pace. He would chase until he was out of sight of the Tinde braves. The canyon narrowed, and Desan noticed the white man round a bend and disappear. Maybe not all was lost. The white man might trap himself in the shrinking canyon. The quarry ran with great skill and although Desan doubted it, the white man might stumble.

Doc knew he had to end the chase, and soon. His energy was failing. He'd been pleased when the Indian sped up, as he wanted the most distance possible between the warrior and his group. However, the increased pace quickly surpassed his lungs' ability to harvest the thin oxygen. Exhausted, Doc rounded a bend in the canyon and knew he'd found what he wanted. He slowed his pace and allowed the trailing Indian to close the gap without knowing he did so. Doc loped ahead searching for a place to stop.

Gunsi and Toh-Yah staggered to a stop, bending over to grasp their knees and gasp for air. The others had already fallen out. Only Desan charged on. A half mile away the white man raced from sight around a bend. Desan appeared willing to follow him. Drawing a deep breath, Gunsi ignored the searing pain in his chest and shouted for Desan to halt. Toh-Yah retched violently.

Reaching around, Doc grasped the rifle and loosed it from his shoulders. He glimpsed a slim trail up the now shallow side of the canyon and went for it.

Desan rushed past the bend and saw the white man turn for the canyon side. The warrior failed to understand the gun in the hands of his quarry until the white man slid to a stop and lifted the rifle.

Doc took a deep breath and exhaled slowly to steady his pounding heart.

Desan's eye's flared wide, his arms and legs flailing as he tried to stop.

Toh-Yah struggled upright and Gunsi looked at him.

The boom of the rifle shattered the stillness of the canyon.

CHAPTER FOUR

At the last instant, Desan dived to his right. Stretched horizontally three feet off the ground, Desan took the heavy ball in the leg, which spun him twirling into the rocky surface. The impact knocked the breath from his lungs and fear surged through him, followed by pain.

When at last his breath returned, he twisted his head to look for the white man and found him standing two feet away reloading the heavy rifle. Their eyes locked and held as Doc finished. Hatred and uncertainty alternately shared space with ever-present pain in the eyes of Desan. Doc noted with admiration that the Indian showed no sign of fear and although he doubted the bleeding man could move at all, he laid the rifle well out of reach before kneeling down and removing Desan's tomahawk and knife, hesitating before slipping them into his own waistband. Twisting around, Doc yanked several large tufts of grass and rolled the bundle into a ball. He then lifted Desan's head and gently slipped the grass underneath.

"You are a brave man and a fine runner. I'm sorry to have shot you in the leg, but you're too fast to leave with two good legs. I gave you the best I had, and still you came on."

Doc felt the heavy pounding inside his chest as his heart and lungs recovered. If Doc were fully acclimated to the altitude, Desan would be a good opponent, but not a true threat. He'd run well in the thin air, better than he had any right to expect, but Doc knew that he'd been lucky, for he was not yet fully acclimated. Doc cocked his head to the side and a curious smile pulled his lips apart. "I think you might have caught me."

Desan didn't know the words, but he understood the white man didn't intend to kill him and that fact roused his own curiosity. Doc stood upright at a noise from down the canyon, staring at the bend. "You'll be all right, they're coming." He lifted his hand in farewell and scrambled up the sloping side and into the trees.

Lying faceup, pain swept Desan in a current of agony. His lungs burned from exhaustion, his leg from the fire of the wound. Blood ran into his eyes and he tried lifting his hands to wipe it away. With horror, he realized he lay atop one of his arms.

Gunsi was the first to reach him. At the sound of the shot, he'd run for the bend of the canyon, surprising himself with the sudden burst of strength. It took longer than he had anticipated; Desan had pulled far ahead before disappearing around the bend. The huge Apache couldn't keep the shock from his face as he looked at the tattered warrior. He knelt down and rolled Desan to his side, freeing the broken arm. Sweat poured from the wounded Apache but he made no sound.

"The coward!" growled Gunsi. "When he couldn't escape you, he shot you down! He will die, Desan, I promise."

Desan rolled his head back and forth in a painful shake. "No. He set a trap . . . for me . . . I was too . . . foolish . . . to see it. Shot me . . . from that rock." His eyes pointed the direction. "Then went up . . . the side."

Toh-Yah heard the last of Desan's statement as he staggered near, followed by most of the others. Gunsi rose to speak with him.

"When he realized he couldn't escape, the white coward shot Desan."

Toh-Yah nodded his head in agreement, though the statement didn't quite fit what he'd seen. Up to now, the white man had killed effectively, and he looked at the rock Desan indicated. This was an easy shot, yet he had missed the kill. Desan was hit, but he should be dead. Something touched at the edge of Toh-Yah's consciousness, and he shuddered. Also, Toh-Yah noticed what Gunsi seemed to have missed—the pillow of grass beneath Desan's head.

"I believe the white man is clever," he said.

"Bah!" spat Gunsi. "He is a coward!"

"Think of it, Gunsi. If he had killed Desan we would be one less," Toh-Yah replied. "But with him wounded, we will be two less for now one of us must carry Desan home."

Gunsi spun around to look down at his cousin. It was his responsibility to care for his family and Toh-Yah's words hit him hard. If forced to follow tribal custom, he must see to Desan's safe return to the village. He must abandon the chase! An ugly notion prowled the dark corners of his thoughts. If only Desan were . . .

"Cousin. I free you from . . . your obligation . . . to me," the battered Indian whispered. Desan then struggled to make his voice stronger. "I want Gunsi . . . to continue . . . to honor his oath. Leave me here . . . where I have . . . fallen."

Toh-Yah stepped forward and spoke. "No, Desan. You will return home." He lifted his eyes to the solemn men, all of whom had now straggled near. He must phrase his request in way that would allow the volunteer to save face. "Which of you will sacrifice his own glory, to save the life of Desan? Is his glorious chase to end here, buried in this canyon of rock?"

The gathered men exchanged sideways looks. One spoke. "I will take Desan home."

Gunsi stared hard at the speaker and again Toh-Yah felt the touch brushing past his mind. "Wasagah! Why must it be you?" Gunsi demanded.

"It must be done, and I will do it," the brave answered.

Pulling the travois that carried Desan, Wasagah rounded the bend, and out of sight. Toh-Yah was worried. Wasagah, at twenty-five, was the oldest of the warriors. He was respected and skilled, the best hunter and archer in the village. Toh-Yah and Gunsi had intended for one of the younger men to take Desan home. The loss of Wasagah was a blow to their strength—and morale.

An hour later, Wasagah looked into a narrow, but deep and rocky, chasm. He'd walked along the edge in hope of finding a gentle crossing for Desan but it was not to be. He fretted over the choice of dragging the wounded man through the gully or doubling back and finding another way. The chasm might kill him with its roughness, but the delay in reaching help might also kill him.

"We'd better hurry. I don't have much time."

Wasagah spun at the sound and produced a knife from his sash. The white man stood there with his hands empty, his rifle slung across his back. He bent down and grasped the poles at the foot of the travois.

"Hurry," he said.

Wasagah didn't speak the white man's language, but he didn't fail to understand. He glanced at Desan.

"Put the knife away, Wasagah. He has courage . . . and though he is foolish, we cannot kill him for helping you."

"It is not me he helps. He pays tribute to you, Desan."

The knife disappeared and Wasagah raised the head of the travois, wondering at what must have passed between Desan and the white man for him to act in this manner. Once across, Doc held on as the two carried the wounded man several hundred feet past the chasm. They crossed over a four-foot-wide ledge of rock, and then a few yards farther Doc lowered his end to the ground on a second, much wider ledge.

He placed the knife and tomahawk into Desan's hands, faced west, and examined the surface of rock, leaving his back exposed to men supposed to be his enemies.

Doc bolted into a run along the rock. After a dozen strides, he gathered himself into a leap, landing on the first, smaller ledge. Taking a second to erase the sign of his jump, Doc walked back along the rock toward the two Apaches. With a smile and wave, he passed by and continued to the east.

Desan was grateful for the return of his weapons. It would bring him great shame to have them used against his friends. He knew the white man would die; there was no escape. But Wasagah and Desan would sing a song of his courage—and cunning.

"They let him *go?*" thundered Gunsi. "Why would Wasagah not kill him? Is he afraid?"

Ka-a-e-tano had tracked the white man to the chasm. The mingled prints were easily read and understood by all, even the young Hok'ee.

It took the young warrior's candor to say what they, with the exception of Gunsi, were thinking. "The white man's spirit is strong."

"No!" shouted Gunsi. "It is not! He is a white man, weak and cowardly."

Hok'ee shrank away from the venomous words. Toh-Yah said nothing. The boy was right, of course. The white man was strong and his spirit was strong. Toh-Yah knew Gunsi well enough to hear the uncertainty in the shouted declaration. The big Apache always strengthened his volume when his argument weakened. It did not matter to Toh-Yah that the white man had power. In fact, it pleased him. No warrior gained esteem from killing a hapless enemy.

The gathered faces revealed both shock at Gunsi's foolishness, and anger at his claim of fear by Wasagah. They knew of Wasagah's bravery, had heard songs of it. Some had seen it for themselves in battle. Gunsi, noting the flintlike stares and set faces, let his anger slip away and regained his command.

He lifted his head and spoke to the sky, "Forgive me, Wasagah. I grieve for Sotli." Returning his gaze to the braves, he looked at each one in turn as he said, "Toh-Yah asked for a man who could set aside his own glory for Desan. Wasagah proved his honor in abiding by his promise. Had he fought the white man and been injured, Desan wouldn't get home. He used the slyness of the wolf in accepting the white man's help, for now, Desan will live to fight again!"

Nods and grunts of approval evidenced that he'd accomplished his objective. A glance at Toh-Yah found the warrior staring back. So, the dramatics failed to fool his friend. No surprise, he thought. But Toh-Yah had Kitchi to answer for, and he would see it through.

"Ka-a-e-tano, take us after the white man. When we find him, we can test his courage." Thirty minutes later, they figured out Doc's ruse and followed the narrow rock ledge to the east. Frustrated at the delay, Gunsi had held his tongue. He would have a private talk with Wasagah. The warrior should have left a sign pointing out the direction of the white man.

Doc stared down the steep cliff and knew he'd made a mistake. For the last two hours, he'd followed a game trail that clung to the top of a thin finger of land towering above two parallel canyons. Confidence at the start of the trail turned to nervousness when he never found a point where the path descended into one of the canyons. He stood at the end of the finger, five hundred feet above the junction of the two valleys, and the trail led right over the edge! It was a game trail all right. Not for deer or elk; they could never scale the face. But the bighorn sheep that made the path could.

He might climb down the face, although it would be dangerous and slow. He gave quick thought to doubling back and searching for an easier passage. No—that was too risky. He didn't know what kind of lead he had and running into the Apaches while returning along the finger would leave him trapped.

Doc leaned out and studied the slope below him. Ragged boulders jutted from the face at all angles. He pulled the tail of his shirt from his pants and tore a wide strip from the bottom, wrapping his hands with the material. Checking the straps on his powder horn, pouch, and rifle, he swung them all to the middle of his back. Seating himself on the trail at the edge of the slope, he swung his legs over the side and pushed forward, sliding three feet down to the first boulder.

Careful in his turn, he spun around to face the cliff. Edging along the face for ten feet brought him to the end of the boulder. Just below was another smaller boulder and, taking a deep breath, he let go and dropped onto it. He felt a slight shift in the rock and his fingers seized the cliff face as panic tripled the beating of his heart. He cast a longing glance at the top of the cliff, then looked down to pick his next boulder.

An hour of mind- and muscle-numbing effort saw him to a point forty-five feet above the canyon floor. And he was stuck. He'd chosen the rock upon which he sat because of its size. The boulder immediately above had offered two routes down, but both required a ten-foot drop and he'd opted for the larger landing area. He had three options: climb back up and try to drop on the smaller boulder, climb across the face of the cliff to the smaller boulder, or slide down the cliff to the bottom.

He lifted his hands and looked at the torn and bloody flesh. Their strength was almost gone. His entire body was one laceration on top of another. His shirt and pants were in tatters. A jagged stone had cut the leather strap to his powder horn and the horn had fallen. He hoped the plug had stayed in place. On foot was bad enough. No powder was scary.

Doc finally admitted that he couldn't go up or across—he had to go down. Fifteen feet almost straight down and then thirty feet of steep talus to the bottom. He sat on the edge of the boulder and swung his legs out for the last time. Taking a moment to prepare his mind for the tearing his back would take, he pushed out into space.

Time seemed to pause as he hung beside the boulder, and then he slowly fell. He looked across the wide combined canyons to a point where Raton Creek should be. He thought he could make out the green shape of trees along its banks. A turkey vulture, or buzzard, drifted in wide lazy circles above the canyon. His back didn't hurt, and oddly, he felt nothing at all. Then his feet hit the talus and everything moved faster—much, much faster. Doc's legs whipped forward in a helpless, uncontrolled run as he flew down the slippery talus. Near the bottom, he felt his torso leaning too far forward and he flipped over, striking the slope with his shoulder, continuing the roll. Airborne for a moment before his feet touched the slope, he felt himself flipping frontward again.

Doc lost count of how many times he tumbled before hitting flat on his back, unconscious on the stone floor of the canyon. The buzzard altered its course to fly over the still form. Interested, it banked into a tight circle and hovered on the currents, waiting.

In his dream, Doc lay in a soft bed warmed by a thick, down comforter. He lay under the comforter, covered from head to toe. Someone at the foot of the bed began to pull the comforter from him. He sensed light and felt pain as his head was exposed. The pain flared down his body as the cover slid ever lower, finally piling on the floor at the foot of the bed. His eyes opened to a fuzzy flickering light as an object passed back and forth between him and the bedside lamp.

He combated the pain by focusing on the object. A few minutes later the buzzard blocked the sun as it swooped into clear view and awareness returned fully, painfully. Move! His mind screamed the command. Every joint, bone, and muscle resisted the roll onto his stomach, but he continued and, drawing his knees beneath, he stood. Spreading wide his legs, he fought for balance. The nausea ebbed away, leaving behind a pounding in his skull.

He lifted his arms, bending his elbows and flexing his hands. They were battered and bruised, but not broken. And he *was* standing, so his legs weren't broken. A feel of his head found no punctures. He'd made it. Sort of.

Doc dropped back to his knees and crawled about, gathering his strewn belongings. Another brutal effort saw him stand once more. Licking his bloody tongue across puffy lips, he tried to think. What now? He looked down the canyon toward Raton Creek and knew he couldn't make it yet. He stared at the fallen slab of rock for several minutes before he understood why. Part of his mind still worked, and in patience, it had waited for his thoughts to catch up.

The slab was huge and tilted in a manner that created a large, natural lean-to. Under the slab was the protection he needed while resting. Doc lifted his leg and strode forward, falling when his ankle buckled. Terror wiped away the remaining fog and clarity of mind returned. His ankle! Had he broken something after all? How had he been able to stand?

These were his thoughts as he scrambled on hands and knees into the cool refuge of the slab. He removed his boot and stared at the swollen purple mass that was his ankle. It wasn't broken, but it was badly sprained. Feeling defeat coming from all sides, he laid his head back onto the rock and closed his eyes.

"He went down there," pointed Ka-a-e-tano.

Gunsi was shocked, but he could read the signs. The white man had escaped him again. Following the tracks onto the towering fingerlike ridge and seeing no returning prints, to a man they believed their quarry had trapped himself. The Llanero knew this place well. Situated up the canyon to the north was a campsite they occupied every couple of years. The high, prominent finger provided a majestic setting for ceremonies. It was also a strategic lookout during the times their Ute cousins raided the Tinde.

As far back as the combined memories of the gathered warriors recalled, no one had ever attempted what the white man had done. Gunsi sprang onto an overhanging boulder and peered down the craggy face, searching for a body. He must be dead. During ten minutes of silence, he studied every spot where the white man might have fallen. There were several places a body might lie hidden from view, but Gunsi now doubted the white man lay in any of them. Unbidden, he felt respect. Until now, Gunsi denied the obvious and saw in his quarry only what he wished to see. He hated the white man and longed to kill him, but respecting the man's courage might save some Apache lives.

"Come, we will take the village path down into the canyon," said Toh-Yah. "We must hurry if we are to pick up his trail before dark."

Gladdened that Toh-Yah had spoken of it first, but hesitant to agree, Gunsi stared into the canyon. Was this fear he felt? He was relieved that Toh-Yah thought it wise to spend the afternoon circling around the danger. But relief at facing away from danger meant fear—didn't it? Gunsi wanted to scale the cliff and prove to himself that he wasn't frightened, and he started to voice it to the others. He felt the pounding of his heart. Could the others hear it? In his ears, the beats sounded like thunder.

"Yes, we must hurry." Gunsi was surprised at the sound of his own voice saying the opposite of his intended words.

"I will go down."

Toh-Yah looked at Hok'ee. "No. We will take the trail."

"I too will go," spoke another young voice. Viho was the same age as Hok'ee, but he was short and heavy, while Hok'ee was tall and lithe.

"Viho, you and Hok'ee are brave, but there is no need to climb down," Toh-Yah explained. "If we all attempt to descend at the same time, the rocks we dislodge will fall onto those below us. It will take no longer for us to use the trail than it will for us to make our way down the cliff one or two at a time. It is better that we take the trail."

Toh-Yah was right, Gunsi admitted. They could kill themselves climbing down and Toh-Yah, thinking through the situation without emotion, had settled on the best strategy. Gunsi had let passion guide his thoughts and he would have to be more careful. His friend thought and acted like a leader, and right now, Gunsi knew he did not compare well with Toh-Yah in the eyes of the warriors.

Viho looked at Hok'ee and spoke. "Then we will go alone."

Toh-Yah saw the boys were frightened and yet he knew they would go. He must end their argument now; if allowed to continue, the young fools would talk themselves into a corner.

"No! We will speak of this no more!" He started down the trail without another word.

Gunsi walked after him and the others fell in behind. All except for Viho and Hok'ee. Hok'ee sat down on the edge and, much the same as Doc had done, dropped to the first boulder. He walked to the end and selected his next move—a quick jump down to a small boulder, followed by another drop to a third. He felt a slight shift on the small boulder as he bounded past, landing on his hands and knees on the large rock.

Standing, he looked up to Viho and motioned him to follow. Viho regretted his decision now that he faced the descent. He swallowed once and gathered his courage, slipping over the edge to land on the first boulder. Encouraged by the ease in which he accomplished the first step, always the hardest, he moved to the end and readied himself to follow Hok'ee's quick jumps and join his friend.

Fear seized Viho as he leapt for the small boulder. Sudden and unexpected, it washed from his mind the carefully timed movement. He dropped hard onto the small boulder and felt it move! The shifting rock altered his balance and Viho flung himself at the cliff face, digging his fingers into the small cracks. Frozen with terror, he felt the rock move again!

From far away he could hear Hok'ee yelling for him to jump, and then the boulder was gone and he hung from his hands! A horrifying instant later, his fingers slipped and he plummeted down the cliff. Viho's terrible scream echoed across the canyon—cut short by the impact of a boulder. Hok'ee watched Viho bounce from boulder to boulder. Spinning and tumbling with arms and legs at incomprehensible angles. A sickening thud accompanied each hit until his friend fell too far for the sounds to reach him.

"Hok'ee! Hok'ee, grab the belt! Hok'ee, listen to me!"

Numbed, the boy turned to look above him. Gunsi's head and arm were visible at the lip of the cliff. From his hand dangled the wide leather belt.

"Boy, you grab that belt. If you make me come after you, I'll throw you off the cliff after Viho!"

Gunsi would do no such thing, but the boy was like a statue and he had to say something to jar him loose. Hok'ee made one feeble attempt to grasp the belt, then turned and sat on the rock.

Wild, Gunsi jumped up and looked around. "Remove your sashes. Braid them together to make a rope! Move, you lazy dogs . . . hurry!"

Toh-Yah looped the makeshift rope twice around a protruding rock and dropped the rest over the side. The tail of the rope curled near Hok'ee and he knew it would be long enough. Gunsi grasped the rope and threw himself over the side, sliding down to land beside the young Apache. He hauled the boy erect and looked down into his eyes.

"You are Tinde! Even more, you are Llanero! Do you ask that I, Gunsi, should waste my time with a timid woman?" he fairly shouted at the stupefied boy.

The insult breeched Hok'ee's fear and he gave a slow shake of his head.

"Then climb, Hok'ee! Prove your courage."

Horrified, Toh-Yah spoke. "Gunsi, tie him to the rope and we will haul him up!"

Never taking his eyes from Hok'ee, Gunsi snarled, "Shut up! Hok'ee is a warrior. He will climb out as any warrior would."

Thrusting the rope into the boy's hands, Gunsi backed away. "Climb, Hok'ee, or I will leave you here!"

CHAPTER FIVE

Doc awoke, too confused to realize the danger he'd courted in allowing sleep to overtake him. He had heard—what? A brief horrible scream pierced the canyon—and then silence. They must have found his tracks! Reaching for his rifle a faint sound came to him, followed by another, louder sound. Doc's mind traveled several paths at once. He listened, he prepared his rifle, and he considered the scream. For it had been a scream and not a shout of discovery. Mere seconds had passed since he awoke, and now he focused on the odd sound. It came from above, and it was coming closer!

For the briefest instant he thought it had stopped—then the Indian smashed into the ground fifteen feet from Doc's shelter. Within the shadows, he sat and stared at the body framed in the triangle of light at the opening of the lean-to. From the length of time between the scream and the body striking the ground, Doc knew the Apache had fallen from, or near, the top. Vacant eyes stared at Doc from a face strangely devoid of damage. The dead Indian was young, he noted.

Doc snapped rigid with the realization that the boy didn't hunt alone and his ears strained for sounds of others climbing down. Hearing nothing, Doc eased to the opening and peeked upward. He was near the base of the talus slope and could see the cliff all the way to the top except for the areas blocked by jutting boulders. He watched as an Indian climbed over the lip, followed by the huge Apache. No other Indians were on the cliff face. He slipped back into the cover of the lean-to and relaxed.

Gunsi led down the trail at a fast trot. It would take three hours to reach Viho. The Apache flashed a look at the sun. Once in the canyon he would increase the pace. If the white man's tracks were to be found today, they must hurry. Already the angle of the sun extended shadows markedly to the east.

Ferguson walked to the edge of the Trail and stared into the mountains. How many times had he done this, he wondered? A loud curse and the crack of a whip announced the arrival of the last wagon. The other fifteen wagons already waited at the top of the pass.

Ferguson found it hard to believe, but he actually regretted the easy ascent. Not one bit of trouble—amazing! He'd been over the pass eight times before and each had been a nightmare of loose rock, broken wheels and axles, injured men and livestock, and runaway wagons. The company was a full day ahead of schedule and that meant one less day for Doc.

"Ferguson! Take a look here."

The wagon master turned to the speaker, Todd Bracken, a rugged Louisiana man with fair hair and a tellingly dark complexion. In New Orleans, they called folks like Todd mulattoes. Ferguson called him friend. And if he had one, Bracken would be his second-in-command.

Ferguson trailed the ox driver to the rear of the big wagon where, tied to the tailgate, standing on trembling legs with head hung low, was Doc's mustang.

"Over here," said Bracken.

Circling the horse, Ferguson saw the bloodstain on the mustang's shoulder.

"Had an arrow in 'im," the driver reported. "Went in 'bout six inches deep, though at a shallow angle. We pulled it out and poured in some alcohol. Poured some on his forelegs too."

Ferguson bent down to look at the horse's legs. Several lacerations covered by a mixture of dried blood, dirt, and grass ran the length of its legs. Ferguson didn't bother to ask about Doc; Bracken would have told him of the missing scout right off. "Where'd he come from?"

"Up our trail. We'd just started the team when Hamilton looked back and seen him comin' along slow."

"It's a mite early, but we'll camp up here tonight," Ferguson decided. "Who knows? Maybe Doc'll come stragglin' in."

Bracken and the other men showed their doubt. Ferguson doubted it also, but he refused to give credit to the wayward thought. He liked Doc, and he'd hold out as long as he could. And he'd give Doc all the time he could.

Now that he wanted it, Doc wasn't able to sleep, but he did rest with his foot propped up on a melon-sized rock. After an hour, he tore another wide strip from his shirt and placed a tight wrap on his sore ankle before slipping the injured foot back into his boot. He guessed the Indians would need at least two hours to reach him. On his trip along the finger, too late to do him any good, he'd learned the first possible way down was two miles back.

It was time to go and yet he hesitated, unwilling to test the ankle. When he outran the Indians earlier, it was in his mind to keep running. He'd proven he could travel faster than they could follow. All he needed to do was reach Raton Creek and run up the Trail toward the advancing company.

Now that option was gone and the severity of the injury would determine whether he lived or died. He crawled from the rock and stood, flinching when he tested the ankle with his weight. Tentative, Doc shuffled a few steps forward. The ankle hurt, but held. From the dead Apache, he removed a tomahawk. Spotting a bow several feet up the talus slope, he also took the boy's arrow quiver, discarding two that had broken during the fall.

Upon reflection, he bent down and picked up the broken arrows. The points and feathers could be useful. He hung the quiver and bow over his shoulders and, using his rifle for a walking stick, headed out of the canyon. He was far away and traveling in a deep, gravel-bottomed wash when the Indians reached the dead boy.

Gunsi looked once at Viho and turned away. The fall was an ugly death. None of Viho's close family was among the braves, so Toh-Yah suggested they all attend the boy's burial. Other than the mountains, which they would not take the time to climb, the nearest high point was a low rise to the east. Gunsi allowed Hok'ee to carry the boy.

The tracks of the white man around Viho's body bothered the lesser warriors. Some mumbled that he must be a shadow warrior, able to vanish and reappear at will, for all of them had looked down the cliff and none had seen the white man. The foolish talk subsided when Ka-a-e-tano found the lean-to. Though not as strongly voiced, murmurs about the white man's power were whispered among the Apaches.

Gunsi didn't like the whispers, but he could no longer deny that the white man was a capable enemy. Yesterday they were nineteen warriors, Gunsi reminded himself. Tonight they were twelve. Seven Llanero were gone: four dead, one wounded, and two returned to the village—and still the white man lived.

The solemn Apaches trotted from the hill, following the trail left by the white man. The prints told the story as plainly as if they saw him with their eyes. He was hurt. One foot left a print that slid forward before lifting, and the steady imprint of the rifle butt explained why.

Doc lay on his belly, his face immersed in the water as he drank from the clear pool. He stripped his boot and stuck the sore ankle into the icy coolness of the spring. The sun was below the western peaks and the gray of dusk settled in. High clouds had blown in over the last hours and the night promised to be dark. He hoped so. He could use the help.

The wind had picked up; now and then, a gust would blow dirt into the wash. Twelve feet deep with near-vertical sides of crumbling dirt, the wash limited his view of the sky to a narrow band. His pace was too slow and he harbored no doubts of his capture if he continued along the water. When he stumbled onto the wash, he'd taken to it right quick. The gravel bottom muffled his trail somewhat and there were rounded imprints of animal passage as well. The tracks he'd left out on the canyon floor couldn't be helped. He'd needed distance and the sore ankle didn't allow the time or agility to hide tracks. The Apaches could follow his sign on a dead run through the canyon.

Doc had tried some ruses in the wash that might slow them down. At every point in the wash that offered an obvious path out, he'd tried some little trick. On some, he scuffed the dirt along the edge; at others, he tossed a handful of gravel in a way that looked like a foot may have kicked them exiting the bottom. At one particular cut-down where a smaller wash intersected, he walked several yards into the small gully and broke the limb of a dried sage bush, leaving it hanging in a way that he hoped would catch the notice of the Apaches. With a second, smaller branch taken from a less noticeable shrub, he brushed his trail while he backtracked into the main channel.

None of it would slow them down for long, but they would have to check each possibility, and it hadn't cost him much time to try. Rising, Doc replaced the boot and started down the wash. The soft gravel bed was less jarring to his ankle and he quickened his pace.

Stopping short, he stared while his mind worked the possibilities of what he saw. Up ahead the gully made a turn and floodwaters had carved an arc from the canyon. A large tangle of brush lay piled in the bend, and across the pile, reaching to the top of the wash, was a log big enough for a man to walk on. Better yet, it left the wash on the left side, the north side, and he wanted to head north and meet the company.

As it was near dark, he'd almost missed seeing the brush pile. In fifteen minutes, he doubted that he would have seen it at all. If the Apaches tried to track him all night, chances were good they would pass right by, not realizing until morning that he'd left the wash. There was a risk they would see it and investigate, and there were many eyes in that group to fool all at once. If they got wise to him, they would run him down on the open floor of the wide canyon.

Doc looked around. He had to do something different. If he stayed in the gully, they would catch him, and if he cut north for the wagon road and they found where he left the wash, they would catch him. Overhead, the wind whipped with the fury of a building storm. Flashes of light danced through the clouds far to the south. To his right lay a moderate slope covered by thick shrubs, and Doc knew what to do. Fifteen minutes later, he hobbled across the canyon once again. If his plan worked, he would live. At least until tomorrow, he admitted.

The last of the Apaches to file past the pile of brush, Beshe saw the log. He heard some small noise and stopped. As he peered into the darkness, the faint outline of the brush and log emerged. He called out and the warriors turned back. Ka-a-e-tano moved to the log and studied the surface.

Toh-Yah kindled a small fire and, when it burned well, placed a limb from the pile into it. Soon, Ka-a-e-tano examined the log by the light of the burning limb held overhead.

"He climbed out," the tracker reported. He pointed to the log with an outstretched arm. "See, here and here, are the scuff marks of his boots." The scout climbed the log and handed down a small piece of Doc's shirt. "This snagged on a small branch."

That piece of cloth bothered Toh-Yah. Trailing the white man down the wash had taken more time than expected, due to the man's cleverness. How could such a man make a mistake so simple and dangerous? He recognized that the log was an excellent means of escape. It was only luck that they'd found it in the dark at all. Had they seen it the first time they'd passed, it would have saved them two hours.

Even so, Ka-a-e-tano's instincts were the reason they turned back when they did. The tracker felt something was wrong and insisted on doubling back. Gunsi had argued with him, concerned that the white man might be ahead of them. He'd surrendered to Ka-a-e-tano's instinct when the tracker pointed out that the wash was running south. He reasoned that the white man would not want to go south, and would try to use the dark and wind to escape to the north. If the white man was still in the wash heading south, they could afford to give him a few hours' lead as there was no refuge for a hundred miles in that direction.

On top were the remnants of boot prints near the edge. It seemed the white man had great difficulty climbing from the log. A few faint tracks led to the north, then nothing.

"The wind," guessed Ka-a-e-tano, "has wiped them away."

To be heard over the wind, Gunsi spoke in a loud voice. "Spread out," he ordered.

Without tracks to look for, the Apaches trotted rapidly north, heads turning, eyes searching the night.

Two miles away, Doc came upon another gully and dropped down to the bottom. The journey across the wide canyon was slow and painful. The combination of his ankle and walking into the howling wind had been difficult and now, in the protection of the wash, he realized he couldn't go on in the gale. The gully seemed to run southwest toward the mountains, and northeast toward the wagon road. The latter option tempted him and it was several moments before his earlier resolve returned. Doc sighed, and moved up the gully toward the mountains.

Twenty minutes of travel sapped the last of his strength and he began looking for a spot to rest. He found a place where the flow of a past flood undercut a large willow, toppling the tree into the gully. When it fell, the roots pulled up a huge chunk of earth and the hollow left behind created a snug shelter, one that would allow Doc to build a small, protected fire.

With fingers trembling from cold and exertion, he gathered dried twigs and leaves that had blown in among the roots and become trapped. Flint from his pouch sparked a flame and Doc fed in larger twigs before adding small branches. Leaving the shelter, he walked across the canyon, away from the tree. The glow of the fire was invisible unless you were within twenty feet. Satisfied, he returned.

Chewing the last of his venison, he leaned back and allowed his tired muscles to relax. There was no reason to push on now, he thought. The trick had worked, or it hadn't. If it failed, they would find him soon and it wouldn't matter to the Apaches if they caught him on the flats or behind the tree. It did matter to Doc, here was warmth; out there was wind and cold. If the trick succeeded, the Apaches would be miles away, searching in the wrong direction.

He felt his eyelids sag, and sat up. The dirt-encrusted roots and the opposite wall of the hollow reflected the heat from the fire, trapping the warmth inside the small depression. Doc added several more branches to the hungry flame before falling asleep. Three more times during the night he awoke to feed the fire and listen. Once, he ventured onto the canyon floor for any sounds carried on the wind of the now dying storm.

Dawn found the Apaches in a surly mood. The morning broke clear and the air tasted sweet and clean. Although lightning had flashed and distant thunder had shaken the ground, it hadn't rained in the canyons or valley. During the night, the rain fell everywhere except the area they searched. Some had grumbled that it was the work of the white man's power, for the wind hid his tracks from the Apaches. With fresh prints pressed into the moist earth, it was simple to track a man after a storm; but the clouds held their rain and protected the white man.

All night, they'd pushed north, hunting without success. They searched well past the point where the injured man could have gone, then doubled back to hunt again. Gunsi stalked the perimeter of the small camp, stopping often to stare across the brightening valley. They rested at a point beyond the junction of the wide canyons, well out into the valley of Raton Creek. Ten miles to the south lay the Canadian River.

Gunsi fumed; the white man had escaped again. His anger came in small part from frustration. The bulk of his rage grew from embarrassment. The white man had proven himself a cagey and able adversary; but now he was injured—virtually a cripple, Gunsi roared to himself—and still he evaded capture! The huge Apache believed the others viewed him as a fool and unworthy of leadership. In truth, they were as perplexed as Gunsi.

"Where has Shadow gone, Ka-a-e-tano?" questioned Beshe, receiving only a shrug in response.

Gunsi's will battled for control and he managed to resist the wild urge to smash Beshe, though the fool deserved it. He must not lose control. To do so meant the loss of leadership, and the warriors were already beginning to look to Toh-Yah as often as they did to him. References to the white man as Shadow began shortly after leaving the deep wash. Throughout the night they used the name with more frequency until, now, Shadow was the only name they used.

"He has fooled us," said Toh-Yah. "Back at the wash I believe. We should return there."

Wordlessly, the men arose and prepared to leave. Gunsi stepped to the front, asserting command, and set a fast pace toward the wash. Protected from the wind, several prints remained beneath the log and Ka-a-e-tano squatted and studied them.

"They are too deep and ragged," he said at last. "Even if Shadow jumped from the log, which his injury should not allow, the prints wouldn't be so deep. They are ragged because his feet shifted slightly as he pressed down."

The tracker rose and faced Gunsi. "He made these prints to last. He wanted us to find them. I didn't notice under the light of the torch."

It wasn't an apology or an excuse. Ka-a-e-tano stated a fact.

"Then he went south or east," stated Toh-Yah.

Gunsi, at last, found the tracks. The white man—the warrior refused to think of him as Shadow—had left a false sign on the log knowing the Indians would readily believe he went north. North is where the white man's friends were coming with the wagons. Instead, he had gone south after pushing through the thick brush-covered slope on the opposite side of the wash. Toh-Yah grunted in admiration as Gunsi pointed to the tracks. Hidden beneath the thick brush, the tracks were difficult to see. Knowing what to look for, Toh-Yah's eyes followed Shadow's path through the brush. Several branches were broken during his passing and many more had been disturbed in a way that left the lighter underside of the leaves exposed to the bright sun.

Toh-Yah walked to the top and looked across the flats. He didn't bother to search for tracks. He knew, as Shadow had known, the wind would remove them. Instead, he freed his mind to reach out for Shadow, to think as he thought. Toh-Yah knew Shadow fled south or east, or some point between, but which? They were now at least a half day behind and this time they must guess correctly.

CHAPTER SIX

A RUSTLE AND A TRICKLE OF SAND roused Doc from sleep. Above his head, a ground squirrel peered at him from the lip of the shelter, vanishing when Doc stirred. Sitting up, he stretched arms and legs, working the kinks from them. He poked his head up high enough that he could see over the edge and scanned the canyon. Nothing moved and after a moment, he sat back down.

There was time and enough light, so he wiped the rifle clean and checked the weapon. The rifle was known as a Lancaster, and was made by Henry Harris. Harris lived in Lancaster, Pennsylvania, along with dozens more gunsmiths. They all turned out quality flintlock rifles and pistols known commonly as Lancasters. In one of those inexplicable mysteries, at least half of the gunsmiths in the country lived in or near Lancaster and had for the past sixty years. For that matter, the state of Pennsylvania was home to nine out of ten gunsmiths. Even the so-called Kentucky rifle came from Lancaster and Doc held one of them in his hands.

The rifle's barrel ran forty inches and the stock was made of curly maple. Other than the flintlock, which was case-hardened steel, the patch box, butt plate, and other fittings were made of brass.

Shaking his head, Doc reached into his pouch for a flint. At some point yesterday or last night, the flint had fallen from the hammer. Without the flint, he might as well have thrown the rifle at an attacking Indian. His hand groped the contents of the pouch as his mind refused to accept the message. The pouch was empty!

He turned up the pouch and dumped it onto the ground between his legs. It wasn't completely empty; he had flint and a whetstone—and two balls. The remaining contents had fallen from a thumb-sized hole ripped into the bottom of the leather. It seemed as though the cliff had robbed him of more than his ankle. Doc tore off another piece of his shirt and laid it in the bottom of the pouch, covering the hole. The patch would have to do until he found the time and material to stitch and mend it properly. Counting the one seated down the barrel, he had a total of three balls.

"Old son," he said aloud, "this is shapin' up to be a right lively soiree."

Doc twisted the round-topped hammer screw and raised the cap on the hammer. He inserted a piece of flint and lowered the cap. The hammer of a flintlock was actually three separate pieces comprising a hammer screw, a cap, and the hammer itself. The screw raised and lowered the cap over the hammer, much like a small vise. The flint lay on the hammer and the cap was screwed down, squeezing it in place. The whole mechanism then moved as one during firing.

Five minutes later, after another long look at the canyon floor, he was moving down the wash. He'd taken a dozen steps before he realized he could step without using the rifle for a walking stick. The ankle was sore but it felt stronger and he slung the weapon over his shoulder. If he got the opportunity, he'd practice some with the stolen bow. He'd had playmates among the Osage and Omaha as a boy and from them had learned to hunt with a bow, make arrows and points, and throw a tomahawk, but that was years ago and practice might make the difference between a hit and a miss.

❋ ❋ ❋

"Roll 'em!" shouted Ferguson, and the ox drivers started their teams.

He'd loitered over breakfast, hoping against reason that Doc would show, and now it was time to be moving. Before he turned away, the wagon master stood looking into the green peaks until long after the last wagon passed behind him.

Last night's rain had pounded the mountains and the Trail was slippery. Several times an ox slid and went down, often dragging along his yoked mate. They traveled across the top of a series of high ridges and Ferguson hoped the ground dried out before the Trail led down into the valley. If not, they'd be using double teams and ropes to control the wagons on the descent. Thoughts of Doc diminished as the men strained to keep the wagons upright and rolling straight.

Doc left the wash at the base of the mountains and stopped to rest under a grove of pinyon pines. Collecting a handful of nuts from the trees, he sat down to eat and think. His trick had given him the time to reach the mountains. After the injury, Doc reasoned that his only chance was to do what the Indians would least expect—turn away from all help and hide in the mountains. There was always the chance that he'd lost them for good.

Angling up the side of the mountain and climbing a painful two hundred feet above the valley, he found a spot where he could sit and watch for pursuit, and rest his throbbing ankle. Fearing inactivity would stiffen the ankle, he stood thirty minutes later and placed a testing weight on his foot. It held, and with less soreness than he'd expected.

Picking a tree forty feet away, he unslung the bow, nocked an arrow, and drew the string taut. Movement behind the tree snap-focused his vision twenty feet farther and a deer stepped into view. Without thought or hesitation, Doc shifted the bow, drew back farther, and let fly. The doe took two stumbling steps and fell. The joy of finding food didn't overshadow the certainty that he'd made a lucky shot.

He'd lost his knife, so he honed the tomahawk on his whetstone and set to work on the doe. As he worked, he reconsidered his luck. When he'd lined up on the tree it was in his mind that he would miss. He'd expected to fail because it had been years since he last used a bow. Upon seeing the deer, he'd merely reacted and shot true. It was something to remember.

A check of the valley detected no movement so he chanced a small fire and broiled some of the venison. Sitting with his back against the trunk of a pine and his foot propped on a fallen log, he ate his fill. The rain had fallen on this spot in the mountains and Doc enjoyed the fresh, damp smell of the pine and grass. The birds were pleased also. Overhead a couple of jays cackled at each other in their loud varied calls. He heard and saw meadowlarks, robins, and tanagers. The tap-tap-tap of a lewis's woodpecker, distinguished by its pink belly and green-black wings, added to the chorus. Doc was still sitting there when the Indians appeared far out in the valley.

Staying among the trees and moving fast to cover the doe's carcass with brush, he slung on his weapons and grabbed the deerskin bundle containing his meat. Picking a difficult path through the forest, he went straight up the mountain, using the trees and branches to haul himself upward.

"He went there," Toh-Yah said, pointing southwest toward the mountains.

"Why? There are no whites in the mountains," Gunsi argued. "He went toward the settlements, or the wagon road."

"He has never done what we anticipated," Toh-Yah replied. "Why should he do so now?"

Gunsi, believing it to be another trick, refused to accept Toh-Yah's opinion and it was decided to split into three groups, each searching a different direction. Ka-a-e-tano led to the east, Gunsi to the south, and Toh-Yah toward the mountains. If no sign was found by dusk, Ka-a-e-tano and Toh-Yah would head for Gunsi. If one of the two of them found tracks, they would wait there while the other joined Gunsi and together they would travel to the waiting party.

After two miles, Toh-Yah knew that he was right. Shadow went to the mountains. He squatted on his heels where he'd dropped to examine the faint print. Only one side of the heel's impression remained but Toh-Yah recognized it. He had followed the tracks for two days now and could identify Shadow from his print as easily as if he looked up and saw the white man standing there.

A few yards farther lay another print and Toh-Yah found enough to lead him to the hollow under the tree. Knowing Shadow had been here, the Apache was able to distinguish the carefully brushed-out sign and find the buried fire.

Toh-Yah led the little group down the wash at a fast trot toward the mountains. Climbing out of the gully on Shadow's trail, he noticed the hunted man no longer used his rifle to help him walk. If the injury had not been severe, why hadn't Shadow chosen to go to the wagon road?

He could be at the Trail by now, Doc thought—maybe even heading up it to meet the company. But then, he admitted, there was no way to know that the ankle would recover as soon as it had. Besides, they might have caught him last night if he had gone north. The injury bothered him less with each passing hour and he was making good time.

He'd sprained the same ankle once before as a boy while running to school. His father had cut a crutch, and Doc had followed the doctor's orders and kept weight from the leg for five days. It took another five days to work the stiffness from the joint. Yesterday's sprain might not be as severe as the first, but it was close and Doc wondered if his forced use of the ankle aided its recovery.

All of the Apaches regrouped at Toh-Yah's position two hours after nightfall. Before the light faded, Akule, one of the warriors in Toh-Yah's group, had found the deer carcass and clear sign of Doc's trail up the mountain. Toh-Yah shared his opinion that Doc's injury had lessened and that he was moving faster. Tomorrow they would need to rise early and close the distance. Gunsi was sullen and Toh-Yah wondered whether it was fatigue or being wrong about the white man's direction that blackened the mood of the huge Apache.

Topping the mountain, Doc paused and turned to scan the flats. The tree-covered slope below blocked his vision close in. Five slow minutes of scrutiny failed to reveal any sign of the Apaches so he figured they were already near the base of the mountain. The setting sun shone on Doc, but the flats were already darkened under the mountain's shadow. Would they come on in the dark, he wondered? They had before and he assumed they would again.

He was tired, in spite of the fast recovery of his injury, but he was far from whole and the ankle was sore. Doc knew he couldn't risk pushing too hard, for another misstep in the looming dark might damage the ankle further. He followed the northwest curve of the mountain ridge until sunset when travel through the shadowy forest became difficult. Making camp behind a wall of brush beneath the spreading pine trees, he built a fire the size of a tin plate—which would have been nice to have—and broiled some of his venison, holding the hot meat with stinging fingers while he ate. The smoke from the fire diffused rapidly in the dense brush and overhanging tree limbs; still, he smothered the flames after cooking. He cut several pine boughs with the tomahawk, crawled beneath them, and curled up in a tight ball to sleep.

"Your man's alive," stated Shep Knorr, "leastwise he was yesterday."

The mountain man wandered into the company camp a few minutes earlier just as he had the time before, appearing from out of the dark without warning. It unsettled Roland Ferguson to know someone could enter the camp at will undetected. He always posted a guard, two of them since Doc disappeared, but Shep came and went without so much as a challenge.

Shep squatted by the fire, blowing on the coffee cup he cradled in both hands. The wagon master stared across the flames, stunned by the casual comment.

"Alive! Where is he?"

"Over west a-ways, and a little south. Near the Canadian River by now, I s'pose."

Confused, Ferguson took a minute to gather his thoughts. "Is he hurt? Why don't he come in?"

"Can't. 'Paches got him on the run." Shep peered over the cup at Ferguson. "Your man's in trouble. That Llanero I told you 'bout before, Gunsi, well, your man done kilt his brother. He's got the whole bunch after his hide." Shep reached for the coffeepot. "I 'spect they'll get it too"—he paused and chuckled—"though they's paying a sweet price for it."

The wagon master rose to his feet, "How do we get to him? Can you take us?"

Shep gaped up at Ferguson in disbelief. "You can't and I won't! Mister, you best understand this, if'n you go into those hills you'll be dead. Not one of you, not some of you . . . but ever' man jack of you. Those 'Paches are out for blood, your man's fer sure, but they'll take any white man they can get along the way. 'Sides, if you walk off and leave these big wagons, they'll be gone a-fore you're out of sight."

Ferguson knew the mountain man was right about the wagons, but it didn't help much. That he liked the scout only added to his frustration over not being able to help one of his men. Jamming his hands deeper into the pockets of his thick wool coat, he paced to the edge of the firelight and stared into the gloom. Doc was alive! But what could he do to help? Ferguson wasn't skilled in tracking and neither were his men. That's why

Doc was made scout; he was the only one who could read sign. Still, there must be something.

Suddenly he turned to the fire. "What would it cost to have you go and get him?" he asked Shep.

"More 'n these wagons are worth."

Shep's response had been truthful, Ferguson observed with shock. The cargo held in the wagons represented both necessary and luxury items for the isolated town of Santa Fe, and their value was enough to make two men wealthy—three or four men, if you continued on to the California settlements and sold the goods there. Yet the mountain man hadn't the slightest interest in his offer.

In answer to Ferguson's unasked question, Shep said, "A dead man can't spend a thousand dollars any better than he can a single dollar."

"Is it that bad?" Ferguson voiced the question in a low whisper.

"Now you're catchin' on. It's as bad as you think and then some." Shep drained the cup and stood. "Your man was a fool to go up there. I tried to warn 'im."

The mountain man slipped on his gear, cradled his rifle in his arms, and said, "I appreciate the coffee, and I hope I ain't caused you no grief. Just figured you might want to know what happened."

Shep walked away from the fire and into the darkness.

"How did you know about all this?" Ferguson asked into the night.

He shivered when Shep replied. It was eerie to hear a voice so close by and not be able to see the speaker.

"Word gets around. Them hills ain't half so empty as a body might expect. They's Indians, both good and bad, though even they tend to switch around from time to time. They's more like me, hunters, trappers, and such. Of late, a few miners have wandered in lookin' for color of one sort or another. Mostly, they's men who like traveling the lonely trails. Up there a body can look down on the eagle, he can reach out his hand and touch the sky. For a man who's prone to it, once you get in 'em, the mountains won't let go."

Ferguson heard the soft scrape of leather on brush as the mountain man started away.

"Did you know that your man was a runner?" Shep's voice sounded farther off yet carried easily in the crisp air.

"What do you mean?" Ferguson asked.

"A runner. A footracer. Story is he ran off and left them 'Paches in his dust." A light chuckle reached the wagon master's ears. "Now I would have liked to seen that. Yes sir, I surely would. Them Llanero pride themselves as runners."

Before walking away, Shep spoke one last time. "Most men I wouldn't give no chance a'tall. But your man might do it if any could. He's kilt four of 'em so far."

Four! Ferguson didn't know if he was shocked because so many men had died in only a few days, or if it was the thought that the small scout had killed them. He'd judged Doc to be a capable man, but not one so formidable. Well, he decided, Doc's got his back against it and I hope he does whatever it takes, even if it means killing every mother's son of them.

Awakening at daybreak, Doc broiled more meat and ate while waiting for the sun to pierce the canopy of the forest. Soon after, he was on his way. During breakfast, he'd changed his plan. His intention to hide out until he recovered was no longer necessary as the ankle felt even stronger this morning. He could now circle wide and head east for the Trail. The question was, which way? Should he circle north or south?

If the company was on schedule, they would have cleared the pass and might now be far into the valley. Doc had lost an accurate feel for his position during his rushed escape and night travels, but he knew enough to figure he was south of the wagon train. But how far south? In the valley, the wagons could set a good pace, maybe two miles an hour. Slower, if the rains turned the ground too soft.

If he were to hit the Trail in front of or behind the train, it'd be better to be in front, he reasoned. If he went north and hit the road behind the wagons, the Indians could wind up in the middle and cut him off. No, he'd circle south, then east, and hit the road ahead of the company.

Beshe glanced at his brother-in-law and smiled. Ce-col-quin returned the smile and backed out of the brush. The two Apaches slipped from their camp three hours before sunrise and climbed the mountain. At first light, they were trailing Shadow, finding his camp among the brush thirty minutes after Doc left.

"He is near," Ce-col-quin stated. "We will catch him!"

Both men were in their early twenties, strong and eager to prove themselves worthy of being among the privileged rank of all Llanero warriors. Each had killed enemies in battle and enjoyed the esteem accorded them, but now they wanted Shadow. To capture him would secure the friendship of Gunsi and Toh-Yah, one of whom was sure to become chief. It must be a capture and not a kill. Gunsi had claimed the life of Shadow and to deny him his oath would be dangerous.

Confident, the two advanced through the forest on silent feet. Slowly at first, as they worked out Shadow's trail, then faster as they became confident that the man fled west. At the edge of the tree line, Beshe raised his hand and Ce-col-quin stopped behind him. Beshe pointed through the thinning foliage at a bald ridge. On the far side, their quarry reentered the forest. The Apaches whispered an exchange then separated. Beshe remained as his brother-in-law ran through the trees to get around Shadow and trap him. When he felt the time was right, he rose and trotted across the open ridge.

CHAPTER SEVEN

Astonished, Doc watched the Indian emerge from the trees and come straight for him. Doc glanced around, listening for sounds of others. He had stopped soon after entering the trees to look at his low-heeled boots. The beating they'd taken climbing down the craggy cliff had caught up with them, and the sole of one now hung half off. He'd cut a strip of hide from the deerskin and bound up the toe of the boot. Slipping the boot back onto his foot, he'd looked up as the warrior ran from the trees across the ridge.

Where were the others? The Indian was halfway across the open space and yet the forest and ridge behind him remained empty. Doc knew the Apache had seen him enter the trees, for the man ran straight toward the spot. The carelessness of his advance told Doc the Indian had no idea that he sat there and watched. Reaching over, he picked up the rifle, and then put it down. From his back, he took the bow and fitted an arrow; there was no sense in giving away his position by firing the gun.

The warrior closed to fifty feet and Doc let him come. The Indian slowed ten feet before the trees and the arrow took him square in the chest. The Apache looked down, astonished to see the arrow protruding from his breast. He sank to his knees and his head lifted, seeking his attacker. A sight he was never to see, for Doc held to his cover and waited until the Indian pitched forward. The impact drove the shaft through his body to leave the red-tinged flint point high above the warrior's back.

The wagon scout held his breath and listened. Curious, but satisfied that the warrior was alone, Doc crawled out and tugged the body into the trees. He stripped the Apache of his deerskin shirt and moccasins, changing them for his own shirt and boots. He put what was left of his shirt into the pouch, tied the boots together with a rawhide strap, and hung them around his neck. The moccasins were a little snug but Doc figured they would stretch out. The shirt fit well. He eyed the dead man's leggings and then his own tattered pants. The man was a warrior, and Doc couldn't get comfortable with leaving him naked. It just didn't seem right.

Adding the dead brave's arrows to his quiver, Doc slipped deeper into the forest. He moved from tree to tree, squatting often to look and listen. The third time he paused, he saw another Apache moving through the forest. The Indian advanced with deliberate movement as he studied the forest. Doc waited motionless, his breath shallow.

The Apache looked only forward, never turning to glance behind. Was he alone also, Doc wondered? Human nature would have caused him to check the position of any friends he had with him. Doc sat immobile as the brave passed by and disappeared in the direction of his dead companion. Knowing he had to move, Doc angled away from the Indian's path. Not knowing whether the Apache was alone, he couldn't chance running into any warriors straggling behind.

The forest ended on the lip of a steep canyon and Doc hesitated, scanning to his right and left. Should he stay in the trees and hope they weren't full of Apaches, or risk crossing the canyon where he might be seen? For five minutes, he listened to the sounds of the forest, straining to hear anything out of place. The second warrior must have found the dead Indian by now, yet there was no sound, no shout for help or warning. Why? Where was he?

He would stay in the trees, he decided, and standing, he turned to the right. A brushing of leaves sounded a late warning as the second Apache leapt a low shrub and drove Doc over the canyon rim. The warrior clung tight with fierce determination as the two men tumbled down the slope. Yielding to the Indian's grappling maneuvers, Doc relaxed his body to reduce the impact the ground inflicted with each wild tumble. The rolling slowed as the slope flattened out near a creek in the bottom of the canyon. Instantly, Doc reacted with a hard-driven knee into the Indian's groin. The grip loosened but did not break.

Desperate, Doc placed both palms against the warrior's chin and pushed back. As his neck bent over, the Apache growled and squeezed harder. His arms were pinned, and Doc felt his own elbows crushing into his sides. His breath came in short gasps and each time he exhaled the Indian squeezed tighter. Black spots floated before his eyes and Doc knew he would soon pass out. Powered by fear, Doc shoved with all his strength and the Indian's head extended farther back.

Just as he thought he would black out or that the warrior's neck would break, the Indian released him and spun quickly to the side. Leaping up, he aimed a kick at Doc's head. Doc rolled away and took the blow on his shoulder. Scrambling to his feet, he reached out his arms to feel for the Indian. With vision impaired by lack of air, all he could see was a blurry form. Ignoring the pain in his ribs, Doc took several deep breaths and circled.

The warrior lowered his head and dived at Doc's knees, cutting his legs from under him. Moving fast, Doc rolled away, fighting off the Apache's attempt to wrap his arms around him. Both men stood at the same time. Doc's sight cleared and he saw blood flowing freely from a gash along the warrior's scalp. The Indian lifted an arm and wiped at the blood with the back of his hand. They sidestepped around a small invisible circle, arms extended, looking for an advantage.

Lunging forward, the Apache dived again at Doc's knees. Pivoting away, Doc felt a twinge in his ankle. Until then, he'd forgotten about the injury. Determined to be more careful, Doc shifted his weight to the other foot as the Apache rose from the ground and circled once more. The warrior had both a knife and a tomahawk in his sash; why didn't he use them? Unconsciously, Doc's own hands felt along his belt and came away empty—his weapons were gone.

The Indian grinned knowingly and reached forward, fingers spread. He's set on wrestling, Doc realized. Suddenly, the Apache lowered his head and feinted a dive at Doc's knees. Backing rapidly, Doc slipped and almost went down. The Apache charged forward, gripped Doc's shirt, and yanked to the side. Rather than fight the throw, Doc tucked and went with it, rolling twice before he sprang back to his feet. Again, the Indian bent low and Doc set his feet. Feinting toward the knees, the Indian stood and reached for Doc. On impulse, Doc's left fist shot forward and smashed the Apache's mouth. Stunned, the Indian backed a step.

"Okay, then," Doc said aloud, "you can wrestle, but can you fist-fight?"

Understanding the taunt, if not the words, the Apache roared and leapt forward. Doc fired a straight overhand right that caught the Indian coming in and cut his cheek to the bone. He backed a step and then darted forward in a low tackle that surprised Doc. The force of the move drove them both into the creek. The icy water ran less than two feet deep but the current was strong and the Indian lost his grip. Doc stood and felt for balance with his feet. Tiring, and bleeding badly from his head wound, the Apache faced Doc. His hand dropped for the knife at his sash and Doc dived at him. The move caught the Indian flat-footed and both men went into the water. Doc clasped his hand around the Indian's wrist to keep him from drawing the knife. With his free hand, the warrior clawed at Doc's eyes and thrashed wildly to shake him loose.

Doc lost his balance and dropped his hand to steady himself. His fingers closed around a smooth stone. As the knife cleared the water, Doc swung the stone in a wide arc that ended at the Apache's skull. The blade slid from lifeless fingers and sank below the water. Doc staggered to his feet and waded from the creek to drop in the deep grass. When his breathing slowed, he sat up to examine a stinging pain in his side. The Apache had managed to use the knife before he died and Doc inspected the six-inch-long cut. Long, but not deep, he noted with relief.

For the first time, Gunsi admitted to the feeling. Doubt. Great frustration and rage shook him and as though crushed in the embrace of an enormous bear, his chest tightened and forced him to fight for breath. All thought numbed as the fury sought release toward the object of destruction. The warrior's anger flared at dawn with the discovery of Beshe and Ce-col-quin's absence. It simmered throughout the morning as he and the others rushed after them. A building anticipation that the two might capture the white man was all that prevented an uncontrollable wrath.

The anticipation died as he stood over Beshe, leaving in its place a black maddening hatred. Now, staring at the half-submerged body of Ce-col-quin, the spirit of the huge Apache faltered. Was the white man a shadow warrior? Why should he seek to destroy me, Gunsi wondered? The would-be leader of the fierce Llanero had never known uncertainty. Gunsi's strength and ability had failed him, and he cursed his oath to Sotli for revealing such a weakness.

An image of his young brother stirred the embers of Gunsi's heart, rekindling the passion of his spirit. With sudden clarity, the Apache knew the white man was only a man. A cunning man, and dangerous—but not a ghost. With the insight, Gunsi had a vision of a wolf streaking through the grass to snatch a rabbit in its teeth. With a savage shake, the wolf broke the neck of the rabbit and dropped it to the ground. The wolf trotted away, turning once to gaze at the dying rabbit.

The warrior found power in the vision—he would kill the white man! Against a wolf, a rabbit had little defense. It could run, and try to hide. But, as Gunsi knew, a hungry wolf could not be deterred. He embraced his loathing for the white man and, with the hatred, a craving for revenge. He pushed the rage into the far reaches of his spirit and left it there to burn. Like the wolf, he would hunt his prey using patience and cunning. Denying the rage its demand for immediate vengeance would sweeten the satisfaction to come at the capture, and death, of his enemy.

Toh-Yah watched as Gunsi stood in the creek with his eyes closed, swaying against the current. Sunlight sparkled from the water as the stream flowed past. Nothing else moved. Even the forest grew quiet and waited. When at last his friend's eyes opened, they were cold and flat like those of the snake. The remaining Apaches stood back from the creek, whispering among themselves. Toh-Yah and Gunsi lifted Ce-col-quin from the water and laid him on the bank. Ka-a-e-tano and Hok'ee approached and told Gunsi they would stay but the others wanted to return to the village.

"Leave, then!" Gunsi growled at the group. "Run home to your mothers! This is a place for warriors, not children."

The six braves recoiled from the wicked slur. Gunsi continued speaking, now low and deliberate. "We will bury Beshe and Ce-col-quin and then we will kill the white man. You may wait here or leave as your pride permits, but I will not dishonor these brave warriors with the touch of your cowardly hands."

The four warriors carried the two dead men into the forest and when they returned, the shamed warriors were waiting. Ka-a-e-tano picked up the trail at once and Gunsi, Toh-Yah, and Hok'ee trotted after. Without as much as a glance their way to see if they followed, the six warriors fell in behind.

Shep Knorr rested at the bend of the Canadian. During the morning, he had tired of chiding himself over his decision to locate Doc and admitted that he wanted to know how the lost man fared against the Apaches. It wasn't an issue of white against red for Shep; he had more friends among the Indians than he did among his own kind. And why not, he thought? He preferred the unfettered lifestyle of the Indian.

Warriors ate when hungry, slept when tired, and spent the rest of the time doing as they wished. Far from lazy, the life could be brutally hard, especially for the women who must prepare meals, tend crops, raise kids, skin game, and tan the hides for trade. The men filled their days with hunting, fishing, raiding, or exploring—and that was Shep's life. There was always company if you wanted it, a woman, shelter, and fire on a cold night. If one desired solitude, that most important aspect of the mountain man, it lay just over the mountain or across the next river.

Like all men living in wild country, the mountain man was a part of it. He felt the peace of sunrise, the rebirth after a summer rain, the serenity of doing as he did now, resting beside the rushing waters of a river. He accepted these conditions as naturally as he did the forbidding side of the wilderness, for every hour in the mountains was a battle of survival by all forms of life.

In the lush beauty of a tree-covered mountain, the pines and firs grew tall and wide enough to block the sun from the aspen and low-growing shrubs. The soaring flight of an eagle or hawk was, at its base, a pending ambush for a rabbit, squirrel, or pika. Shep often marveled at the sight of a brown bear poised in midriver, deftly wielding a massive paw to toss fish from the water. A stirring sight, but not for the fish, or for a man either if he got too close.

There was no right or wrong to nature except where man was involved, and only then in his dealings with other men. Man might take something, including a life, to gain profit or advantage. He could be motivated to kill by such contrary reasons as hate and love. Many animals are capable of wanton, even impulsive killing, but they don't do so for justice, revenge, or honor. Predators kill because they are killers. Although perhaps they enjoy the hunt as much as man does. It is impossible to miss the timbre of excitement in the howl of a pursuing wolf or in the shriek of a diving eagle.

The struggle between Doc and the Apaches was no different from that of the bear and fish, Shep thought, and it was something he wished to see. The mountain man rose and started west along the river. Shep Knorr was a man who considered himself unequaled in woodcraft and capable in every way of surviving in the mountains. Had he looked deeper into his reasoning, he would have found the real question of his interest. Was Doc lucky, or was he that good?

Doc left the creek and the dead Apache and clambered up the far side of the canyon. A throbbing ache warned that he had overexerted his ankle. Favoring the leg, he entered the trees. A short distance later, he came up against an impenetrable wall of brush and angled off his course to find a way around. Not knowing where the other Apaches were was constantly on his mind. Had the two dead warriors been sent to drive him in a certain direction? Perhaps toward a trap set by the others? If that were true, then why had they pursued so quietly?

The fight thinned down the ranks of the Apaches, but it also forced Doc to abandon his plan to circle back to the wagon road. He intended to stay atop the far side of the canyon and follow the contour west until he found an easy route that would lead him south before doubling back east. With no way to hide the bodies and all signs of the fight, he knew that he must make his move now. Cutting south from the creek took him to the top of the tree-and-shrub-choked ridge. Bleeding from several cuts and scratches, Doc dropped onto a fallen log and rested. Sunlight shone through the branches and the air in the thicket was still and hot. A chipmunk poked his head from beneath the brush and crept forward to search for seeds.

The animal disappeared into the dense growth when Doc lifted a hand to wipe the sweat from his brow. Placing his elbows on his knees, he cradled his forehead in his hands and forced himself to think. Concentrating against fatigue, Doc fought off the exhaustion. He must assume the Indians would find the dead Apaches and be on his trail. They would be coming fast and he needed to find a way out of the thicket and a place to rest. Doc's body jerked and his head came up. He'd almost fallen asleep!

Rising, he shook his head and swung both arms to clear the drowsiness. There were no sounds of pursuit, but he decided against going back to clear the thicket. If the Indians were close, and he must always take for granted they were, they could spot him as he doubled back. Bending low to avoid the branches, he resumed his tramp through the forest. Several times, he was forced to lie flat on his belly and snake through the brush. An hour later the undergrowth cleared and Doc was able to walk upright. He had made less than a half mile and his back and legs ached from the effort of moving crouched over through the brush.

While burrowing through the thicket, it was impossible to keep his bearings, so Doc followed the thinning forest to find an opening and check the sun. Before clearing the last of the trees, he saw another canyon opening before him. Standing on the rim, he glanced at the sun. It was late in the morning, and judging from the slant of the shadows, he now faced—north? Movement on the opposite slope drew his eyes to four Indians making their way into the canyon. Six more Apaches stood together in a small group along the banks of a creek. The same creek where he had killed the last Apache! Doc groaned and dropped to the ground.

He hadn't made it through the brush after all. Unable to keep a straight heading, the brush had slowly turned him back to a point five hundred yards from where he'd entered. Too tired to run and too exhausted to plan, he merely watched the scene below with detached curiosity. As he'd suspected, they picked up his trail without trouble and headed straight up the slope for the forest. Doc twisted around and looked behind. The thick blanket of pine needles hid his trail from the brush. That they might be able to follow the tortuous route through the thicket wasn't in doubt. There would be broken branches and numerous scuff marks to point the way. The question was, would they choose to follow or would they separate and scout the edges looking for his exit point? If they chose the latter, they could be on his trail in a matter of minutes.

Doc considered dropping back into the canyon and following the course of the creek. It meandered east and the going would be easier and faster. It was a risk. If the Apaches should find his trail too soon, they would have no trouble spotting him in the canyon. Looking to his right, Doc saw only more of the same dense forest as lay behind him. To go that direction might leave him trapped. He surely couldn't go back or left, and all that remained was the canyon.

Doc crawled forward onto a large flat rock and rolled onto his stomach. Sliding both legs over the side, he gripped the rock with his hands and swung down. Letting go, he dropped a few feet to the sloping side of the canyon. At the base of the rock, he saw a narrow cleft perhaps three feet high and ten feet wide. Fearful of disturbing a snake or badger, Doc carefully stuck his head in to determine the depth. The opening sloped downward on a slight angle for about five feet. A call from somewhere above sent Doc scrambling into the fissure. Reaching out, he brushed away the marks of his landing, sifting a handful of sand over the spot before easing farther back from the opening.

CHAPTER EIGHT

AKULE NOTICED THE RAGGED HOLE IN THE BRUSH and bent down to investigate. Certain that he'd found Shadow's trail, he called for the others and drew his tomahawk. Hok'ee and Ka-a-e-tano were close enough to hear the call. Hok'ee was sent to gather the other searchers while Ka-a-e-tano set to the task of trailing the white man. True signs of the white man's passing vanished in the covering of the forest floor so it was more by guesswork than skill that the tracker stood on the large rock overlooking the canyon when Gunsi joined him.

"Why would he do this?" Gunsi asked.

"I do not know," Ka-a-e-tano replied. "To return to this spot with us so close behind seems foolish, and Shadow does not make foolish mistakes."

Toh-Yah and the rest of the group drew near and listened. Gunsi asked, "Where did he go?"

"It is a guess, but I believe he went down the canyon." Ka-a-e-tano pointed at the ground. "There are no tracks in the deep leaves to follow. He could have dropped from the ridge anywhere along this side."

Gunsi ordered the warriors to fan out along the ridge overlooking the canyon and, when all were in place, he waved them to begin their descent. He stood on the large rock and watched as his men slipped over the ledge to hunt for tracks on their way to the bottom. Satisfied the search would cover as much ground as possible, Gunsi bent down and leapt from the rock.

Doc listened to the conversation that took place above him and wished for an understanding of the language. His nerves settled as the sounds of retreating footsteps reached his ears. Two feet clad in moccasins thumped suddenly to ground just outside the opening and Doc recoiled and rammed his back into the rock at the rear of the fissure. In his terror, the narrow cleft became a coffin. Doc held his breath and stared at the unmoving legs.

Gunsi stood and watched the warriors. He expected one of them to cut the white man's sign even though Ka-a-e-tano was unsure of where the trail might be. Most of them were halfway to the bottom, moving slowly as they scoured the ground, yet no call had come. His own eyes dropped to scan the dirt at his feet as he commanded his legs into motion. The legs remained rigid as Gunsi snapped his head up and around to scan the rock above him. He examined the portion of the forest that was visible to him while he sought to home in on the feeling. The white man watched him, Gunsi was certain. It was the same feeling he'd experienced on the banks of Raton Creek when the white man sat under the pine and watched them search. And now, he did so again.

The Apache returned his vision to the canyon and probed every rock, swell, and tree. The white man could not be behind him on the ridge, Gunsi knew. Not after the thorough search they'd made. He must be in the canyon—but where? The warrior closed his eyes and opened his mind to the answer.

Toh-Yah paused and looked along the line of searching Apaches. At the gap created by Gunsi's absence, he turned his head upslope to see the warrior standing in front of the large rock. From his vantage point below,

Toh-Yah could not see the dark, thin opening of the cleft at the base of the rock. As Toh-Yah watched, Gunsi's head ducked forward in a slow movement until his chin rested upon his chest and his shoulders folded inward. Toh-Yah felt the icy touch brush along his consciousness—Shadow was here!

Unable to shake free of the feeling the white man was behind him, Gunsi opened his eyes. Far below, Toh-Yah stared up at him. As understanding flashed between the warriors, Toh-Yah nodded his head and turned slightly as if to look downslope. Gunsi bent over and dashed twenty feet to his left then stood to look down the canyon. After a brief moment, he again moved in a hunched run twenty feet farther and stood. Gunsi made deliberate movements with his head toward the canyon floor. Toh-Yah watched the trees beyond the ridge from the corner of his eye.

Both Indians avoided looking directly into the trees. Gunsi's strange movement was meant to confuse the white man. In order to see the purpose of the crouching run Shadow might reveal himself by a sudden movement. Twice more, Gunsi tried the tactic and always he moved left. If the white man were up there, he lay in tight cover as he observed the search. Such cover would not allow a wide view and at some point, he must shift position to keep Gunsi in sight.

When Gunsi stood the fourth time, the feeling was gone. He ran up the slope and into the trees as Toh-Yah did the same. Three hundred feet separated the two as they bolted over the ridge. The Apaches carefully scoured the pine and brush until they stood together on the large rock overlooking the canyon.

"I know he is here," Gunsi muttered, "or was here . . . I felt him."

"So did I," Toh-Yah replied. "But he has vanished again."

Gunsi cast a disapproving glance at his friend. "You too, Toh-Yah. You believe the white man is a spirit?"

"No, but he is strong. I would not have thought one man could cause the death of so many Llanero."

"Strong or not, I will catch him," Gunsi stated.

The warriors dropped from the rock and joined the waiting Apaches at the creek where, after a quick discussion, they moved down the canyon.

Doc waited, unable to take a breath until the legs suddenly bolted away. He watched as the Apache ran several paces crouched over. Once the warrior was far enough from the fissure to see him clearly, Doc averted his eyes to watch peripherally. He recognized the huge Apache as the Indian from the creek, the one who had felt Doc's eyes before. The Indian stood and stared into the canyon, then repeated the process three more times before he ran uphill and disappeared from sight.

Several minutes later, his heart again beat faster as he listened to the guttural conversation taking place overhead. When both Apaches dropped before the opening Doc was certain they had found him, but even before panic could set in, the legs trotted downslope. The slight shake in his arms turned into a full tremor as realization set in. They hadn't found him after all! Surprised and confused, he saw that he held a knife and tomahawk in his shaking hands. Doc couldn't recall drawing the weapons.

An hour later, he crawled to the opening and looked out. An elk stood at the creek, head turned down the canyon. A moment later, the head dropped to the water for a drink. From the trees across the canyon, three more elk appeared and started for the creek. Doc slid back into the cleft and relaxed. There were no Indians in the canyon. He let another hour pass before he felt safe enough to crawl from the fissure and climb atop the ridge.

Doc reentered the brush through the same hole he'd exited earlier. Picking a tree trunk ten feet away, barely visible through the dense growth, he crawled toward it. At the trunk, he turned and lined up the opening and tree, then picked out anther trunk along the same line. By crawling from tree trunk to tree trunk, he traveled, more or less, in a straight line.

In thirty minutes, he was tired and sweating. The bramblelike growth grabbed at the rifle, bow, and quiver on his back and the branches tore at his face and hands. Ten more minutes passed, then twenty and still the growth surrounded him. As he pushed past the large trunk of a ponderosa pine the brush thinned somewhat, then stopped altogether as Doc scrambled free.

He rolled onto his back and stared at the patches of blue sky visible through the pine branches. Breathing deeply of the clean, clear air, he allowed his tired legs and shoulders to unwind. There was a sudden darkening in the forest as the sun hid behind a blowing cloud. Doc flicked his eye toward the patchy sky and took in the black, boiling cloud. Rain right now would be a blessing, he thought hopefully. He'd separated from the Indians for a time, the canyon held no tracks of his, and the Apaches were now down to cutting his sign by luck. That is, unless one of them decided to come back and crawl around the brush for fun.

The way out of the canyon where he'd lost the Apaches led to the east, but where they might have gone from there was a guess, and for Doc, trusting to luck was becoming mighty chancy. The way he looked at it, he'd used up three lifetimes of luck in the last few days. He needed to be sure which way they'd gone, and then he'd go the other direction.

Sitting up, Doc dug in his pouch for the last of the venison. He built a small pile of the driest wood he could find and sparked it to life with the flint. The wood gave off little smoke, and what there was was quickly lost in the branches and darkening sky. He broiled and ate the meat before stomping out the fire. Satisfying his hunger left only a nagging thirst to deal with. Doc's last water came just after sunrise and the long day and belly crawl through the brush had used it up. He gathered his gear and checked the weapons. Not willing to trust his life to a rifle battered by the grappling brush, he carefully inspected the gun. Setting it aside, he examined the bow, then the quiver of arrows. He cut the points from three that had damaged feathers and discarded the shafts. In addition to the pair of knives and tomahawks taken from the Indians, he had three balls for the rifle and twelve arrows for the bow. It was enough; he'd counted ten Apaches in the canyon.

Doc moved out along the top of the ridge. A brief scout after his meal revealed a second canyon that paralleled the one he'd left, and he figured the ridge was less than a quarter mile wide. If this ridge held to the pattern of the surrounding country, those two canyons would join up somewhere to the east, he realized. With any luck—there's that word again, Doc thought wryly—the ridge might jut out far enough that he could use it for an observation post and spot the Indians.

Most would have seen the situation as one man against ten, and just four days ago Doc might have felt the same, but now, he viewed things differently. He had ten enemies and fifteen chances to kill them if they insisted on it, more if he recovered additional arrows. Since his fight with the last two Apaches, a slow anger began to build. Many men had lost their lives while others were wounded for no good reason that he could see. At the mountain park where it all started, hadn't he tried to flee? He made no challenge over the deer and offered no threat to the Indians. Yet they had attacked him, and continued to hunt and attack.

Doc knew on his first day in the mountains that it was a dangerous place and he accepted the risks. The Apaches lived here and knew the high country better than he did. They were determined to run him out of the mountains, or kill him, and Doc realized he had no intention of leaving. With every step he took, he became more a part of the land and it a part of him. No, he would not leave, or be run out. There was room enough for all. He didn't begrudge the Indians their right to live here and he claimed the same right.

Some said the Indians viewed the white men as conquerors, and there was a heaping measure of truth to that. The United States was growing and land in the East was shrinking fast. To the many who sought bigger opportunities, ample land, and wide spaces, the West called to them from across the prairie. Doc didn't believe the Indian must leave for the white man to flourish. In Missouri, he'd known the Iowa, Illinois, Kansa, Omaha, and Osage. They had fought at first, but over time they adjusted to each other. From the whites, the Indians learned more of farming and gained access to better tools and weapons. From the Indians, the white men learned to live with the country, to coax a harvest from the soil instead of struggling for one.

In this manner, both cultures took the best the other had to offer and made it their own. Not as individual peoples, but as one people. For neither remained as when they first met. Both changed, and both became better. There were and always would be among the Indians and white men those with hatred for the other, those men and women for whom change was deemed unnatural. It was not unique to the red or white conflict, for both fought savagely among themselves, and had for centuries. More often than not, land was a result of a conflict and not the cause. Most wars occurred over religious or philosophical differences and the combatants' unwillingness to tolerate those differences. To focus on the negative aspects of your neighbor denied you the opportunity to enjoy the positive. Some men fought to build empires to satisfy an overblown image of their worth. It happened in the Americas just as it did in Europe, Africa, and Asia.

Many whites pointed to their manufacturing, exploration, and great cities as proof of superiority and intellect. But to Doc, it had more to do with population. The Indians sparsely inhabited two vast continents during a time when Europe grew crowded. All men were clever, and when you piled them together in a small area, they were going to come up with ways to trade for or make what they needed in order to survive. *Civilization* was just a high-toned word for having enough farmers, hunters, fishermen, and traders so that other folks had the opportunity to build their dreams and imaginings into commerce.

The western tribes warred over the white man's custom of buying deeded land. They held a belief that no one could own the land; it was the land that owned all people. As individuals, that held true for the Indian, but the distinction blurred somewhat when they viewed it collectively. Tribes migrated, and when they found a country they liked, they had to fight the tribe that already occupied the land. Call it what you will, ownership, occupation, possession, or control; it all amounted to the same thing. If you had it now, it's only because you took it from someone else.

His feet made no sound on the pine needles that would disturb the natural voice of the forest and Doc reveled in the solitude, though he felt anything but alone. The wind spoke to him of the approaching storm in whispers that grew stronger by the moment. Rabbits and chipmunks rose to peer at him before scurrying under cover and a tassel-eared squirrel paused in his meal of pine twigs to scold Doc for the intrusion. From the canyon came the shrill whistle of the small pika. The peculiar call of the turkey mixed with those of a dozen other birds. All of the creatures spoke, but not at once. As if by some agreed-upon politeness, the calls were sporadic, seemingly intended to convey messages without disrupting the serenity that they all enjoyed.

The trees came to a stop a hundred yards from the end of the ridge. A littering of rocks and a few shrubs were all the cover that remained. At this point, the ridge was less than sixty feet wide and tapered rapidly to a blunt tip maybe ten feet across. From within the last of the pines, Doc surveyed the canyons and the larger valley into which they emptied. When he detected no movement, he hunched over and moved down the center of the ridge, dropping to his belly and crawling the last few yards to the edge. He peeked over the side and saw a wide ledge just below the lip. On impulse, he slipped over the side and sat on the ledge with his back to the rock. The deerskin shirt he wore blended in with the rock face and Doc felt better about this spot than he did leaving his head outlined atop the ridge.

Struggling against the building storm, the midafternoon sun cast a shadow over the eastern face where Doc sat, making it that much harder to see him. Black clouds continued to gather overhead and their passing between earth and sun released large dark silhouettes to roam across the valley floor. Doc relaxed in the shade and coolness of the rock and scanned the valley, now fully open to inspection beneath him. It was several moments before he spotted them, over a mile away and working to the east. From his height and distance, the Apaches were small and might have been indistinguishable except for their movement. But once he found them, the crisp mountain air made it easy to keep watch. Spread out in a ragged line almost a half mile wide, far too wide for a concentrated search, the Apaches were sacrificing thoroughness for speed.

Even as he began to relax, some loose thought nagged for his attention. Doc idly watched the retreating Indians as he allowed his mind to grope for the elusive thought. Having no luck, he pushed aside the vague notion and laid his head back to rest against the rock. The tension slid from him as he watched the Indians recede farther. He let his eyes close as a cool wind played over his face and triggered his thirst with the scent of rain. Suddenly, his eyes snapped open and his head lunged free of the rock. Leaning forward, Doc peered at the distant Apaches. Eight! He counted again—there were only eight men moving in the valley. A slight movement is often easier detected with the corner of the eye than by direct observation so, for a long moment, he watched the horizon above the searchers. Two of the Indians were not in the valley!

Doc cocked his ears to listen for sounds of movement. He heard the thrumming wings of a hummingbird and the twittering song of cliff swallows. Then the whistle of a pika in the canyon to his right echoed up from the canyon floor. Several more whistles followed and Doc knew something, or someone, was moving in the canyon. Only six to eight inches long, the pika had thick fur and stubby legs, ears, and tail. Like the marmots, which often lived nearby, the pikas lived in colonies and used a warning system of whistles and sharp squeaks to spread an alarm among the group. When several sounded at once, it meant they feared danger.

Doc crawled to his right along the ledge, careful to keep his head low. When the canyon opened to view, he stopped and watched. The pikas were gone, hidden among the rocks or beneath their piles of cut grass and flowers. A fly lit on his cheek and Doc caught himself before he waved a hand at it; instead, he blew lightly from the corner of his mouth until the fly moved on. A click of stone on stone preceded the sight of the Apache as he moved from a sun-soaked slope toward a shaded area. Apparently tired of waiting in the still heat of the canyon, he'd decided to find a more comfortable lookout.

So, there was number nine, thought Doc, and number ten would be near the mouth of the canyon to his left. He crept back to his original position and climbed quietly to the top of the ridge. A loose stone at the top gave way under his hand and Doc feared it would fall. If it did, the spotters would know right where he was. His fingers tightened around the stone and held on while he struggled up and over the lip one-handed. Safe on top, he lifted the loose stone and laid it back from the edge. He hunched over and sped across the open ridge to the trees, where he straightened up and without pause trotted through the pine and fir until he encountered the brush.

Making a choice to skirt the brush on the south side, he hurried along the top of the canyon. He would follow the rim to the beginning of the canyon then loop around it. If the contours were favorable, he would head south and east from there. Assuming he could pass the Apaches, it was too late to meet the wagons by heading due east. By the time he could get to the Trail, the wagons would be long past and Doc still intended to meet the wagon road somewhere out ahead of the wagons and let them roll to him. He would have to range farther south to make that happen. A few large drops of rain struck him and he raised his face to the sky. The dark clouds tinged with green. This was not a good night to be on the mountain. Far to the north, the cloud bank lit briefly and then again as lightning raged within the storm. No more drops fell, and Doc hurried on.

CHAPTER NINE

Tar-he flicked his eye toward the canyon rim overhead and wondered what movement drew his attention. At the upper end of the canyon, there was little cover among the boulder-strewn sides and bottom, so he stood still on the shadowed side of a lightning-struck pine trunk and waited. Shadow appeared briefly as he drifted among the trees atop the canyon. Tar-he gripped his bow and pulled an arrow from the quiver.

Suddenly, Shadow stopped and looked into the canyon depths. Tar-he had known fear his entire life, but never like this. Adrenaline coursed through his body, raising every hair to stand on end. Surely, Shadow could not see him, he thought, not if he didn't move into the sunlight. His frightened mind asked a question he couldn't answer—could a spirit see into darkness?

The range was well within his ability with a bow. The exposed white man was an easy target and he could fit the arrow and release it within seconds. Still, he could not move. The bow and the arrow shook from the tremors in his hands and Tar-he could not tear his gaze from Shadow.

The Apache was a lowly warrior who had never killed an enemy, at least not one hale and standing on two feet. He had taken two scalps from men he'd finished killing after another warrior had injured them and moved on. One of the two had been unconscious when Tar-he found him. He was not a brave man and he knew it. It was why he stayed on the fringe during the few battles in which he'd been involved, moving in after the bulk of the danger had passed. Tar-he never volunteered to participate in raids and only went along after being called by name in front of others.

The Apache had been glad to volunteer for the duty that thrust him into this unexpected position for he, like all the others, believed Shadow was far away to the east. When Toh-Yah had thought to search the small connecting canyon for sign, Tar-he stepped forward quickly to accept the task so that he could stay away from the expected danger out on the wide valley. None of the other warriors offered to stay, though Tar-he knew several who where as frightened as he. They were fools, he'd thought, in letting their pride outweigh their safety. Gunsi had to order Akule to stay at the canyon mouth. Akule had saved face among the warriors, but Tar-he knew the Indian was relieved at being left behind.

Now his cowardice seemed to mock him and he longed for the safety of the distant group. His fear refused to listen to the feeble bravery in his heart calling for action. Then he locked eyes with Shadow!

Doc stopped on the canyon rim and snapped his focus onto the rocky ground below. Someone watched from down there, he could feel it. He fought the instinct to step back into the trees or to drop lower, for the movement might give him away if he had not yet been located. Instead, he let his eyes wander over the boulders, searching for whomever, or whatever, watched him. He had accounted for all ten of the Apaches, and the probability that it was a cougar, mountain goat, bear, or some other creature that attracted his attention was possible.

A flash of white drew his gaze to the tall, charred trunk. A moment later, the flash reappeared and Doc saw clearly the white-tipped eagle feather blown by a slight wind. The area, obscured in the evening shadows of the cliff, and the trunk itself, was difficult to probe. He focused his sight at the place where he'd seen the feather and stared. Slowly, as his eyes adjusted, the dim outline of the warrior took shape. Doc followed the shape upward until he detected the dim white spots of the Apache's eyes.

Had they joined forces with more Indians? He knew, or thought he knew, the watcher was an Indian because of the bow. No, he reasoned, this must be the tenth Apache. He had assumed they guarded both canyons, but there would be no need to watch the one they'd just searched. Instead, one had searched the smaller canyon while the other waited at the mouth in case the search flushed him out.

These thoughts passed his mind in an instant and left him wondering. Why hadn't the Indian attacked? The tree was less than one hundred feet away and only twenty feet lower than where he stood and there was no way the warrior could fail to see him. As Doc, motionless, stared hard at the shape, the Indian retreated from the shadows, then turned and fled down the canyon. Confused, Doc resumed his trek to the south. No longer concerned with stealth, he set off at an easy run along the dim ridge. They would pick up his trail after the warrior reported his sighting and he wanted to separate from them with as much distance as he could before dark.

"He saw me and disappeared," Tar-he lied to Akule. "He was too far for my bow or I would have killed him."

Akule doubted Tar-he's boast, but not that the Apache had seen Shadow. The panting warrior was clearly frightened. Akule bent and gathered a pile of cut grass, thanking the hardworking pika for the supply and apologizing for the need to destroy the animal's home. With two pieces of flint, he soon had a fire blazing high enough that the searchers in the valley would see it. An hour later, the group trotted to the fire.

Not trusting Tar-he, Akule spoke first. "He claims to have seen Shadow."

Tar-he had regained his composure and in the comfort of the crowd, he told the story he'd prepared while waiting. His version added distance between him and Shadow, and told of a dangerous and silent approach made to capture the white man.

"Somehow, he must have seen me," Tar-he said. His face revealed a look of dejection any stage actor would have admired. "When I reached the place where I could wound him with an arrow, he was gone. I would have followed him, but I knew that you"—he glanced at Gunsi—"would want to know, so I came here to light the signal fire." Akule threw a hard look toward Tar-he at the untruth of the fire, but Tar-he avoided looking at anyone other than Gunsi or Toh-Yah.

Gunsi nodded at the warrior, and then looked up the canyon. He knew Tar-he, and he knew the fainthearted Indian would never track the white man on his own, but at least he'd seen him. It's just as well, Gunsi thought; the white man would have killed Tar-he with ease. By ending the fruitless search in the valley, they had saved valuable time. The lesser warriors were growing tired of the hunt, and ever more fearful. Had the white man killed Tar-he, worthless as he was, it might have been all the weak ones needed to abandon the chase.

Toh-Yah, in a move to get ahead of Shadow, led four warriors out of the canyon and into the valley where they turned south and traveled rapidly along the flank of the mountains. Gunsi and the remaining braves went up the canyon to follow the white man's trail. The tree-covered mountains hid the storm from the view of trailing Apaches and it hit them hard without warning, a howling wind driving great sheets of rain that pelted the warriors and sent them scurrying for cover under the trees. Moments later, they fled for the rocky crevices of the canyon as fist-sized chunks of hail shredded the forest canopy.

* * *

Ferguson saw the approaching storm and sighed. A huge storm, it stretched across the northern sky with a wide, gray sheet of rain hanging below the boiling black clouds. Such a storm would turn every draw and ravine into a roiling death trap. He eyed the short distance from his camp to Raton Creek and judged it enough. They camped on a low hummock covered with grass and no trees. Lightning stabbed the earth with frightening regularity. Eerily, there was no thunder; the only sound was the increasing wind pushing a strong scent of rain. The wagon master rubbed his chin and looked about. There was no place to go, no place to hide. They were too far from the mountains to hope the high peaks would draw the lightning and there were no trees of any height to help in that regard. The soil in the valley ran from three to six feet deep over the underlying bedrock and trees couldn't grow. His alternative was to move the camp to low ground.

Todd Bracken rose from his spot beside the fire and wandered over. "Looks like a bad night comin'."

"Way I see it," Ferguson said, "we got us two choices. Though it seems like we got no choice a'tall. We can stay here and hope those wagons don't draw the lightning, or we can head for lower ground and hope the water don't wash us away."

"Be best to stay put, I'm thinkin'," replied Bracken.

"How so?"

"The ground in this valley is likely to be a sea of mud come mornin' and it'll just be worse in the low spots. You'd have to double-team the wagons to get them to high ground, if a'tall." He raised an arm and pointed. "It'll be slow goin', but we can stay atop this hogback and foller it east a-ways. Ground gets a bit rockier over that way and the ox'll have a better time of pullin' them heavy wagons."

"What about the lightning?"

Bracken lifted his eyebrows and shrugged. "Cain't be helped. It's goin' to be a miserable night up here or down yonder and that's fer certain sure. We can stay here or we can move; either way, it's a guess and men might get kilt. But when mornin' comes, those of us still livin' have got to pick up and move on. Be a whole heap easier startin' from up here than down there somewhere."

The wagon master exhaled sharply and removed his hat to rub his forehead with a powerful hand. Replacing the hat, he spoke with resignation. "Makes sense, Todd." Ferguson felt a slight shiver, uncertain whether it was from the dropping temperature or the detached manner in his friend's tone. "What if we moved downslope just far enough to get the wagons under the crest of the hill?"

"Good idea," Todd replied. "I'll see to it."

Ferguson looked back to view the storm. Astonished at the speed of the oncoming squall, he ran to help the scrambling men. They finished the move in the teeth of the biting wind and rain, and just had time to cower under the wagons before the hail hit.

The only man in the country who'd been happy to see the approaching storm, Doc was about to change his mind. Drenched and cold, he huddled beneath a deadfall of spruce, victims of some long-ago disaster. He was partway down a steep slope that faced away from the storm, but it offered little protection. The onslaught of large hailstones had been brief, but not so brief that it hadn't been painful. Doc had pressed on through the rain and sought cover only when the hail began. It took but a minute to find and crawl beneath the deadfall, but it was time enough to take three direct hits and several glancing blows from the hard ice.

He bled from a gash on the back of his head; the force of the hit had knocked him to the ground. He was still woozy from the impact and hoped he'd avoided a concussion. More troubling than his head was the blow that hammered his left arm below the shoulder. Numbed at first, the feeling in the arm was beginning to return with sharp stinging pricks racing from bicep to fingertips.

Doc opened the neck of the buckskin shirt and pulled it down over his shoulder to look at the arm. The large dark bruise revealed itself with each flash of lightning. He flexed the arm a few times and learned it wasn't broken, but it hurt. The injury wouldn't have much effect in shooting the rifle, but he could only hope he would be able to grasp and hold the bow while he drew the string. With just three balls for the rifle, the bow was now his main weapon. He continued to work the arm while waiting for the rain to slacken. His ankle had recovered quickly from use; maybe the arm would too. The high country was proving to be a demanding mistress, he thought grimly. She aided him by sending the storm to erase his tracks, then took payment in the form of the bruised arm and injured skull.

Still, the Apaches would not be able to track him any longer; they would have to find him again. Having an idea of his direction might narrow the ground they must search, but it would still slow them down. Abruptly, Doc decided to head east. The Indians were behind him now, somewhere between his deadfall and the canyon, and that left open the way to the wagon road. If he did hit the Trail north of the wagons, it wouldn't be by much and the muddy ground would clearly show the passing of the wagon train. If he saw nothing on the Trail, he would wait, but if he saw deep, fresh ruts, he would turn and follow them. With the thought of reaching the wagons, Doc was excited, and suddenly anxious to return to the company of men. He longed for a place to sleep without fear, for a place to walk without pursuit.

As he watched the muddy flow of water over the ground, he wondered if the previous disaster was a mudslide. The few remaining trees and sparse vegetation on the slope weren't enough to anchor the soil. Doc glanced down toward the bottom of the slope to see a massive mound of earth blocking the canyon. Barren limbs and trunks from a forest of timber lay jumbled among the mound like the exposed and shattered ribs of a great beast. Shuddering, he stared at the carnage. He'd move now; the slope was no place to be during a heavy rain. Slogging across the hillside, he hunched his shoulders against the rain and set a line for the closest timber. He had one consolation—at least moving during the frigid rain would wipe away the sign of his sudden change in direction.

Doc covered two weaving miles through the drenched forest, scrambling over fallen logs and beneath brush. The storm intensified, and if not for the canopy, travel would be impossible. Treetops whipped violently in the blasting gusts of wind, while rain fell in the scattered openings and ran freely from the limbs overhead. At ground level, the forest broke the wind. And the rain, though cold and persistent, wasn't blinding. He paused at a spot where a view of the wide valley should have been present, but all he saw was the slant of rain and gray mist.

A sudden prickle of his scalp propelled him into a lunging face-down dive for the mud. The prickle grew to a vibration followed by heat and a crackling explosion. When he lifted his face from the mud, the top forty feet of a towering ponderosa pine, sheared in half by the lightning, toppled toward the ground a dozen yards in front of him. Smaller trees briefly held the great weight before they too splintered, then buckled and fell. The bolt had traveled through the trunk until the sap and moisture overheated and exploded, leaving a frayed trunk thirty feet tall. As the rain washed the mud from his face, Doc rolled to a sitting position and watched the rain douse the flames atop the trunk. The air, previously heavy with moisture, now felt thin and smelled heavily of sulfur.

He'd seen bad weather before. During the prairie crossing, two violent storms had forced the men to abandon their wagons, run back along the Trail for fifty yards, and lie prone in the bottom of the ruts. They'd fared well, though, as the lightning passed by without striking the wagons. One night in Missouri, when he was twelve, a bolt of lightning blew away part of the stone chimney of his house. But before there had always been shelter—a house, or a low spot on a barren prairie to protect him from the worst of the lightning. Here there was nothing. The low spots, ravines, gorges, and canyons lay beneath a frothy rush of water, and all about him the tall trees beckoned for a strike.

Lightning hitting the trees was bad enough, but the explosion terrified him. If the bolts made it closer to ground before the trunk overheated, the flying shards of wood and bark would be deadly to any creature on the ground nearby. There was nothing else to do except keep moving. That and be ready to drop if he felt his scalp prickle again.

Gunsi led his bedraggled band from the crevices and boulders at the upper end of the canyon and guided them over the top. Their shelter protected them from the hail, but not the rain. There was no relief from the downpour, and as the hail seemed to have passed, Gunsi decided it was better to be wet and moving than simply sitting in the rain and mud. His men were sullen. He spoke no words of encouragement to them, words that should come from a leader. Inwardly, he sneered at their weakness. Wasn't he also hungry, tired, wet, and cold? With the loss of his brother, hadn't he suffered more than they had?

Gunsi dwelled on these questions and vowed that he would not tolerate such weakness when he became chief. He would lead many raids, he thought. He would train his warriors to be tireless, fearless, and merciless to their enemies. It didn't occur to Gunsi that such brutal men might tend to be harder to control. Or that men bred for battle and conquest would become a threat to his continued leadership. The group trudged south in silence.

* * *

Toh-Yah found cover for his men under an overhanging shelf of rock. They suffered through the hailstorm, exposed to its fury with no place to hide. After they'd pushed fast through the hail, then through the stinging rain, the shelf was a welcome respite for the downcast and wet warriors. Under the overhang, the men saw to their many abrasions. Ka-a-e-tano was hobbling from a hailstone that struck his knee, laying open the skin. Akule removed his shirt to reveal two large bruises on his back. They were painful but not debilitating. The third warrior, Alchise, and Toh-Yah escaped serious injury, but each rubbed the tender areas where hailstones had grazed him.

The overhang, located at the junction of the canyon and valley, was open on three sides. Toh-Yah squatted, staring into the gloom. A gust of wind covered him with a fine spray of cold rain yet he did not move. He peered into the dull gray curtain, trying to find signs the storm might be waning. His mind was ever more occupied with a growing unease. Alchise discovered a pile of dried brush and twigs, remnants of some small animal's home, and prepared to light a fire. Near the overhang, he broke several branches from a fallen tree and dragged them inside. The wet wood sputtered and hissed as the flaming kindling licked at the damp bark.

The storm increased its intensity and Toh-Yah withdrew to the feeble warmth of the struggling fire.

CHAPTER TEN

THE COMING SUN TINGED THE THIN LAYER OF WISPY CLOUDS a pale pink. Doc awoke and rubbed hard at his eyes. Four hours before, the rain had stopped and he finally gave in to exhaustion. Finding a place to sleep, he'd curled up and dropped off. He recalled being uncomfortably cold, but even the night air and damp clothing had not been enough to overcome his sleep. The mud dried on his face, leaving a thin crust that covered his eyelids. Using fingernails to scrape away the last of the mud, he winced at a sudden pain in his left arm. Tugging down the deerskin shirt, Doc was stunned to see a huge purple-black bruise extending from elbow to shoulder.

Gingerly, he began to flex and stretch the arm. The movement created sickness in his stomach, but he clenched his jaw and continued to work the injury. Scared, he spoke aloud. "Well boy, you may have got yourself killed now. Chances were slim enough before, but there ain't no way a one-armed man can pull a bowstring." He placed his left hand on a nearby tree and rubbed the trunk. The feel of the rough bark was a relief. "At least it ain't numb." He didn't know if the sense of touch was unusual for an injury of his type, but he did know that a dead, numb limb wouldn't be a good sign.

Slowly, the stiffness began to ease and the pain, though persistent, seemed to slacken. Another ten minutes of steady movement removed the stiffness and made the pain tolerable. Reaching out, he grasped a large heavy stone with his right hand and, turning it palm-up, hefted it a few times, feeling the weight. Closing his eyes, and whispering a silent prayer, he switched the stone to his left hand and lifted. The stone rose easily.

Joy washed over him, and he tossed the stone down the slope. It was the ugliest and deepest bruise he'd ever had, ever seen for that matter, but that was all it was—a bruise. He'd have to pay close attention to the arm to keep it limber and ready for use. Somewhat rested and wildly relieved, he led his mind back to the pursuing Apaches and considered his options.

They would be coming, of that he held no doubt. Whatever bee he'd put under their bonnet wasn't likely to fly away because of the storm. Those Indians wanted him dead. A sigh escaped him. Why was he so important to them? There were other white men in mountains. Not many perhaps, but enough so that the Indians knew they were here. What was it that made him so different? Some of those men, like Shep Knorr, had been around for years.

Was it more of the Croft luck? His father, as good a man as lived, seemed snakebit nonetheless. He always walked just one step behind prosperity. Close enough to see it, but never quite catching up to it. No, he reasoned, it wasn't bad luck that dogged Doc through the mountains. If anything, he had an angel resting on his shoulder. By all rights, his scalp should be hanging on a bow or lance right now.

Forcing his thoughts to the problem of escape, he pushed aside the puzzle of why and focused instead on the how. How to stay alive and how to get back to the company. The Indians were close behind him, but they had no trail to follow. Like a chalk rag over a schoolroom slate, the storm wiped the mountains clean of all tracks. He'd been traveling south when the Indian spotted him atop the canyon and they would follow right along. The Apaches would expect him to turn toward the Santa Fe Trail, but now, they wouldn't know when or where.

After he'd turned east at the deadfall on the barren slope, it continued to rain for several more hours. There would be no sign on that hillside, if the hillside still existed at all. Doc remembered the sheet of water flowing ankle deep down the slope, turned brown by the topsoil it carried away, further weakening the mountainside.

Lost in his dark thoughts, Gunsi reached the lip of the slope and stepped down without pause. He'd taken two steps when the soil shifted under his feet and both legs flew into the air. The warrior landed flat on his back and began to slide rapidly down the steep slope. Hok'ee, Tar-he, and the others watched in shock as Gunsi sped from sight. No sound came from below and the four men looked at each other.

"Let's go," said Hok'ee, and he turned and placed his foot on the slope. The young Indian settled his weight by working his foot into the mud. He took several cautious steps before he realized the others weren't following. Looking up, he repeated, "Let's go."

Tar-he spoke quickly. "If we all go down together, one could slip and take down everyone. I will find another route. That way at least one of us will be sure to make it uninjured."

A look of scorn from Hok'ee caused Tar-he to defend his statement. "Gunsi may be hurt, and it will do him no good if we are unable to help him." Without waiting for a reply, he spun and moved off along the canyon rim.

Hok'ee's gaze switched from Tar-he to the two other warriors. Neither spoke.

"Go with him or come with me, I have no more time to waste," said Hok'ee as he lifted his foot. A few yards farther downslope he paused and looked up. The two men were nowhere in sight. Lucky for all three of them that it was not them lying at the bottom of the canyon, he thought. Gunsi wouldn't have bothered to help them at all.

The young Apache picked his way with care, pausing to rest at the deadfall that had sheltered Doc. After a moment, he resumed and reached the bottom of the canyon. A quick scan left and right failed to reveal Gunsi. The rain, though lighter, fell persistently and the heavy cloud cover deepened the darkness. Both made it difficult to see far in the bottom of the canyon. Tar-he and the others would be coming from the left, so Hok'ee angled to the right.

The bottom of the canyon was a jumbled pile of mud, rock, and shattered trees—remnants of a prior slide. With difficulty, Hok'ee made his way over and around the jutting logs and branches. Five minutes of clinging to branches and sliding through mud brought him to the edge of the slide. Gratefully, he stepped onto the grass-covered canyon bottom and slid down to rest against a tree trunk.

Gunsi must have tumbled to the left of his search, he reasoned. Tar-he and the others would find him. Hok'ee realized that he didn't care whether the huge Apache was found dead or alive. He'd had enough of Gunsi's bullying leadership and obsession with Shadow.

To the east, Tar-he and the two Apaches stood at the canyon bottom peering through the rain across the ravaged slope. "We should go look," said Elu, a broad-faced warrior, short in stature and esteem. Elu was experiencing a newfound interest in his rank. His father, a worthy warrior with many songs, died during the winter leaving Elu, at eighteen the eldest son, as the head of the family. Elu's father had nearly as many children as he did songs and now suddenly the young man could no longer live prosperously in his father's lodge. He had his mother, four younger brothers, and four sisters to care for. Smart enough to see that leadership of the tribe would one day fall to either Gunsi or Toh-Yah, Elu had chosen to support Gunsi.

Over the last several weeks, he had worked hard to impress Gunsi. He laughed at the large warrior's jokes and strutted along behind wherever Gunsi went. The old men laughed at the sight, for Elu's head reached barely to Gunsi's elbow. Elu knew they laughed, but Gunsi had taken an interest in Elu's oldest sister, and with luck would take her as his first wife. The old ones would be afraid to laugh when his brother-in-law became chief.

Neither Liwanu nor Tar-he moved and Elu considered what to do. He was almost family with Gunsi and these two should obey him, at least now that Hok'ee was off somewhere else. Tar-he was a coward, but he was cunning. He was also taller and stronger than Elu.

"Liwanu! I said get moving!" His choice made, Elu barked at the equally small, and two years' younger, warrior.

Liwanu glanced at Tar-he, and then back to Elu, who let his hand drop menacingly to his war club. Young, and one of the lowest-ranking warriors in the group, Liwanu realized he had no choice but to obey, and he stepped forward.

"Hurry!" said Elu as he grasped the young man's shoulder and propelled him out onto the slope. As they started up the canyon floor, Elu didn't bother to look back. Tar-he would follow. He couldn't afford to be the only one not present when Gunsi was found. Elu hoped the fool would remain behind. If he did, Elu would make sure Gunsi knew, and that would be one more warrior Elu would have placed firmly beneath his status.

Toh-Yah rolled over, looking out from beneath the overhang. The rain had slackened while he slept, and as he watched it stopped altogether. The fading storm left long furrows of stars shining through the dissipating rows of clouds. He ducked under the low overhang to the bed of coals and fed in twigs and logs to rebuild the fire. The men slept well. The area beneath the outcrop was snug and dry with the heat reflecting from the low roof and back wall. They could travel now and Toh-Yah considered waking the others. Deciding to wait, he moved out from the shelter and sat on a flat rock, content in the early morning to breathe in the rain-soaked pine and grass. Even the dust of the valley floor smelled fresh. He listened to the crickets call to one another in an endless song.

The moon, low on the horizon, revealed itself as a thin cloud drifted past. His contentment deepened. Suddenly the moonlight flickered and the warrior glanced up. He saw no cloud blocking the moon, nothing that would cause a shadow to fall over him. Shadow! Just like the man; one minute there, gone the next. Toh-Yah knew it was a sign, but he didn't understand its meaning.

His reverie broken, he arose and stirred his men from slumber. In minutes, they were trotting south under the gray-black sky of predawn. Toh-Yah's apprehension deepened. With a certainty, he knew the men with him would not be returning to their homes and families and he considered giving up the chase. These men trusted him and it was his place to lead them. How could he lead them to certain death?

Ka-a-e-tano surged past him and swung into the lead, followed by Akule and the others. Toh-Yah realized he'd let his pace slacken as he brooded over Shadow, and Ka-a-e-tano, thinking him to be tired or lost, had quietly assumed the lead. These men would not turn from their quest. Toh-Yah felt pride for them, and shame for himself. Not because he wanted to turn back, but because he lacked the words to convince brave warriors to follow him home.

He felt death around him now as easily as he felt the damp night. It surrounded him, cloaked him, and he breathed it in. He exhaled with a snort and shake, trying to give a physical sense to the feeling, and thus perhaps rid himself of it. But it did not leave. Death plagued the Llanero with an insatiable hunger since Sotli and Kitchi attacked the white man.

The moon flickered again, but Toh-Yah didn't look up. No, he realized, he couldn't look up, for Death was ready to feed again and to look into its face was to die.

Elu saw the crumpled form and his heart plummeted. Gunsi looked dead and so did all of Elu's plans. He shoved Liwanu aside and bent over the still warrior. Laying his hand atop Gunsi's chest he felt the air fill, then empty his lungs.

"He's alive," Elu said. "Help me pull him from beneath the log."

"So Elu, it is you that finds me."

Liwanu, startled by the words, fell over backward to sit in the mud.

Gunsi laughed a dark, ugly laugh and rolled into a sitting position. "Poor little Liwanu, so easily frightened," he taunted. "What will you do if the white man comes for you? Will you run and hide?"

Gunsi shifted his gaze first to Elu, then to Tar-he. "I am surprised to see you here," he said scowling at Tar-he. "I am also surprised that Hok'ee is not here. He alone is the one I expected to come."

"I am here," spoke a voice from the darkness and Hok'ee climbed over a massive trunk to join the group. Like himself, Hok'ee was covered in mud, and Gunsi guessed the young brave was the only one of the four to risk coming straight down the slope to look for him.

Gunsi drew his legs beneath him and began to rise. Halfway up, his knees buckled and Elu's hand shot out to grasp him. Gunsi found a branch to brace against and slapped away Elu's hand. A moment passed before the huge Apache was ready to leave.

Hok'ee led the way along the canyon floor, sinking into mud above his ankle with every step. The rain continued to fall and the mud pulled at his calf-high moccasins. He looked at the pile of earth and mud that in some past time had slid from the mountain, and then with eyes tightened by apprehension he glanced at the slope above. Unconsciously, the young warrior increased his pace, struggling to lighten his steps by lifting his feet before they had time to sink deep.

From the quickening sloughing sounds behind, he could tell that the others were now moving faster. He felt a vibration and the mud around his feet shifted, then settled. The five men stopped and stared at one another. As one, they looked up the mountain and listened. Several minutes passed in quiet as soft rain fell into wide, unblinking eyes.

Suddenly, Hok'ee started for the edge of the slide less than fifty feet away. Within two steps, he was laboring in an agonizing run. Dropping down to place his hands on the mud, he began crawling on all fours to spread his weight. Oddly, it was hard to crawl in a straight line; he had to keep adjusting his path upslope. The sensation grew stronger . . . what was . . . ?

"It's sliding!"

The hoarse scream rang with terror. Gunsi didn't know who voiced it. Tar-he and Liwanu were both behind him, Elu floundered directly ahead, and farther up Hok'ee was scrambling off the slope and into the security of the trees. Irritated with Elu's pace, Gunsi grasped the smaller Indian and threw him back, propelling himself forward. Reaching up, he grasped Hok'ee's outstretched arm and was yanked from the mud.

Spinning about, Gunsi helped Hok'ee wrench Elu to safety. The mud visibly moved now, and ripples appeared as sections began to slide at different speeds. At a deep rumble from higher up, Tar-he's already wide eyes opened further and he began to crawl wildly for the trees. He fought against the slide, crawling almost straight uphill.

"Go with the slide!" shouted Hok'ee. "Crawl downhill and angle for the side!"

For once, Tar-he did as told without hesitation and it saved his life. He rolled into the trees twenty feet downslope as the entire mountain rushed past. Liwanu, hands out, clawlike fingers mere inches from Gunsi's hands, was swept abruptly, violently, away. His mouth opened in a scream, but there was no sound other than the roar of the dying mountain. The mud surged to the canyon bottom, covering the debris pile of the previous slide, mounding upward before spilling out along the sides. The four remaining Apaches were forced to scramble up through the trees as the bottom half of the slide filled the canyon, leaving no room for the top half of the devastated slope, which was forced to spread outward along the narrow course of the canyon. And then silence—and the rain. Falling to the ground, bodies trembling, the survivors drew deep breaths, filling empty lungs and trying to steady ragged nerves.

A game trail led Doc along the finger of a ridge that jutted far into the valley of the Canadian River. At the tip of the finger, the trail rounded a boulder and disappeared over the side. Bending low to merge with the boulders, he stopped at the lip and nestled in among the rocks to survey the valley. He saw the wagons at once, off to the north at the far left of his field of vision. Only four miles out, if that far.

The Santa Fe Trail led down the east side of Raton Creek as it descended from the pass. It then followed the south-flowing creek until the vicinity where the Canadian rushed from the western mountains and made its sharp turn to the south. There, the Trail crossed over the creek to run along the east side of the river. Around Eagle Tail Mountain, a high point on the east bank of the river, the Trail cut across and traveled along the west bank. The company had already crossed over the Canadian and was plodding south for the junction of the Vermejo and Canadian Rivers.

He didn't need a telescope to know it was his company. The clear air and altitude added miles to a man's vision. The lead wagon, like always, had that ornery spotted ox in the front yoke. And Todd Bracken's huge frame and bright red shirt would have been recognizable from ten miles.

Doc leaned back against the boulder in wonder. He'd made it. "Well, almost," he whispered aloud. It would take a half hour to get down to the valley floor, then an hour to walk across. A half hour if he waited until the wagons came farther south, and then trotted to intersect the Trail. He would wait, enjoying the sight of the approaching train. Slowly, he began to scour the valley floor, examining every copse of trees, gully and wash, or mound large enough to hide an Indian. Finally, he picked a spot in the middle of the valley and focused there, freeing his peripheral vision to detect any movement.

A half dozen antelope grazed in a tight bunch to the southeast and several buzzards circled in wide loops beyond the Trail, but the rest of the valley was empty. The wagon train continued its steady progress and was now very near to the low rise Doc had picked for his starting point. Another slow scan of the valley and he rose to start down the path.

At the bottom of the ridge, he paused to reposition the bow and quiver that became unsettled during the descent. Then, with a chuckle, he removed and dropped them to the ground. There was ammunition aplenty in the wagons. After four steps, though, he stopped and looked back. The bow was a good weapon. He'd depended upon it twice, once for meat, and once for protection. That he'd eaten well and remained alive said a lot about its usefulness.

A strange gratitude made it hard for him to leave the bow. Finally, he realized that if he was to return to the mountains to hunt, and he would return, the silent bow would hold advantage over the musket. Reaching down for the bow, he lifted, and in doing so dumped the arrows from the quiver.

He was wasting time. Standing, Doc checked on the company's progress and saw that the wagons had stopped rolling. Some problem with a wagon or harness, he figured. Reassured, he knelt to retrieve the arrows, and then slung the quiver and bow over his shoulders. The wagons were moving again and he eased into a steady run that would close the distance.

A mile to the north, traveling single file along the flank of the mountains, Toh-Yah and his band matched pace with the slow wagons. The wagons were too far for them to see whether Shadow was with them. If he was, the chase was over. An attractive target, there were too many men, all with guns in hand, or near to hand, for Toh-Yah to attack. Not even with Gunsi's men would such a move be wise, tempting though it may be.

If Shadow was not yet with the wagons, at some time he would try to get to them. The Apache had only a vague idea of Shadow's whereabouts. To the south certainly, but how far south was a guess. And he could have been moving east since the storm hit.

Running through a shallow depression, ten acres in size, Doc lost sight of the wagons. He had covered more ground than he anticipated, so he sharpened his angle northward in order to hit the Trail closer to the slow-moving company. Back on level ground, he saw the wagons directly ahead. Fifteen minutes? Maybe a little more, he thought.

"There he is!" shouted a stunned Ka-a-e-tano, pointing at the small running figure. Toh-Yah snapped a look to the wagons, then back to Shadow, judging the angle and distance.

"Go!" he said and began to run.

Doc caught the movement and swiveled his head. He leapt forward in an all-out run across the uneven ground.

Roland Ferguson enjoyed the warmth of the sun on his shoulders. After the last night's rain and hail, he'd wondered if he'd ever be warm and dry again. All in all, he mused, the outfit had come through better than he'd expected. There were no injuries to men or stock, and only minimal loss of goods to the rain when one of the canvas tarps tore loose. Thanks to Bracken's suggestion about avoiding the low ground, the company had rolled at a good pace since daybreak. Enlivened by his cheery assessment, Ferguson stopped and drew a deep breath of crisp morning air. The wagons continued their rumbling course as he squinted at the sun. Figuring there was an hour before noon rest, the wagon master drew another breath, holding it in to relish its flavor.

"Indians!"

The air burst from his lungs and Ferguson swept his eyes across the valley—nothing. Then what—?

"Other side, Boss!" shouted Bracken as he ran toward the wagon master.

Ferguson darted around a wagon and looked west, seeing the Indians immediately.

"I count five," Bracken said, sliding to a stop. "'Bout a mile off, looks like. They sure ain't trying to sneak up."

"They're in a hurry, but they don't seem to be coming at us. Least, not directly."

"There's another one!" A shout from the lead wagon.

Bracken and Ferguson spotted the single Indian running at them from the southwest.

They watched in silence as the distances narrowed.

CHAPTER ELEVEN

WHY DIDN'T FERGUSON OPEN UP ON THEM, Doc wondered? What was he waiting for? Then, as if the wagon master heard his thought, eight men raised their muskets and fired. The ground before him erupted in two plumes of dirt, and he felt the whiff of a ball as it flew past. Doc slowed and watched in disbelief as the shooters knelt and began to recharge their weapons. Six more men stood behind them, rifles at the ready. He saw Ferguson drop his arm, and then saw powder flashes from the muskets.

Throwing himself to the side, Doc rolled awkwardly, coming to rest hard against a rock. Again, the dirt exploded around him as the balls missed their mark. Jumping up, he shouted and waved his arms, then pointed to the Apaches.

"Not me, you black-hearted ox pushers! Them! Shoot them!"

But the distance was too far or the confusion too great, for the first eight men stood and raised their muskets.

At the first volley from the wagon men, Toh-Yah believed Shadow had beaten them. The white men were setting up a covering fire. Then he saw the dirt fly up in front of Shadow just as it did around him and his warriors. The wagon men were shooting at Shadow. He watched as Shadow dived to the ground, followed by the sound of the second volley. Though the wagons were still almost a half mile distant, the long muskets had gotten the range.

Balls thumped into the ground. Alchise yelped and went down. Akule swept a hand down and lifted the fallen Apache. Turning away from the wagons, he helped Alchise run for the mountains. Toh-Yah, Ka-a-e-tano, and Nahama shared a quick look, and again ran toward Shadow.

"Keep firin', boys!" yelled Ferguson, pleased to see two of the Indians withdrawing. "Don't let none of 'em get no closer in."

Poking his head above the grass, Doc watched the two Apaches, in a stumbling run, head for the mountains. Three others came straight for him. They were now as close to him as he was to the wagons, and he knew that he would get no closer to safety. At least Ferguson was firing at everybody. Forcing himself to lie still as the Indians raced closer, he waited.

A crash of musket fire from the company caused him to flinch, but this time no balls came near him. Down in the grass, he wasn't a target, so all eight had fired at the Indians they could see. It was why he'd waited. Springing to his feet, he began to shout at Ferguson, waving his arms wildly.

Nahama wrenched around violently and died without a sound. Toh-Yah felt a ball bite his calf and he staggered forward, managing to stay on his feet. Ka-a-e-tano thrust his head under his friend's arm and guided him away.

Toh-Yah watched over his shoulder as Shadow stood and waved at the wagons. He grunted with satisfaction when Shadow spun and ran back along his path, followed by the crack of musket fire, the balls spraying the earth at his heels.

* * *

"Well done, boys!" cheered Roland Ferguson. "Save your powder and let 'em go if they're goin'."

He grinned at Todd Bracken, who forgot his penchant for stoicism and grinned right back.

"What do you think, Todd?"

"Got one for sure, like as not we hit some others. Looked like two from that first bunch was needin' help to run away." His face clouded over. "Beats me what they was up to, though. Seemed almost like that bunch was after the other one, and not us."

"Yeah, it was odd, I'll grant you that," replied the wagon master. "What do you reckon that lone Indian was up to?"

"I dunno. If them others were after him, could be he wanted some help. I guess you could say we did help. We shot 'em up pretty good, and he 'peared to get off okay."

Taking the shirt from the dead Apache turned out to be a bad idea, Doc thought gloomily. When the company fired at him, he hit the ground in confusion and found himself staring at his outstretched arms. Arms clad in buckskin. No amount of yelling or waving helped. Between the Indians and the quick-shooting company, he'd been unable to get close enough to be heard or recognized. To the men at the wagons, he'd looked like another Indian.

Doc set a fast pace back toward the finger-shaped ridge. He would be invisible among the boulders and trees scattered along its slope, and it afforded him a high spot to watch from while he planned his next move. The company had mangled the band of Apaches. He'd seen at least two of them escaping with obvious wounds. How serious the wounds were was the question. Would it stop the Indians, or just slow them?

Settling among the boulders near the top of the ridge, Doc gazed into the valley. The wagons were moving. He knew their pace was the same as always, but somehow it seemed much faster now that he would have to catch up to them, rather than meet them. He shifted attention to the north to look for the Indians but saw no movement. The low foothills were much closer to the Trail where the Apaches had disappeared and they'd entered the mountain's cover long before he reached his own. They could be anywhere within a mile of him, resting and tending to their wounds, waiting for another chance.

Sitting bolt upright, Doc scoured the ground along the base of the foothills, thinking fast. Why not go now, before the Indians were ready? He could slip down the far side of the ridge, hug the flank of the hills as the Apaches had done, and, when the distance between the hills and the Trail lessened, make a dash for the wagons. He sorted several alternatives as he continued to search for movement from the Indians, but no plan formed that caused him to change his mind. He still needed a way to keep the company from shooting at him, but he'd work on that problem as he trailed the wagons. Maybe Ferguson, Bracken, or one of the others would separate from the wagons to scout or hunt. He felt much safer approaching one man rather than risking being under twenty guns.

Slipping down the ridge, he set off along the base of the foothills.

Hok'ee was troubled. Something was dangerously wrong with Gunsi. At first, when they'd found him under the log, Hok'ee thought Gunsi's snappish words were from humiliation. After all, his wild slide down the mountain had been careless and Gunsi was a warrior who took great pride in his strength and coordination. But the big Llanero had continued to speak with cruelty whenever words were spoken, and so for the last hour, none had been. Hok'ee decided he'd had enough. It was one thing to avenge Sotli—and all of the others, he added glumly—but to be browbeaten while doing so, well, he was also a Llanero warrior and not a dog for Gunsi to curse. More important than Gunsi's abuse, Hok'ee could not shake the approaching feeling of death.

He'd leave tonight, he decided, while the others slept. He wasn't slinking away; he just didn't want Tar-he going with him. If they knew he was leaving, Tar-he would find some reason to go along, and Hok'ee despised Tar-he. He'd fight Gunsi at the village if it had to be that way, but he'd taken no oath, nor lost any of his family's blood to Shadow, and he owed nothing to the sulking Apache. He'd fight if he had to—if Gunsi made it home.

The prideful warrior inside the young Llanero began raising many reasons to stay, but his resolve to leave remained unshakable—until he realized he knew where Shadow was going! The random thought was one of many fired during the battle between will and pride. Hok'ee could not ignore the thought that struck its target with such force and clarity. Before now, he believed he had nothing to gain. If they caught Shadow, he would share in small part the collective trophy. If he died, it wouldn't matter how many shared that fate, he would still be dead. Knowing where Shadow was going, where Shadow would be, changed everything. He had much to gain. The inner battle renewed in earnest now that he had a reason for staying as potent as the feeling of death that urged him to leave. Either way, if he left or if he faced Shadow, he intended to do so alone.

As Hok'ee thought of Shadow, somehow Gunsi didn't seem so powerful. A picture entered his mind. An image of the proud warrior sliding and spinning from sight down the muddy slope, legs and arms spread wide, mouth open, though too frightened to scream. Overcome by the memory, and the realization the great Gunsi had been afraid, Hok'ee laughed aloud.

Gunsi spun and glared at him, but Hok'ee continued to smile and even laughed again. Unable to force Hok'ee to break their locked gaze, Gunsi frowned and turned away, his forehead creased in thought. Gunsi had always seemed large and bold, but now—what? wondered Hok'ee. He was as tall and broad as he was yesterday, and all the days before. His great strength hadn't abandoned him. Why then did he sense smallness in Gunsi? The smile eased slowly from Hok'ee's face as he considered the question, and his belief that he could, on his own, capture Shadow.

Soon, thought Gunsi. Very soon, he would have to turn his attention to Hok'ee. He didn't know the cause of the young warrior's laughter, but he saw clearly the lack of respect as Hok'ee returned his stare. Gunsi was used to having the warriors wilt under his burning look. Except for Toh-Yah, of course. He had never been one to surrender to Gunsi. Toh-Yah was always there, ready to fight with or against Gunsi, depending on the situation. The two men were close in many ways: strength, cunning, and bravery, among others.

Toh-Yah was the only man Gunsi called friend, and that didn't bother the big Llanero in the least. Toh-Yah was the only warrior of sufficient stature to be his friend. Recalling the clumsy efforts of Elu to win his favor twisted Gunsi's lips into a sneer. He knew Elu was contriving to have him marry his sister, which Gunsi would do. Nah-hi-mani was beautiful, by far the prettiest maid available, and he deserved no less. The woman was aloof and feigned disinterest, but he would have her and more like her when he became chief. If Elu thought to gain by the marriage, so what? He would learn better soon enough.

The thought of Nah-hi-mani annoyed him. Lately, she had spent much time with Toh-Yah, without the aloofness. He was sure that she was needling him, but trying to force him into marriage now would not work. He was ready to marry, but until she showed the proper respect— he would be the one to decide when. Gunsi would never act at the behest of a woman. Maybe Elu was directing her to spend time with both men. It would be like Elu to stand in the middle and wait to see which warrior rose to leadership.

A disturbing question arose. Why was Toh-Yah spending time with her? The entire village knew Gunsi and Elu had reached an understanding about Nah-hi-mani. It was odd that he'd never thought to blame Toh-Yah for the interference. Such was not the behavior of a friend, he realized. He must speak of this to Toh-Yah, so his friend would stop talking with Nah-hi-mani. Further reflection revealed many things he must say to Toh-Yah. More and more of late, he had stepped forward to take charge while Gunsi considered a course of action. It was beginning to confuse the warriors, Gunsi reasoned. They were uncertain of the leadership. It was likely the very reason so many of them were sullen.

Like all men wrapped in a cloak of self-image, Gunsi saw the world only as he chose to see it. The way it should be, must be, in order to suit his purposes. Had he seen clearly, he would know that Toh-Yah possessed an ability to unearth meaningful issues and quickly determine the best solutions. Whereas he had one friend, Toh-Yah had many. It would have shocked Gunsi to know that Toh-Yah considered him the least of his friends. Whereas Gunsi led by fear, Toh-Yah led by respect. But Gunsi couldn't see clearly, for to him, respect and fear were one and the same.

Shep Knorr sat quiet on the rim of the mountains, his rifle sight lined on the neck of a bighorn when the animal swung its head to stare into the valley. Cautious, Shep held his shot and strained to see what had caught the ram's attention. He soon picked out the wagons trundling along the banks of the Canadian. The bighorn seemed content to stand by and watch, so he lowered the rifle. He was two hundred feet downwind from the ram, well hidden, and knew there was no danger of the animal detecting him.

For a few minutes, he watched as the company rolled south. When he returned his focus to the ram, it was staring straight down the side of the mountain. Several times its body twitched. Shep was familiar with the movement. It was the result of conflicting impulses over whether to stand or flee. Something else had the bighorn's attention, something much closer than the wagons.

Abandoning all thought of the sheep, he moved to a spot on the rim where he too could see down. A party of five Apaches ghosted along the base of the hills, keeping pace with the wagons. Shep thought to thank the ram, but when he swiveled his head to look, the animal had disappeared. "Smart critter," he whispered. "I should be so smart."

He glanced about, his eyes probing every tree, boulder, and shrub for anything out of place. Listening intently, he searched for sounds that didn't belong, and then listened for the presence of sounds that did. Everything seemed in order and his cover was excellent. Curiosity overrode his caution, and he pulled his spyglass and settled in to wait.

It didn't take much waiting. When the Apaches were directly beneath his position, one shouted and lifted an arm to point down the valley. When hunting, or being hunted, movement is never quick, so it was with ingrained care that Shep allowed his head to turn in the direction the warrior indicated. Even with the distance, he knew it was the lost man, Doc. The mountain man knew Indians well; sometimes as friends, and at other times as enemies, but always as people to be respected.

As such, he had studied their habits, tendencies, and mannerisms. The lone man, even if he wore Indian clothing, didn't move like an Indian and therefore wasn't one. And since he was running, quite fast Shep noted, straight for the wagons, the company was the obvious objective. No Indian would attack so many men single-handedly, and only someone in trouble would approach at that speed. It was Doc. Shep didn't even feel the need to confirm his supposition with the spyglass.

Once the Apaches were under way and at speed, he did a quick estimation of Doc's chance of getting to the wagons before the Indians got to him and determined the lone man should make it easily, barring some accident. When he saw the wagon men lift their weapons, he lifted his telescope. Stunned, he watched as the men prepared to fire. "Blamed fools!" he breathed. Couldn't they see their man would make it without the need for killing? Okay, sure, if the man tripped or came up lame, they could shoot. And if smart, they'd shoot over the Apaches' heads. No use killing one unless you had to. That type of activity had a way of stirring up big trouble. It was precisely the type of activity that had the lone man running for his life.

Or did they recognize their man, and were so daft as to believe five Apaches would attack a large and well-armed party? He saw puffs of smoke from the rifles three seconds before the sound reached his ears. Having risen to his haunches during the building tension, Shep plopped down on his backside in disbelief. He had been both right and wrong—the wagon men were shooting at everybody.

Shep Knorr placed a palm on the lens of his telescope and collapsed the spyglass. In one smooth motion, he rose and walked south along a wisp of trail that clung to the rim of the mountains. That greenhorn 'bout got hisself kilt, he thought. Though it was the fault of the quick-shooting wagon men, and not anything the lost man had done. Any man who shot a weapon before being certain it was the right thing to do was a fool.

Todd Bracken rose from his spot at the fire and, plate and cup in hand, strode over to the large rock where Roland Ferguson sat. Using his boot to toe a large stone from atop the rock, he sat down beside Ferguson.

"You not hungry, Boss?" asked Bracken after sitting.

Ferguson looked down at the full plate lying on the ground between his feet. He picked up the cup of lukewarm coffee and took a swallow before balancing the cup on his knee.

"Nah." Tiredly, the wagon master pushed a hand through his hair. "I keep thinkin' 'bout that Indian. Somethin' 'bout him has got me flummoxed."

"How so?"

"I dunno, I can't put my finger on it."

"You still believin' he might've been tryin' to signal us?"

"Maybe. I don't think them other Indians were interested in us a'tall. I'm figurin' they was after the other one. Remember, when the shooting was over with, that lone Indian took off in a different direction than them others."

Bracken spooned in a mouthful of beans and nodded thoughtfully. "Well, he was jumpin' and hollerin' to beat the band, I'll give you that. Seems like if'n a man is going to flap arms that hard he ought to be able to fly."

"Yeah." Ferguson chuckled. "He sure was clawing the sky and I . . . Oh, my Lord!" Ferguson stood straight up, spilling the forgotten cup and its contents to the ground. "Bracken! That weren't no Indian. That was Doc!"

Grabbing for his plate upended by Ferguson's unexpected jump, Bracken bellowed, "Doc? What're you talkin' about?"

"That Indian, the one by himself. Think back, didn't you notice anything odd about his arms?"

"No," Bracken said thoughtfully, finally able to look up after securing his meal.

"His arms was white above the wrist, Todd. Every time he raised his arms, his sleeves pulled down and his arms showed white." Ferguson swore. "I'm telling you Todd, that was Doc a-tryin' to get to us."

CHAPTER TWELVE

LEADING HIS GROUP TOWARD THE RENDEZVOUS with Toh-Yah, Gunsi thought of the white man. He must be found soon. The men grew tired of the chase and were beginning to grumble. They had endured many hardships over the past days in pursuit of the white man and yet their quarry still eluded them. The dark thoughts nurtured his hostility for the white man. Though born of his brother's death, Gunsi understood that the heightening hatred resulted from his failure to catch the white man. With a shock, the Apache realized that the white man had beaten him at every turn. Beaten? He had never before failed. Not ever. And failure now would ensure that Toh-Yah became chief.

His stomach sickened at the thought and his eyes blazed. How had this happened, he wondered? In the ten days before the first encounter with the white man, he had led the Llanero on several successful raids. Four times, they ambushed white trappers, killing them, or capturing them for torment. The men were in high spirits then, and spoke loudly of his leadership. Now everything was changing and he was in danger of losing all he'd worked so long to achieve. He would capture the white man—he had no choice. Unconsciously, the warrior's hand dropped to the wide, black belt, and stroked the two fresh scalps hanging from a thong of sinew. When he reentered the village, the white man's hair would hang there also.

Gunsi's brooding distracted the normally vigilant Apache, and though he didn't know it, Doc owed his life to the very thoughts of his death. The Apaches, traveling southwest, had followed the Vermejo River out of the mountains and were just now entering the wide valley. Doc, making his way south along the edge of the tree-covered foothills, stepped into the open and froze. Less than fifty feet away, appearing from within the narrow valley of the Vermejo, walked the big Apache wearing the black leather belt. A second Indian emerged followed by two others.

To move would be to die, and Doc had come too far since the first random encounter to die so haphazardly. He remained rigid, one foot still raised on its toe, a result of his sudden stop in midstride. His partly extended left hand and arm held back a large pine bough. Just before the Apache appeared, Doc had pushed the bough forward through the air, increasing the scent of pine. He didn't notice the tangy smell; his breathing was too shallow.

To fight with either the bow or rifle would mean he must let go of the bough, which he couldn't do quickly for it would then sweep back into his face. If he didn't move quickly, he'd never get his hands on a weapon in time to do any good. Not that he stood any chance against four armed Indians passing by at a distance of fifty feet. He was careful to keep his eyes from the big warrior, but he didn't miss the movement of the man's hands to his belt, nor the grisly trophies hanging there. Doc's only move was not to move. That, and pray—and he concentrated to keep his lips from moving.

Gunsi stopped and waited for the others to gather around. They needed encouragement and it was his place to give it. Although to him it wasn't a privilege of leadership, it was a chore. Men should not need encouragement to do what must be done. He resented the waste of time and words, and longed for the day when, as chief, his warriors would think and act like men. For now, he needed these men, such as they were, and he would do what was necessary.

"We should meet Toh-Yah soon, and then we'll go on."

The square faces remained impassive, the eyes dull. He cursed himself. Of course! These fools didn't want to continue, they wanted to go home. Home to their mothers. The loathing he felt remained inside, invisible to the gathered warriors.

With effort, Gunsi spoke again. "Perhaps Toh-Yah will bring the white man's hair or maybe the man himself." He forced a smile he did not feel, for the thought of someone else killing his quarry was not a pleasant one. His words had the desired effect, though. Hok'ee and the others brightened visibly. For good measure, and with fervent desire, he added, "Let's hope that he is alive. It will make a better celebration if our enemy is there to share it—before he dies!"

The idea that the long chase could be over, or soon might be, energized the lagging men. Tar-he, joined by Elu, whooped and jabbered about what tortures they would inflict. Gunsi watched Hok'ee. The young warrior didn't speak, but his demeanor lost the last of its hard edge as he observed the others plan their feats. Good, the big Llanero thought. Now perhaps they could continue at a better pace. They would be disappointed when Toh-Yah appeared without the white man, but Gunsi now believed he could manipulate his men whenever he wanted. Besides, maybe Toh-Yah *had* caught him.

Shep Knorr crossed the Vermejo a mile upstream. He'd watched from the woods as Gunsi and three other warriors passed by, heading for the valley. Recognizing the chief's son, and knowing of the Apache's skill in the forest, Shep waited a full fifteen minutes before leaving his cover, crossing the river, and continuing south.

✳ ✳ ✳

The muscles in Doc's arm and leg burned, and both limbs were quivering with fatigue, yet he stood firm. When the Indians first stopped, he thought he'd be discovered, but such was not the case. At least not so far. He had already risked a slight shift of his weight from the toes of his lead foot back onto the foot resting flat on the ground, and it had helped. He couldn't risk moving the leg, though, so it remained poised awkwardly out in front of him. Doc didn't know how long he could remain still; at any moment the knee might buckle.

Letting his eyes stray to the pine bough, he blanched. The limb was shaking! It wasn't a thick branch. At the point where his hand grasped it, it was about the size of a man's wrist. The trouble lay in his grasp along its eight-foot length. Doc's hand was halfway between the trunk and the end of the bough. Any closer to the trunk and he would not have been able to move the limb at all. As it was, he pushed against the limb's point of greatest resistance. The limb began to shake harder as the quiver turned into a tremble.

Wild eyes rolled back to the Apaches. Only one faced in his direction. Could he chance releasing the limb? It was no longer only the motion that worried him; he didn't trust the spasming arm to be capable of a slow, controlled movement. If he started moving—

Suddenly, the Apaches moved away. Doc forced himself to count a slow ten before relaxing his arm. The branch slid smoothly for six inches then snapped back to slap him hard across the face when his arm buckled. He lay faceup on the ground with a savage pain in one elbow, a cramp the length of one leg, and several pine needles sticking from a scratched and bloody face. He couldn't have been happier.

Toh-Yah limped, but his face showed no sign of the blazing pain in his calf. To complain by either word or action was useless. The ball cut a furrow a half inch deep across the back of his calf, and now that it was bandaged there was nothing more to be done. Soon he and his warriors would reach the meeting place, where they would wait for Gunsi. He looked forward to the rest—if his band arrived first.

Doc waded through a ribbon of swift water and sat on the far bank of the wash. It was the second small stream he'd crossed since leaving the Vermejo River. These were intermittent flows, left over from the rain. Under normal conditions, the first stream south of the Vermejo was Van Bremmer Creek, two and a half miles distant. However, today was anything but normal insofar as rainwater and runoff. Every low spot held water and every gully did duty as a river. The small streams were already far below last night's crest, evidenced by the debris scattered well above the current waterline.

Bending forward, he drank. He sat up dragging a sleeve across his mouth and chin, eyes scanning the Canadian valley to the east. Where were they now, he wondered? As frightening and painful as his near encounter with Gunsi had been, Doc was glad the Apaches passed in front of him, instead of the other way around. Had he reached the river before the Apaches exited the canyon, they would have walked right over his trail. In the soft, muddy ground his tracks would have pointed his direction as surely as if he'd stood there and waved them along.

Resting by the creek, he gave thought to his course of action, trying to decide on the next attempt to reach the wagons. Unless there were more of the Indians than the two groups he'd seen in the morning, both north of him now, he should be able to travel south in some safety. Accepting the notion the Apaches intended to have his hide, either whole or full of arrows, Doc assumed the worst and made his plans as if the warriors were already on his trail.

When the Indians he encountered at the wagons met the second group, they would know his only possible path was south. Like as not, they would then push hard for the twin mesas of Rayado and Gonzales, which jutted far out into the Canadian valley. The eastern tip of Gonzales Mesa sat less than a quarter mile from the Santa Fe Trail and was the logical place to wait for the company. There was timber on the mesa and its sides, and the ground was broken, offering plenty of cover. From its slopes, a man could watch for enemies and easily see the traffic along the Trail.

Oriented west to east, the huge Ortega Mesa sat at the base of the mountains. A narrow gap separated it from the smaller Rayado Mesa, itself separated by a narrow gap from the still-smaller Gonzales Mesa. The smaller mesas topped out higher than seventy-four hundred feet each, a thousand feet higher than the surrounding valley. It was a perfect place to hole up and wait. Doc intended to head straight for it, and then keep right on going.

There was no way to avoid leaving tracks in the soft ground, so he would use it to his advantage and travel fast for the small Gonzales Mesa. Once there, he could lose his trail among the rocky, tree-covered slopes. The Apaches would not be surprised by his actions; rather it is what they should expect. The hunt would not be in where he fled—to the mesa— but where on the mesa he tried to hide. If he was lucky, very lucky, the chase might end on Gonzales Mesa. If the Indians spent the time needed to scour the slopes, the search would take a full day, and that was more than enough time to carry out his plan to reach the wagons.

After losing his trail among the rocks, Doc planned to pass through the narrow gap and head for Ocate Creek, eight miles farther south. The wagon road forded the creek and the ground was crisscrossed by washes and gullies ideal for concealment. Doc estimated the distance from his position to Ocate Creek to be twenty-five miles. Considering the rough ground he must pass over and the time needed to lose his trail somewhere on Gonzales Mesa, he should be in hiding on Ocate Creek by the following evening.

✽   ✽   ✽

A pair of sharp eyes identified the lone man emerging from a gully a mile distant. The watcher chewed a mouthful of pemmican and grinned. Of everyone searching, he was the one who'd guessed where to find the wagon man. Finishing the last of the small cake of buffalo meat, fat, and berries, the watcher scooped handfuls of water to his mouth from a small basin in the rock. He dried excited hands on his deerskin leggings and stared at the object of his search. Yes, his idea was working. The man would pass directly beneath him. Twenty minutes, he wondered?

"Where are Hok'ee and Liwanu?" asked Toh-Yah when Gunsi led his group into the rendezvous.

Gunsi looked over his shoulder. Elu and Tar-he, standing behind Gunsi, also turned to look. Gunsi flicked a questioning gaze from one to the other and the two warriors offered a shrug in reply. Hok'ee had vanished during the last half hour. Twenty minutes later, Gunsi led the combined band south. It was his idea to head for the small mesa overlooking the white men's wagon road, but a quick glance at Toh-Yah during the discussion revealed he too had the same thought. The decision was made quickly, but the warriors lingered, giving Hok'ee time to appear. When Gunsi's patience reached its limit, they moved on without the missing Indian.

Doc walked forward, his eyes picking a winding route through the low, scattered pinyons. Several times, he'd paused to climb partway up the mountain to watch along his back trail. No sign of the Indians yet, but they would be coming. It was no longer a matter of if, but of when. Though the reason behind the pursuit continued to elude him, he accepted the fact it would end only with his safe return to the company, or with his death.

He stepped carefully, avoiding noise, yet unconcerned with leaving tracks. He was jumpy, his breathing shallow, and his ears quickened to the slightest sound. Confused, he stopped. Lifting his hand to block the sun, he scanned the terrain ahead. The feeling came upon him so slowly that he hadn't noticed when it started. He was aware of it now—he wasn't alone—but where?

A few hundred yards before him lay a low hogback covered in large part with trees. The mountain loomed to his right, but it was free of timber and provided no concealment. Opposite, the valley extended to the river and beyond. Although it appeared empty, Doc knew a hundred men might lie hidden within rifle shot.

It was the hogback that kept pulling his attention and his eyes returned to scour its dense foliage. If it was an Apache in hiding, Doc would be in bow range in a few minutes. He was already in rifle range, so whoever waited didn't have a rifle, or didn't mean him any harm.

Eyebrows lifting in surprise, the watcher surmised he'd been detected. He held still and waited to see what the man below would do. He allowed himself a small grin as the other man stared into the trees, seeking for his hidden position. He'd selected the spot with care and knew that he was invisible unless he moved. And he did not intend to move, at least not yet.

Still, the man below deserved more credit than he'd thought. Even after everything the white man had accomplished, the watcher had wondered whether it was from skill or luck. Now he knew. The wagon man possessed the eye of the Apache, an ability to see beyond his sight. As such, he was gifted, and a very dangerous man.

Instinct led Doc to seek a route around the hogback and avoid getting any closer to the threat. His mind willed it, but his feet didn't move. He did not doubt the presence of someone waiting; he *knew* someone waited. He just didn't know where. Even as his vision sought and found a safe path around, he'd already decided to go straight ahead. Until now, the Indians had pushed him in every direction except the one he wanted.

He knew roughly how many hunters were behind him. There were the four who passed by while he held back the tree limb. And there were at least as many in the group that cut him off at the wagons, though he'd been too busy dodging rifle fire to get an accurate count. His mind couldn't come up with a number for the Indians killed or wounded. Twelve to fifteen at the start, he figured. No sooner had the number formed than he was struck by the fact that he was still alive.

So many men, yet he lived and many of them didn't. He was tired of being pushed. His anger grew and replaced the edginess. There might be more than one Indian ahead, but somehow he doubted it. Doc dropped both hands to his waistband and lifted the hafts of the stolen knives to ready them. Unslinging the rifle from his shoulders, he checked the load and started for the hogback, every sense alive with energy. It was time he did some pushing of his own.

The only movement on the hogback was a slight lifting, for the second time, of the watcher's eyebrows. Suddenly, he wished he'd picked a spot with more cover. He'd intentionally avoided the trees and picked an exposed spot on the face of the low ridge where his clothing blended into the ground and he had an open field of view. Experience taught him that prey always examined cover, but generally neglected the obvious. His easiest hunts were often from a position like the one he now held. The drawback to the method lay in the ferocity of the game pursued and in the ability of the hunter to kill with a single shot.

He'd anticipated the wagon man would circle around. Instead, the man came straight for his hiding spot. The watcher, sure that the man below was keen to his presence, showed surprise at the unexpected action.

He needed to be careful or the trap he'd set with such care might ensnare the hunter—the wagon man might kill him.

Roland Ferguson was in a foul mood and every man in the company knew it and felt it. None escaped the wagon master's barking orders. Twice, Ferguson mounted up and rode toward the mountains, careful to keep in sight of the wagons. He was more sullen each time he returned. Always hard driving, he was known as a fair man nonetheless. Bracken understood what troubled his boss, for that matter so did most of the men, but it didn't ease the sting left from a whipping by his barbed tongue. The company was ready to revolt so Bracken decided to face his friend.

Ferguson stood with his back to the wagons, fists on hips, staring west at the rugged high country. Bracken noted it was the first time his friend had remained still all afternoon. For the past five hours, Ferguson had marched up and down the line shouting unnecessary orders and insults, ridden out on scout, or paced back and forth, always along the western side of the company.

The wagons were back on hard ground and traveling along a portion of the Trail that received little or no rain in the recent storm. Ferguson should be happy and, in normal times, would be happy. The company moved easy and fast down the dry Trail. The rain had slowed their progress only briefly, the ascent of Raton Pass went off without incident, and he was days ahead of schedule. Things couldn't be going better for the company, and worse for Doc.

It was warm enough under the late-May sun that all the men were sweating. An ox driver's position in the train was discernible from the amount of dusty mud clinging to his face and clothing. The man bringing up the last wagon was almost unrecognizable. Without a breeze to clear the dust, the powder raised by hooves and wheels hung thick in the air. Bandannas tied about a man's face provided relief from the dust, but added the misery of chafing and itching. Wretched conditions at any time, they were unbearable today because of Ferguson. Bracken approached quietly, though not so quietly as to startle his boss.

"What?" Ferguson demanded without turning and before Bracken covered half the space between them.

Holding his reply until he could speak in low tones, Bracken walked on.

"I know you're riled, Roland, but you'd best temper it some."

He found himself staring into the wagon master's fiery eyes. Bracken removed his hat to wipe his head and neck with a clean bandanna kept tucked inside his shirt. He stared back, waiting a moment before he continued.

"The men don't deserve what you're dolin' out and unless you're figurin' on takin' these wagons the rest of the way alone . . ." The driver let his words taper.

"Let 'em go!" Ferguson grunted. "I'll see to it it's the last money they ever make on the Trail."

Bracken saw he'd underestimated his friend's mood. Ferguson was fused dynamite waiting for someone to strike a match.

"You goin' with 'em?" Ferguson sneered, striking the match himself.

Bracken slammed his hat back onto his head and stepped forward hard. Chest to chest he forced the wagon master to give ground.

"We've too many miles together for you to go talkin' to me that a-way," Bracken hissed. "So yeah, I reckon I'm goin' too."

The driver, three inches taller, looked down on his angry boss. The difference in height meant little, as both men weighed the same at two hundred and twenty pounds. Moreover, Bracken was under no illusions of Ferguson's fighting ability. The wagon master liked it rough and tumble all the way. "Keep at it till one is done . . . no rules, no mercy," was Roland's fighting creed. Bracken had held Ferguson's coat on countless occasions while his friend attended to some affront, often imagined if drinking. He'd also fought alongside his friend an equal number of times. Yet, in all those fights, he'd never known the wagon master to lose his temper. Ferguson *enjoyed* a scuffle. To fight the man now, primed as he was, would be suicide, but Todd Bracken was not a mild man and his boss had pushed too far and too hard.

Somehow, Ferguson restrained his temper and Bracken, after a moment of cold stare, started away.

"Hold on!"

Bracken looked back over his shoulder.

Expelling a heavy sigh, Ferguson nodded. "I s'pose you're right."

The two men talked quietly until the last wagon rolled past.

Upon finding the white man's trail, Gunsi broke into a trot. The pace would be difficult for Toh-Yah, but it appeared the Llanero were a few hours behind and Gunsi wanted to close the distance. Besides, he reasoned, if his rival was too weak to keep up, so much the better. The men deserved to see that his strength and stamina were superior to Toh-Yah's. Such differences in qualities were what made him the better leader.

The white man ran straight for the small mesa. It was a mistake, perhaps one that would lead to his capture, the Apache thought hopefully. The Apache enjoyed his scornful contempt of the white man, for even he had begun to have doubts of ever killing his enemy. But now, the prey led the hunters to a place the Apache knew well—the small mesa. Gunsi ordered Akule to scout for the wagons, and without breaking stride the warrior veered to the southeast. Knowing how far the wagons were from the mesa would tell the Llanero how much time they had to find the white man.

Toh-Yah stumbled then regained his balance; a low groan escaped from the pain he held so tightly inside. Gunsi let his head sweep back and around as if searching the surrounding terrain. Toh-Yah ran at the back of the line. They shared a look that said each man understood the other. His head swung forward and Gunsi increased the pace just enough that Toh-Yah would know. The huge Apache loped on, his face wearing a cruel smile of satisfaction.

CHAPTER THIRTEEN

DOC WALKED TO THE EDGE OF A LOW WASH that ran along the base of the hogback. The rainwater had flowed on, leaving a string of three- to four-inch-deep pools. He turned and followed the wash upstream for twenty feet before stopping. At that point, the wash made a sharp bend, which after countless years and storms had carved into the side of the hogback, forming a grotto several yards deep and twenty feet high.

Across the wash from the grotto lay a large boulder with a flat top and bottom. The right height for a table, and Doc figured it would have served the purpose nicely if a man could have gotten his legs underneath. Dropping to one knee beside a pool, Doc scooped water to his mouth with his left hand. His right hand gripped the rifle, finger on the trigger.

He rose and placed the rifle atop the boulder, angled so that it would lift quick and easy. From his shoulders, he removed the bow, quiver, and possibles pouch. With a quick flick of wrists, his knives lay glinting in the sunlight atop the boulder. He raised both arms over his head and stretched his back, sighing deeply as the arms lowered. Facing the grotto, he hopped to a sitting position on the boulder and stared into the pool.

"I could sure use a bite to eat if you can spare it," Doc said.

The watcher shook his head and chuckled.

"I reckon I got enough," said Shep Knorr. "You like pemmican?"

"Toss it down and I'll find out, but I bet I'll eat it no matter the taste."

Taking half the cake in one bite, which tasted just fine, he thought happily, he looked up at the mountain man still perched above the grotto.

Doc waved to the boulder beside him. "Alight 'n set."

"Obliged, but I'll pass." Shep reared up on his haunches, rifle across his lap, and lifted his eyes to the north. "You've got 'nuff misery for ten men a-follerin' you and I'd just as soon leave it that way."

At Doc's curious look, the mountain man continued.

"A-follerin' *you*, I mean." Cocking his head toward the muddy area around the wash, Shep said, "Was I to drop down there ol' Gunsi'd know it and I might find as how I'd borried some of your trouble. No sir, I'll stay put."

Doc popped in the last of the pemmican and shrugged as if to say, *Suit yourself.* He cupped his hands to catch another small cake as it arced down from above the grotto.

"That's the last of it," Shep informed the hungry man as Doc bit off a mouthful.

"Didn't mean to clean your cupboard, but thanks anyway."

His gaze back on the valley, Shep replied, "I'll have an easier time of rustlin' grub than you will. Leastwise, I will once you've led them 'Paches away."

Shep dropped his head to look at Doc. "Say, how'd you know I was settin' up here?"

Doc licked the crumbs from his fingers and wiped both hands on his tattered pants before motioning toward the sky. "That red-tail gave you away," he said, identifying a red-tailed hawk gliding in slow, hunting loops over the hogback. "He flew low over you once, and then doubled back. That second time, he veered off real sharp. I figure he wasn't sure about you on the first pass so he swung back for another look. When he saw you plain and clear, he lit out."

Shep watched the bird drift from sight over the trees and recalled seeing its shadow as it passed overhead earlier. That was something he'd need to remember. If Doc had been an enemy, he wouldn't have asked for food, he would have taken what he wanted from Shep's carcass.

"I didn't know who you were until you spoke," Doc said. "But I knew you weren't an enemy carryin' a rifle when you let me get inside easy range." He took another swipe at his pants to dislodge a stubborn crumb from his right hand. "I'd sorta let myself get over-riled and had a mind to be available if you was a-huntin' me. Once I got well into bow range, I figured you weren't an Indian, at least not one of them chasin' me."

Doc levered back to lie flat on the rock, staring up into a wide, empty sky. The red-tail took his hunt elsewhere, he saw.

"Nice trick though," Doc continued, "a-layin' in the open like that. I'd have never thought to look there if it weren't for the hawk."

Glad for company after so many harrowing days alone, Doc talked with Shep for ten minutes more. The mountain man nodded his approval while listening to Doc's plan of bypassing Gonzales Mesa and joining the wagons at Ocate Creek. From Shep, Doc heard who was after him and how many Indians there were. He also finally learned why.

"A boy, huh?" Doc shook his head. "I didn't know; it happened so fast." Then as if seeking forgiveness, at least from himself, he added, "Reckon it don't make no difference. He came huntin' me so I fetched 'im."

"Here come the rest of 'em," Shep informed. "'Bout an hour off . . . maybe less."

Doc rose to stand on the boulder and peered across the valley without success. Shep's higher position gave him a longer field of view.

Hearing movement, Doc looked up at the mountain man, who lifted a hand in farewell.

A sudden thought prompted Doc to ask, "Can you spare some balls? I'm down to my last one."

"Wouldn't do no good, your rifle's got a bigger bore than mine." Shep's hand went to his pouch. "Though I can give you some lead so's you can make your own."

"That won't do me any good neither," Doc said with disappointment. He began shouldering his weapons. "I tore a hole in my pouch a few days back and lost nigh everything. Lost my ball mold too."

Shep nodded and glanced up the valley. "Anything else?"

Doc looked along the wash. "Yeah, one thing. If you get close to the company, or run into any of 'em, let 'em know what I'm up against and where I'll meet 'em." He paused; his eye had picked up something and he tried to focus on it. An old pine grew at a lean on the lip of the grotto and he stared at one of its long branches extending out high over the wash. His mind jumped back to Shep. "Oh. Tell those fools what I'm wearin' so they don't try and shoot me again."

"Luck," Shep said and started up the hogback.

The tree? What was it about the tree? "Shep!" Doc shouted as he untied the deerhide strap holding his ruined boots.

Three minutes later, Shep was halfway out the length of the long branch, bending the end to a height that allowed Doc to reach up with his rifle and loop the heavy leather shoulder strap over the branch. Leaving visible sign at the boulder, Doc, wearing the boots, walked along the muddy bank of the wash until, in midstep, he lifted his rifle to full length and looped the branch. Easing both feet from the boots, he left them embedded in the mud. Shep shinnied back up the branch and dropped to the ground next to the tree trunk. Without the mountain man's weight, the thick branch lifted Doc from the ground. Slowly, Doc climbed up the hanging rifle until he could hoist himself onto the branch.

A few minutes later, Doc slipped on the moccasins and shook Shep's hand as the two men parted ways atop the grotto. Walking away, Doc looked down at the wash. The end of the branch was back in its original position, about eighteen feet off the ground. He was satisfied that his care in climbing hadn't left many broken twigs or needles on the ground to give away his ruse.

A deep bed of pine needles covered the area above the grotto and neither he nor Shep left any sign that Doc could see. He was sure a good tracker could find something, but only if the tracker knew there was something to be found, and where to look. It meant he'd hidden his trail before getting to the mesa, but the opportunity here had been too great. He would have to count on his past direction to lead the Apaches toward the mesa, for now he had no reason to go there at all. He could get to Ocate Creek quicker by using the gap between Ortega and Rayado Mesas.

In the looming dusk, a young, but wise warrior knelt to drink then bathe his face with the chilly water of the Canadian River. He rose to gaze north across the river. Every step he'd taken to this point had loosed further the bonds on his spirit and mind. Wading the river, he stood on the opposite bank feeling the last of those bonds drop away. Whether the suffocating darkness he experienced on the far side came from Gunsi, Shadow, or the many deaths over the past days was unclear. Perhaps it was from all. It was behind him now and with no further thought of the others, Hok'ee headed home.

Confusion added fuel to the fury that overwhelmed Gunsi. Facing the group of frightened warriors, he shouted at them to be quiet. Elu, Tar-he, Alchise, and Akule lapsed into silence, unable to tear their wide-eyed gaze from Shadow's empty boots. Gunsi took a deep breath to steady himself and dropped down to squat beside Ka-a-e-tano and Toh-Yah. Three pair of eyes studied the last footprint.

"Well?" Gunsi was unable to speak more than the single tight-lipped word.

"I do not know," confessed Ka-a-e-tano. "Shadow has disappeared."

The huge Apache's jaw clenched at the name and he battled against a wild urge to strike the tracker.

With quiet thoughtfulness, Toh-Yah asked Ka-a-e-tano what he *could* see. "The answer may not lie in what we cannot see, but in what we can."

The tracker pursed his lips as he considered the statement. "Very well. Shadow approached from the south. We know it was Shadow because we followed the same set of prints from the river to this boulder." Ka-a-e-tano stood and moved to the boulder. "He rested here and ate. There are several small scraps of food." The tracker pointed to a pair of close, side-by-side prints at the base of the rock. "Shadow was on top of the boulder. These prints are together and deeper than the others, indicating he either dropped down or slid down to stand here.

"Also there are scuffs of mud atop the boulder where he stood, perhaps to look for us." A nimble hop propelled Ka-a-e-tano to the top of the boulder where he stood looking at the back trail. "You cannot see far enough from this spot to have warned him in time to escape, so he must have left without knowing we were near."

Hopping down, he continued, "Shadow switched to his boots and prepared to leave. He then walked slowly this way." The tracker followed the short path of prints to the end. "He walked, he did not run. See, his toes and heels are visible in each print. If he had run, only his toes would have driven deeply into the ground."

"Why would he change his shoes?" Gunsi asked.

Akule, unable to help himself, blurted, "So the shadow warrior could vanish!"

Ignoring the outburst and Gunsi's question, Toh-Yah spoke to Ka-a-e-tano. "If he did not know we were close, we should not expect him to run."

The tracker shrugged agreement then said, "From this point we know Shadow did not walk away, and we know he did not run away. Unless he flew away"—and Ka-a-e-tano's tone indicated that he believed the prospect should be considered—"there is only one thing left: he jumped."

"Jumped!" snapped Gunsi. "Jumped where?" As the tracker talked, Gunsi had let the words paint a picture of the white man's movement. He could see him stand on the boulder and peer to the north, could see him walking around and kneeling to drink at the pool. He could see the white man start down the wash, but he couldn't see him jump or fly away! "You have told us nothing new."

"And *you* have told us nothing at all," Toh-Yah said to Gunsi. "If you want to find Shadow, help us learn." The words were neither harsh nor loud, but there was no mistaking they were an order.

The huge Apache quivered with rage. No one had ever dared to speak to him in so bold a manner. Even his father gave him orders couched as suggestions, and his father was the chief! Toh-Yah stood impassive, waiting. His face was void of fear or concern over what he'd said. Over what he'd done, actually. For the statement was a command, a challenge to Gunsi's leadership. This affront must not pass, Gunsi decided. It was time to settle the rivalry.

With Toh-Yah gone, Gunsi knew he could claim all of the glory for killing the white man. He would have songs and stories told of—he would be the one blamed for the many deaths if the white man escaped. The sudden thought cooled his temper.

Not yet, he thought, not yet. Toh-Yah might still prove to be useful. When this was over, whether they succeeded or not, he would find some reason to fight and kill Toh-Yah. As the tension diminished, the two warriors broke their locked gaze. Puzzled by the indifference of his rival, Gunsi wondered. Surely, the man feared for his life.

All the warriors present displayed open amazement when Gunsi nodded his head in agreement to Toh-Yah's statement.

Gunsi broke the fragile silence. "No man can fly, so where did he jump?"

The three men scanned the surrounding area looking for possible options. There were other boulders, all too far away, as was the edge of the wash.

"The pool perhaps?" suggested Gunsi.

An endless number of pools stretched along the bottom of the wash, some separated by only inches. It was a good suggestion and the warriors fanned out to search. A half hour later, they were gathered again by the boulder.

"It was a possibility, though unlikely," said Ka-a-e-tano. He continued, prompted by the curious looks of the others. "The mud Shadow left on the boulder was still soft, so we missed him by a short time. If he jumped into one of the pools, there would be no way to avoid stirring up the muddy bottom. The water would have taken as much time to clear as the mud on the boulder needed for the sun to dry it out. All of the pools are clear, and were when we got here."

"So he didn't fly, and he didn't jump out, then where did he go?" Gunsi asked with sarcasm so light that the tracker, looking straight up, failed to notice.

Pointing overhead, he said, "There is the only remaining possibility."

Shep Knorr leaned forward to steady the telescope on the remains of a stump. He sat a half mile west of the grotto and three hundred feet higher up the mountain. Taking up his position as the Indians arrived at the wash, he'd pulled his scope and watched. He'd admired the cleverness of Doc's idea and wanted to see for himself how the Apaches reacted. The mountain man knew Apaches were a superstitious people and felt sure the empty pair of boots would spook some, if not all of them. Although now, it looked to Shep like the Indians might have figured it out.

"Up there?" Even Toh-Yah couldn't keep the disbelief from his tone.

"I'm not saying Shadow went there," Ka-a-e-tano stated. "I'm saying it is the last possibility."

"But Shadow would have to fly to get that high," whispered Tar-he. "Why wouldn't he just fly away?"

Gunsi remained rigid and silent. The whimpering fools, he thought. Let Toh-Yah deal with them. But Toh-Yah ignored them, instead looking from the ground to the limb, measuring the distance. His eyes followed the limb to the trunk and then down to the base at the top of the grotto. He knelt to examine the ground beneath the limb and started to pick up two fresh pine needles before he noticed another one poking from the side of Elu's moccasin. He then saw several more stuck in various spots on the assembled warriors' clothing.

No, he realized, without more than two needles, he couldn't be certain where they'd come from. Knowing the answer before asking the question, he said, "Do any of you think you can leap to that branch?"

No one spoke. Then slowly, Akule stepped forward. "I will try."

The warrior walked to the boulder and turned around. His face lifted to the limb while he rocked his body in preparation. Suddenly, he sprang forward and ran four long strides before launching himself upward, fingertips clawing for the green needles.

Shep Knorr laughed aloud. He laughed again as the sheepish Apache, covered head to toe in mud, lifted himself from the bank of the wash. It had been a mighty leap. One to be proud of in a game of skill, but in this more sinister game, the Apache failed to get within eight feet of the limb.

The thick mud could not hide the embarrassment on the face of Akule. Without a word, he walked to the nearest pool and began to wash.

Toh-Yah stifled a laugh and managed to say, "It was a good attempt, Akule. It was not necessary for you to reach the limb. It was more important that we see how close a man could come."

Akule looked over his shoulder at Toh-Yah, wanting to be certain the Apache was not mocking him.

"We know now that the white man did not jump to the limb, for he would have done it while walking, and leaping from one leg." Toh-Yah hesitated to let the words have their effect. "The white man has tricked us. It is a trick we will learn from him when he is captured."

Speaking to Gunsi, he added, "I do not see any reason that he would change directions; the small mesa is still the best spot for him."

Realizing that Toh-Yah was showing the warriors he still thought of Gunsi as an equal, the Apache cleared his throat and replied, "I agree. We will head for the mesa."

Ka-a-e-tano led the way down the wash and Gunsi brought up the rear. Only the two leaders were able to walk past the empty boots without casting a last fearful glance. It didn't matter to Gunsi what the others thought and Toh-Yah should have known it. As long as the band continued the hunt, and moved in the direction he felt was right, he no longer cared who led them. When the time was right, he would kill the white man, and then he'd kill Toh-Yah.

From his spot at the rear, he overheard Tar-he and the others whisper of Shadow's strong medicine, of his ability to appear and disappear, and to fly. They actually thought the white man could fly! The one thing Toh-Yah said that interested Gunsi was of learning the trick after capturing the white man. That would be something Gunsi would seek to learn in private. Such a trick would be useful to know, especially if it could be used to make full-grown warriors believe Gunsi could fly.

Shep was still laughing as he slid the telescope into his pouch. Doc had shaken the Apaches from his trail and was now free to make a dash for Ocate Creek. Only on rare occasions did Shep become involved with other people, much less their troubles. He found in Doc a kindred love of the mountains and a man worthy of friendship. Shep intended to help his new friend. He was going to the wagons to deliver Doc's message.

On the valley floor, well out of sight of the Indians, the mountain man set off in a fast lope for the Trail. He headed due east to avoid going anywhere near the Apaches. Though he'd traded with both Gunsi and Toh-Yah, and probably most of the others, he was wise enough to know an irate Apache doesn't have any white friends. Once he struck the Trail, Shep planned to turn south and catch the wagons. He figured he would overtake the company a least a half day before they rolled across Ocate Creek.

Somewhere north of the Cimarroncito River, Doc burrowed into a mound of pine needles he'd gathered for a bed and went to sleep. Overhead, hidden by the dense canopy of pine boughs, stars filled the black sky, providing the only light in the absence of a late-rising moon. It was cold, but he didn't chance even a small fire that might give away his position. Doc slept soundly for the first half of the night, exhaustion blocking the effect of the cold until the very early hours. Too dark to travel and too tired to rise, he drifted in and out of fitful periods of sleep until just before dawn when at last he gave up and brushed free of the needles.

CHAPTER FOURTEEN

SHEP KNORR HAD TRUDGED THROUGH THE COLD NIGHT across the short-grass flats of the Canadian Plain, determined to reach the Trail before he camped. Believing that he was at least five miles from the Apaches, he built a fire and fell asleep as soon as he lay down snuggled into a hollow. The sun was a half hour high before he awoke the next morning. A quick look was all he needed to confirm the wagons had passed by early the day before. The company was farther along than he and Doc believed. "Get a move on, Doc," the mountain man spoke aloud. "It's gonna be close." Two minutes after rising, Shep Knorr was trotting south a quarter mile from his campsite.

Gunsi, Toh-Yah, Ka-a-e-tano, Elu, and Akule had an hour start on Shep. Rising before the sun, the five Apaches awoke to find Tar-he and Alchise had abandoned camp sometime during the night. The reason for their absence was clear to the five warriors, so no discussion occurred. With no trail to follow, Ka-a-e-tano waited for Gunsi to lead out, dropping in behind the large Apache. Akule followed next, then Toh-Yah. Gunsi noted with dissatisfaction that his rival was better able to keep pace this morning. It would be a long day, Gunsi thought. A long day that would drain

Toh-Yah's strength. Today they would reach the small mesa and should find the white man. Later, there would be time for Toh-Yah, and Gunsi wanted the wounded Indian tired.

Doc ran down the valley at a fast lope. It was a brutal pace for the distance he must cover, but there was no helping it; his roundabout path would be half again as far as the wagons would travel. The Santa Fe Trail, like all trails, followed the easiest route and the most direct route when possible. Once the Trail crossed the Canadian River, it was a straight shot to the Ocate Creek crossing. The course Doc had to travel followed the curve of the mountains as they made a large bend to the west away from the Trail before looping back to the east.

In spite of the danger, Doc felt *good*. His ankle and shoulder were free from stiffness and his lungs pumped the mountain air as though they'd drawn their first breath in the high country. Just after dawn, he forded the Cimarroncito River without slowing and splashed through Urraca Creek an hour later. Another hour brought him to the north bank of the Rayado River, flowing east to west beneath the three mesas.

Twelve miles to the east, he could see Gonzales Mesa; just beyond its eastern crown lay the Trail. He waded across the Rayado and paused for a brief rest. After a long drink followed by a liberal splash of the refreshing water over his head and shoulders, he wondered if the Apaches were now scouring the tumbled slopes of the small mesa.

The easy part of his route was behind him; from now until he made his way through the pass and the tangle of canyons south of the mesas, the terrain would be one rocky ascent and descent followed by another. The last leg to Ocate Creek would be on more or less level ground, but the danger of being found by the Apaches would make for slow and careful travel. His plan hinged on how long the Apaches would search for him on Gonzales Mesa before realizing that he'd gone elsewhere. If they gave up too soon, they might figure out where he'd gone before the company arrived at Ocate Creek.

To look at Doc as he lay stretched out, basking on the warmth of a sun-soaked rock outcrop, one would never guess at the thoughts running through his mind. He appeared to be a man free of strife or concern, and suddenly he realized he was just that, free. The urgency to rejoin the company dissipated, replaced by nothing more than a wish to say farewell to the friends he'd made as the men traveled west across the prairie. And friends they were, each one. Shared toils and hardships made either friends or enemies of men, and Doc's only enemies were the Apaches.

He would not rejoin the wagon train and continue to Santa Fe. He was going to stay in the mountains. Ferguson would let him trade his coming pay for supplies and then he'd explore the high country. His mind made, he gathered his gear and headed for the gap between Ortega Mesa and Rayado Mesa.

Frustrated over the desertion of two of his warriors, Gunsi stood scowling at the mesa towering five hundred feet above him. As timid as the runaway Apaches had been, he needed their help to search for the white man. Their fear might have even been an advantage in searching; they would have been very thorough, afraid to miss any sign that might save their lives. Their worthless lives, he thought, irritated. What had happened? A week before he'd been the accepted leader of nineteen Llanero warriors, each one proud of his heritage and deeds. Now, as Gunsi looked around, he saw only four men.

One of them, Akule, probably wished that the runaways had told him of their plans so he could have fled also. Ka-a-e-tano was brave enough, but also foolish enough to believe the white man was a shadow warrior. The third one, Elu, was here to protect his future, and lastly, the only man Gunsi had ever called friend, Toh-Yah, was no longer a friend. He *must* kill the white man. There was no other way to right all that had gone wrong. Better yet, he should capture the white man and return him alive to the village where all could see him die at Gunsi's hand.

But before he could kill him, he had to find him, and with five men to search so much ground, they would need more luck than skill. At his order, the men scattered and began working up the jumbled slope of the mesa.

The ground was firm and the wagons rolled smoothly down the valley. Even those parts of the Trail that had been inundated had had the time to dry out from the recent storm. Todd Bracken walked beside the lead team of the lead wagon. True to his morning routine, the spotted ox did his best to cause trouble. Most of the oxen were prone to unruliness when first yoked each day, but the big spotted brute made it a point to carry on his peevishness until the midmorning break. At a little more than twelve hundred pounds, the animal demanded wary attention. If Bracken let his mind wander, the ox might sidle over, step down, and crush his foot.

Bracken, tiring quickly of the game this morning, hoisted his Moses stick and administered a little persuasion to the ox. The Moses stick was a shoulder-length staff of hardwood the driver carried to prod or punish, as was needed, his teams of oxen. The solid thwack had the desired effect and the brute settled down.

Leading the little mustang last ridden by Doc, Roland Ferguson walked up and fell into step beside Bracken.

"Gonna try out your idea?" asked Bracken.

"Figured to."

"Well, Doc and that mustang were cut from the same mold. Neither one of 'em wanted to be where they were. They always wanted to be a-goin' someplace new," Bracken opined. "If'n Doc can be found I reckon that pony's got as good a chance as any to do it."

Ferguson stepped into the saddle and adjusted the thick flour sack full of provisions looped around the horn. A slicker and bedroll were tied over the cantle.

"I've told the men you're in charge," Ferguson said. "I ain't worried, Todd, you're good enough to ramrod your own company."

The driver laughed. "Don't you think I know that? If'n I'm good enough to nursemaid you all the way to Santa Fe and back, runnin' my own outfit'd be a breeze."

Ferguson uttered a lighthearted curse at his friend and rode away. Across his lap, he carried a new Plains rifle, and tucked into his waistband were two pistols. He had another friend in trouble, maybe hurt, somewhere to the west and he'd done all the waiting he would do. Now it was time to go help.

"Will we find Shadow?"

Ka-a-e-tano asked the question of Toh-Yah as the two warriors met atop the mesa. The search had been fruitless, but Gunsi refused to give up. With so few men, their effort was more a pass through than a search. Beginning on the north side, the Apaches worked their way around the east face and were now nearing the end of their hunt on the south face. Toh-Yah was certain Shadow was not on the west side—it was out of sight of the wagon road. Why travel all this way and pick a hiding spot that would not allow you to know when the wagons came near? He felt the search on the south face was almost as pointless, for the wagons would be a mile from the mesa and moving away before they appeared to anyone hiding there.

Toh-Yah stood in silence, his eyes closed and his head lowered while he sought an answer to Ka-a-e-tano's question. Would they find Shadow? Other than Gunsi, did they want to find Shadow? The Apache had worked to keep his thoughts free from his apprehension, but his guard dropped and death settled over him with the suffocating weight of buffalo robes on a hot summer day.

"Yes, we will find him."

Toh-Yah's response surprised Ka-a-e-tano; so long was the pause between question and answer he'd thought Toh-Yah hadn't heard. Surprised him, and frightened him. The words of Toh-Yah were flat with resignation, acceptance of a fate over which he, or they, had no control. The Apache was certain they would find Shadow; it was there in his words, as discernible as was the dread.

"But not here!" Gunsi said. His approach had gone unnoticed.

Toh-Yah lifted empty eyes to Gunsi. "No. Not here," he agreed.

"Then where? Where could he have gone?"

"Maybe the shadow warrior has flown home," offered a meek Akule.

"Or to the white men's wagons," said Ka-a-e-tano.

After staring at the two young warriors with a mixture of amazement and scorn, Gunsi looked at Toh-Yah.

"The white man cannot fly," Toh-Yah said.

Emboldened by a lack of strong response from Gunsi, Akule asked, "How do you know he cannot fly? How do you know Shadow is even a man at all?"

"Because ghosts and shadow warriors are tales mothers tell their little ones to keep them from wandering alone into the forest!" Gunsi barked. "They are stories the old ones embellish to make their frail bodies feel as powerful as their memories of younger days."

He could tell he hadn't persuaded the two warriors. In the absence of a convincing alternative, they were willing to believe in spirits.

"Akule." Toh-Yah's voice was patient. "If Shadow can fly, why did he ride a horse? When his horse was killed, why did he not fly to the wagons? If he can appear and disappear whenever he chooses, why does he not disappear until we give up?"

The Apache paused to let the young Llanero think about his questions.

"But you call him Shadow," Akule argued. "You must believe he is a spirit."

"I call him Shadow because he possesses the qualities of a shadow warrior. He is cunning, brave, strong, and a fierce and deadly fighter but he is not a ghost . . . he is a man."

Ka-a-e-tano and Elu listened intently but said nothing. Akule saw the logic in Toh-Yah's argument, but there was too much he didn't understand.

Toh-Yah continued. "At the cliff where Viho fell, Shadow climbed down and injured his leg. You saw the tracks, didn't you?" Akule nodded. "If he could fly, why did he risk injuring himself by climbing?

"If he is a spirit who seeks to destroy us, why does he flee from us? Because he wants to rejoin the wagon men, yet several times we have stopped him before he could do so. How could we stop a spirit from doing what he wished?"

Akule didn't, couldn't, answer the questions. Ka-a-e-tano straightened his back and faced Toh-Yah. "These are things I should have known myself. I did not want to believe the white man was a spirit, but he has done so many things I cannot explain."

"But what about the grotto where he disappeared?" Akule asked. "You could not find his tracks, only his shoes."

"His sign is there, Akule," the tracker replied. "We just did not know where to look. I believe he reached that limb somehow"—Akule opened his mouth to protest but Ka-a-e-tano cut him off—"and if I'd seen him do it, I could explain it to you. On the way home we will look above the grotto and on the trunk of the leaning pine. We will find his sign, I promise."

Confused, the young warrior fell silent. He was not convinced, yet he understood the older men thought him to be a child and he was embarrassed. Every question Toh-Yah raised had but one answer: Shadow was a man. Although Akule couldn't rid himself entirely of the deep-seated belief and fear, he resolved not to show his uncertainty to the others.

"He done what?" exclaimed Shep. "The blamed fool! I told 'im what'd happen to 'im if'n he went after Doc."

Todd Bracken handed a canteen to the panting Shep Knorr and waited while the thirsty man drained the contents. Shep jammed the cork back into place and tossed the empty canteen to Bracken. Reaching out, he snatched a second canteen from a nearby driver and poured the water over his sweaty head and shoulders. Water dripped from his hair, nose, and beard, and with a hard shake he showered the men who'd gathered in too close.

"How long ago did he leave?"

"Couple of hours back. Just before the midday break."

"I know the spot, seen the tracks a-headin' out, but I figured one of you was just goin' for a scout."

Lost in thought, Shep pushed a hand through the wet mop of hair, and then tried unsuccessfully to tug the hand through his tangled beard.

"Your boss got any experience in them mountains?"

Bracken shook his head.

"I didn't s'pose he did."

The mountain man lifted an empty pouch from about his shoulder and tossed it to one of the gathered men. "Fill that with grub, then go through Doc's kit an' see if'n he's got another ball mold for his rifle."

The driver glanced at Bracken, but before either one spoke Shep snapped, "Rattle a hock boy, I got little 'nuff time as it is and I need to talk to your segundo!"

The man hurried away and Shep grabbed Bracken's arm to lead him from the others. A few minutes later, the mountain man trotted west and the wagons began a slow roll down the valley toward Ocate Creek.

Four miles southwest of the wagons, Roland Ferguson dragged himself into a thin band of shade at the bottom of a deep gully and passed out. The mustang craned his neck down to sniff the still man. At the coppery scent of blood, he tossed his head and blew before backing a few paces away.

The animal ducked his head to bite at the saddle hanging below his belly. He wanted to get rid of the saddle and he needed man for that, but this man made him nervous. The mustang looked east down the arroyo where there were other men and took a tentative step, stopping when the smell of blood filled his nostrils. Ferguson lay in the bottom of the high-walled gully directly between the mustang and the wagons. The blood smell grew stronger. Blowing hard to expel the scent, the mustang turned away, walking up the gully. He paused once, looking back to see if the man would get up, before continuing toward the west looking for a way out of the arroyo.

Doc rounded a bend in the narrowing canyon and pulled up short, six feet before a sheer wall of stone. Retracing his steps, he spent fifteen minutes walking out of the canyon, the third box canyon he'd wandered into. The trip through the gap between Ortega Mesa and Rayado Mesa covered two miles. The narrow gap climbed three hundred feet to the middle before descending and the entire passage was littered with loose stones and boulders ranging in size from a clenched fist to one of Murphy's wagons. The area south of the passage was a maze of deep ravines and canyons, and Doc had made several wrong turns.

The smooth rock faces reflected the sunlight and trapped the heat. No wind stirred within the maze and Doc's skin glistened with sweat, soaking the deerskin shirt. The straps from his weapons dug deep into his shoulders through the damp hide. For the last two hours Doc had tried every ravine that branched south from the canyon he'd followed from the gap, and all led to dead ends. With a tired sigh, he shifted his weapons, rolled his shoulders, and started back for the gap. It would take an hour, but he was now certain there was no other way out. He had to backtrack.

Once he cleared the canyon, he still had fifteen miles of rough country to traverse before he reached the Ocate Creek crossing. His plan to make it by sundown was still wandering lost in the canyon behind; it wasn't going to happen, not even close. If there was a clear sky tonight, he'd make it by midnight; if not, it'd be closer to morning. The sky was clear now, Doc noted; maybe it would hold. He had to be hunkered in good cover before dawn, holed up in a spot where he could hide without requiring much movement for water and shade because he might have to sit for a day or more waiting for the company to roll through. "Assumin' they ain't already crossed and are halfway to the Wagon Mound," he said aloud. Doc lengthened his stride—he had to move!

CHAPTER FIFTEEN

SITTING ABACK A MUSTANG ONE HUNDRED YARDS AHEAD of the lead wagon, Todd Bracken raised his arm to signal the driver. Bracken wanted the camp buttoned up tonight and the large knoll beneath him held room for all of the wagons and stock. The driver lifted a hand in reply and began to turn his team. Waiting for the wagon to arrive, Bracken surveyed the vast Canadian River plain. The dry winter had not affected this portion of the Trail. Plenty of good grazing and water would be welcome relief for companies that opted to cross the parched Cimarron Cutoff.

Glancing southeast, he eyed the distinct shape of the massive Wagon Mound, an isolated mountain that bore a strong resemblance to a canvas-topped Conestoga wagon. East, far across the prairie, he spied the telling sign of a company on the move. It was no more than a low patch of dust-colored haze, but Bracken was experienced enough to know what a wagon train looked like from such a distance. The Mountain Branch, running south from the Rayado River, and the Cimarron Cutoff, angling south-west, converged at the Mora River and re-formed into a single trail. At this point, the two branches were only twenty miles apart. The Wagon Mound lay along the cutoff, itself twenty miles or so from the Mora River.

As the lead wagon rumbled up the knoll, Bracken shook off his musings and directed the man where to halt his team, giving similar instruction to each driver as his wagon crested the mound. In the end, he'd placed the company in a wide circle with room for the animals inside. They would graze the stock on the flats until sundown.

Two miles due west rose Gonzales Mesa, plain to see in the early-afternoon sun, so he pulled Ferguson's telescope and scanned the slopes while the men readied the camp. The Trail, running between camp and the mesa, was empty for forty miles in both directions. While there were places along the route where a hundred men might not be visible, he knew a train of wagons would be easy to spot, and tonight he'd been wishing for some company.

After talking earlier with Shep Knorr, Bracken slowed the wagons to give Doc more time to reach the Ocate crossing. It would also make it easier for Shep and Roland Ferguson to catch up, for the mountain man had decided to go after Ferguson and return him to the company. "A'fore he gits hisself killed," was how Shep put it. Besides, with Doc alive and planning to rendezvous at the crossing, there was no reason for the wagon master to go look for the lost man. It was Shep's idea to camp the company somewhere east of the mesa in case Doc changed his mind about where to meet up. They agreed it was a low possibility, but it gave Doc more time and options.

Bracken doubted the mound had seen service as a campsite before tonight. There was neither the evidence of past fires nor the telltale scraps of metal and leather, discarded after repair or replacement of harnesses and such, that littered the ground of the usual camps. The big drawback to the spot was the lack of water, but he'd picked the campsite with two thoughts in mind. It was a mile east of the Trail, which put it that much farther from the mesa and the Apaches, and it left the company less than twelve miles from Ocate Creek. The mound would also provide the men with a better field of fire, at least during the day. At night, it wouldn't matter; the Apaches were phantoms in the dark.

Tomorrow, they'd roll those twelve miles in time to establish a camp near the crossing with daylight left to burn. Shep wanted Doc to have full light to watch the wagons stop because the scout would likely wait for dark before sneaking into camp. If so, he could use the extra daylight to survey several possible routes; he might need more than one if the Indians were around.

The men were quiet as they went about their chores. Most days when they stopped early, the men were loud and boisterous, glad for the shortened day, but tonight, every one of them knew that Doc's life might be at stake. In short order, the quickest the company had ever set up camp, the chores were done and the cook had supper on. Without instruction, several of the drivers took their rifles and settled into hiding just outside the circle, ready to provide the missing men with armed help if needed.

Bracken ordered a couple of water barrels opened for the stock and a large fire built in the middle of the circle to be kept burning all night. He wanted the light visible from miles away, and he wanted the area inside the circle well lit. Satisfied, he slid open the telescope and made another scan of the mesa.

Concealed two hundred feet up the eastern slope of the small mesa, two Apaches considered the camp as they watched the slanting sunlight reflect from the telescope.

"If the white man does not appear, we will move closer at dusk," said Gunsi.

Toh-Yah nodded his head in agreement and looked toward the base of the slope. He picked out the three prone warriors, each one several hundred yards apart in a line that ran north to south along the Trail. If

Shadow appeared, Toh-Yah or Gunsi would alert the hidden warriors by hand signals, informing the Apaches where to find the white man.

"I do not believe Shadow will try tonight," Toh-Yah said, then added, "I think he is farther south, waiting."

"Probably, but we are here so we will wait and see."

At dusk, the two warriors would descend the slope to join the other three, and then under the cover of darkness the small band intended to close to within yards of the camp. There, they would again spread out and wait. If Shadow appeared, he might not expect them so near the wagons and perhaps one of them would capture him. Only if the warrior could not get to Shadow in time had Gunsi given permission to kill the white man. If the night passed without Shadow's appearance, the warriors would regroup before sunrise and make their way south, hunting for sign.

Bathed in a cold sweat, Roland Ferguson awoke to find Shep Knorr kneeling over him.

"You're a lucky man, Ferguson."

"Lucky?" the wagon master hissed through clenched teeth. "I got me a leg bone . . . stickin' through my pants. How do you figure . . . that for luck?"

"If'n you hadn't broke your leg you might've run into them 'Paches," Shep replied. "Then you'd be dead. I'd call that lucky."

The mountain man had treated broken bones before and he gave Ferguson a quick and capable assessment. The leg was broken midway between knee and ankle, and if he could get it aligned and set, it should heal properly. Settling onto the ground, Shep sat at Ferguson's foot, his own legs straddling the injured leg.

"Hang on to somethin', 'cause this is gonna hurt. Just don't yell out."

Shep used his feet to squeeze Ferguson's thigh, then he gripped the injured leg by the ankle and pulled. Ferguson's eyes flared wide and his mouth opened to scream, but before any sound escaped, the eyes rolled back and the man passed out.

Shep hunted along the bottom of the gully until he found two pieces of straight wood. With his tomahawk, he cut the branches to length and tightly bound them to Ferguson's leg. He worked quickly to finish the splint. He wanted time to build a loop and pull the injured man up the side of the gully before he awoke. The hoist up the side of the gully would hurt an alert man, and it was going to hurt the unconscious Ferguson, but he wouldn't know it if Shep moved fast enough.

After wrestling the wagon master from the gully, Shep dropped back down, climbing out again after he found two poles long enough to build a travois. He found the slicker and bedroll lying in the gully and used them to fashion the litter. When Ferguson came to, Shep handed him a cup of broth. The injured man had slept long enough for Shep to build a small fire in the gully, out of sight of the mesa, and prepare the broth from jerked venison and boiled water. Even though the mesa was eight or nine miles away, a small fire could be seen for twice that distance from its high top and Shep wasn't a man who took chances. The broth wasn't much, but it was something. Ferguson had lost blood and needed fluids.

Shep didn't have a good bedside manner because he didn't have time for one. When Ferguson, half delirious, refused the broth, Shep pried open the wagon master's jaws and poured in two cupfuls. He would have tried for a third cup if Ferguson hadn't passed out again.

Three miles from Shep and Ferguson, near the base of the mountains, the sides of the deep gully tapered back at an angle the mustang could scale. The hanging saddle made the climb difficult and the horse labored over the top. On the flat plain, he dropped to roll, trying in vain to dislodge the saddle. Struggling to all four feet, the mustang shook several times, then crow-hopped along the lip of the gully. Unsuccessful and exhausted, he hung his head, drawing great breaths into his trembling body.

At the base of the mountains stood a copse of pines and, after recovering from the wild attempt to shake free of the saddle, the mustang walked straight for the largest tree. A short time later, side bloody and torn from the rough bark, the mustang emerged from the copse without the saddle. He caught the scent of water and started south.

Doc stumbled and fell hard on the loose rubble of rock. Pushing up to his hands and knees, he waited to regain his bearings. The night sky was little more than a sliver overhead; all that shone above the deep, narrow canyon were a few faint stars. He'd lost count of how many times he'd stumbled, but this was his second hard fall in the last twenty steps. Gingerly, he leaned sideways and sat, using his hips to brush a spot free of stones. The first fall bruised a couple of ribs, the second had barked a shin, and if he continued it would only get worse.

Taking a moment to clear a larger area, Doc lay down and looked at the dark ribbon of sky framed on both sides by the inky blackness of the canyon walls. He couldn't make out any features of the walls but he knew they were there because the stars weren't. His eyes closed and he listened to the far-off call of an owl. Maybe he should lie here and sleep for an hour, he thought. An hour from now the moon might have risen high enough to cast some feeble light into the canyon and he could go on without as much trouble. Besides, there was no sense in pushing on now; his schedule was shot and he'd either make it in time or he wouldn't. To travel without light in the canyon risked an injury that could delay him further.

The next time Ferguson regained consciousness, Shep was pulling the travois down the Santa Fe Trail. The mountain man would have preferred to avoid the wagon road and the likelihood the Indians might be scouting its route, but its smooth bottom made pulling the travois easier on both men.

Ferguson tried to speak, then cleared his throat and tried again. "How about some water?"

"Good idea," the mountain man replied. "Could use a swig m'self."

Ferguson drained half the canteen before handing it back. A good sign, Shep thought. In the cool air, the injured man had stopped sweating and seemed to be resting easy in spite of the jostling ride. The moon hung low in the sky, offering a meager light.

"How long was I out?"

"Few hours."

Shep started to ask the man if he felt good enough to keep going, then realized it didn't matter. Somewhere up ahead the wagons were in camp and he had to get the injured man to safety. A half mile farther down the Trail, a distant flicker of firelight drew his attention, and thirty minutes later he knew he'd found the company. It took more time to reach the camp than he anticipated it would when he first spotted the fire, and as he drew nearer, he understood why. The fire burning in the middle of the circled wagons was four times larger than it needed to be. Its massive size had led him to believe he was close to camp when he was still miles away.

Tracks of wagon wheels veering southeast off the Trail marked the spot where the company left the road. Shep eased the travois to the ground and knelt beside Ferguson.

"We got about a thousand yards to go, but we're gonna have to leave the road and go 'cross the prairie. It's gonna get rough." Shep peered at the injured man, looking for signs of distress. Ferguson had a fever raging, and tightness around the eyes and mouth hinted at the pain, but he was holding up, determined to be as light a burden as possible.

"You're a strong man, Ferguson. I think you'll mend just fine."

"I owe you, Shep," Ferguson croaked. He cleared his throat to continue, and when Shep started to protest, the injured man grasped his arm and said, "No sir! Don't you be duckin' my thanks. My life may not mean much to you, but I'm right partial to it."

Shep Knorr had made another friend, and a good one. Well, he thought, the hills were fillin' up with people and he didn't need any more enemies. Might as well make friends of 'em. He nodded once at Ferguson, then tugged his arm free from the grip and pulled the cork from the canteen. While Ferguson drank thirstily, Shep observed the camp atop the mound.

Bracken had done well. The high spot held all the wagons and he saw the stock lying inside the circle. If the men were moving around, he couldn't see it, and that meant they understood the danger. Lingering a bit to let Ferguson rest before starting the bumpy trek to camp, the mountain man kept his eyes on the mound. Sitting where he was, below the camp, his only clue as to what went on within the circle came from the firelit gaps left between the wagons.

Something, perhaps luck, drew his attention to one of the gaps in time to see a dark shape cross between him and the light, low to the ground and *outside* of the ring of wagons! He glanced down at Ferguson, hoping the man was as tough as he looked. It was going to be a long cold night and Ferguson had just drained the last of the water. Leaning low to place his mouth next to the wagon master's ear, Shep began to whisper.

Three hours before sunrise, the Apaches pulled out. Making their way to the Trail before stopping, they gathered to talk.

"Why do we leave so soon?" questioned Elu. The Apache knew there were two more hours of full darkness remaining.

"He is not here . . . and he is not coming," Gunsi replied.

"But how do you—" Elu started.

"Gunsi is right," Toh-Yah interrupted. "We must make other plans."

When the warriors moved again, two groups went in separate directions. Gunsi and Elu trotted south along the wagon road, and Toh-Yah led Ka-a-e-tano and Akule to the west.

As they ran, Ka-a-e-tano asked, "Where do you think Shadow went?"

"Through one of the passes between the three mesas," Toh-Yah replied. "Probably the far western pass between the two large mesas. He would have risked our discovering his track if he used the pass by the small mesa."

"The land south of the far pass is broken by many canyons," Ka-a-e-tano replied. "Finding his sign will be difficult."

"That is why you are with me, tracker, and not with Gunsi."

Sitting on the slope of the mesa the day before, Toh-Yah and Gunsi discussed their next move should the white man not appear. The two warriors now put the alternative plan into action. Because they had known what they would do, little discussion occurred when they gathered at the wagon road, and Ka-a-e-tano wanted to know what was expected of him. And what he should be expecting.

Concerned that Gunsi and Toh-Yah presumed he could track Shadow across the rocks and barren earth of the canyons, the tracker warned, "It could take days to find Shadow's trail among the canyons."

"We will not travel through the canyons," Toh-Yah answered. "Our search will start at the southern end, where the canyons empty onto the plain."

Ka-a-e-tano shook his head; he should have guessed the maneuver, but instead was so concerned over his possible failure that he did not think of strategy. The tracker was glad to be with Toh-Yah rather than Gunsi. He liked Toh-Yah, but then everyone did; it was more a matter of respect and leadership. Toh-Yah answered his questions while overlooking the limited thought behind them. Gunsi never overlooked an opportunity to build himself up by tearing down someone else. It was the one difference between the two men that many felt would result in Toh-Yah becoming chief.

As warriors, both were fearless and strong and each possessed an intuitive understanding of tactics and cunning far beyond the average warrior. They were long considered friends, though rivals, and Ka-a-e-tano knew that a breaking point loomed near. Gunsi's father, Kos-nos-un-da, was aging and soon there would be a new chief. The hunt for Shadow had brought forth the best in Toh-Yah: his cunning, caution, and his encouragement of men. Gunsi had deteriorated into a surly and bullying dog. When the time came, if they all lived, Ka-a-e-tano knew which man would receive his support.

Doc, awakened by his own chattering teeth, slapped his arms and rubbed muscles made stiff by the cold. Though it was dark, he could now distinguish the rocks and stones scattered over the canyon floor. He wouldn't know how long he'd slept until he had cleared the canyon and examined the moon and stars, but he knew he'd rested longer than he had intended. A few more slaps, followed by a stamping of numb feet preceded the resumption of his journey.

Exiting the canyon, he was surprised to see the gray light of approaching dawn in the east. Another day was beginning, his seventh since riding from the camp below Raton Pass. Would it be the last, he wondered? Free of the dark canyon walls and aided by the increasing light, Doc set off at a trot, angling southeast toward a spot he believed he'd find Ocate Creek. Hunger gnawed at him, a feeling only slightly more demanding than his thirst.

Rather than leave the company after saying farewell, he gave thought to remaining with the wagons for a few days to rest and recover. His sagging pants evidenced the weight he'd lost over the past week and it wouldn't do to begin life in the mountains weak from exhaustion and hunger. A smell of antelope steak sizzling over a fire filled his memory, causing his mouth to water. Doc gave his head a violent shake. "Whoa there, son. You'll go daft if you start imaginin' things."

To keep his mind from hunger, he switched to thoughts of his coming life as a mountain man and began to write a mental list of supplies he'd need to make his start. The long miles passed underfoot and soon after completing his list, weighing the advantages and disadvantages of each item, he found Ocate Creek. At least, what he hoped was Ocate Creek.

CHAPTER SIXTEEN

DOC SLAKED HIS THIRST THEN LEANED BACK against the steep side of the creek bank and closed his eyes, drowsing under the sun. Sleep was not the intent, just a few minutes' rest. Sleep wasn't possible; the pangs in his belly wouldn't permit it. Food would satisfy his hunger, but more important, it would fight off the heavy weakness that settled on him.

At a small sound across the narrow creek, Doc's eyelids lifted to find a mountain cottontail slowly approaching the water. Not trusting his vision, he squeezed the lids shut then popped them open. The rabbit was moving toward the water. Doc sat immobile while his mind raced through possibilities. His weapons lay by his side where he had placed them before drinking. The bow wouldn't do; it would take too long. The rifle meant a sure kill even if the shot would have to take the rabbit on the run. Using the last ball on the rabbit was too big a risk, he would need it if the Apaches showed, and firing the gun would pinpoint his location if the Indians were within hearing.

The cottontail moved to the water's edge and lifted up on his haunches for a quick look around. Doc knew when the rabbit lowered to the water it would drink quickly and be gone. The water was a necessity, but it was also an excellent hunting ground and only predators lingered over water. His right hand reached for the tomahawk at his waist and slowly slid it free. With luck, the broad flat head of the tomahawk would strike the animal with enough force to stun it. Doc would need but a few seconds to cross the creek and secure the cottontail.

Lunging forward from the reclined lean against the bank, Doc hurled the tomahawk in a hard sidearm throw, knowing at once that it would miss. Any hoped-for accuracy was lost because of the awkward sitting position. The rabbit leapt sideways at the movement with all four paws churning the air. Upon landing, it would be at full speed. The hungry man watched in helpless frustration as the tomahawk flew for the water two feet short of the bank. With a clang and shower of sparks, the steel head of the weapon struck a protruding stone and tumbled into the air, slamming into the leaping rabbit.

An hour later, Doc tossed the last bone into the coals and rinsed his hands in the creek. Dragging a moccasined foot through the dirt, he scraped earth over the small fire. He stepped to the lip of the creek bank and shouldered the weapons while studying his back trail. The only movement was the bending of the grass before the wind. With one final look, he followed the running water toward the Canadian River. The creek meandered along an easterly course over the wide mesa. He was headed for Ocate crossing and, if lucky, the end of the chase.

Unlike a typical mesa, which arose from a plain like an island surrounded by water, Ocate Mesa resembled a large porch that ended in a single step down to a street. Its origins began fifteen miles to the west beneath the Sangre de Cristo Mountains. A broad, flat shelf of land broken by a few isolated hills and widely scattered trees extended halfway to the Canadian River before it dropped four hundred feet to the river valley. Viewed from the east, its high steep sides and flat top looked like any other flat-topped hill, but from the top, the western end of the mesa formed the foundation of the distant mountains as it slid beneath the towering crags.

Ocate Creek surged down from the high country and onto the mesa where it flowed east for its junction with the Canadian. Five miles from the mesa's rim it began a slow carving descent through the depths of the plateau, forming a long canyon that emptied onto the Canadian Plain a short distance from the Santa Fe Trail. Somewhere within the rugged canyon or on the nearby steep slope of the mesa, Doc would wait for the company.

"Why in blazes didn't Doc just come with you?" Ferguson demanded. "All this mess'd be done with if'n he had."

The sun was up and the camp fully awake before Shep Knorr thought it safe to rouse the company's attention. He did so by waving Ferguson's white handkerchief. With plenty of hands to carry the travois to camp, the wagon master avoided a rough dragging across the prairie. After Ferguson received what medical attention the company could provide—a liberal pour of whiskey over the wound, followed by a large dollop of liniment used by the wrangler on the stock—he voiced the question.

Ferguson thought to ask after his fifth deep pull on the bottle of whiskey. It was stout whiskey, Shep noted. Ferguson already had a slur to his words. The wagon master sat with the leg propped atop an overturned bucket, his face drawn and pale. The whiskey didn't relieve the pain, but the injured man had drunk enough that he didn't care.

"We talked 'bout that," Shep replied. "But there weren't no way of knowin' I could make it back, and Doc figured his best chance was at the crossin'. I was only gonna head this way if all the 'Paches passed by. If'n they was scattered all over, I would've drifted back into the hills. Takin' Doc up into them mountains with me wouldn't have got him back here to you boys."

The wagon master, eyes closed, lay still and Shep wondered whether the man rested, or slept, or passed out, the whiskey bottle empty at his side. In case Ferguson was awake, he continued, addressing his remarks toward Bracken and the gathered men. There hadn't been time to explain when he'd caught up to the wagons the day before.

"Doc knew he had most, if not all that bunch behind him, but what we didn't know was how strewn out they might be. If'n he'd tried to cut across to the Trail, they could be some a-waitin' on 'im. So, he figured to keep headin' south, keep the 'Paches behind, and let the Trail come to him."

"You say you saw them that was followin'?" asked one of the men. "How many was they?"

"That's a right curious thing," Shep replied. "I seen but five and I got no idea where the others might be. Could be they up 'n quit."

"Well," the man continued, "I reckon five ain't so bad."

Shep snorted and eyed the speaker with disdain. "No, five ain't so bad as twenty," he said with slow sarcasm. "But it's still too many. To my way of thinkin', a hundred-year-old blind and crippled Jicarilla woman is too many when she's after your hair. And them *five*"—he cast a sideways glance at the man—"are all prime buck warriors. If'n you think they ain't so much, sashay on out there and give Doc some help."

The speaker's face and neck colored, but he held his tongue.

"Shut up, Muldoon!" Ferguson barked without opening his eyes. "What's next, Shep?"

After hearing the rest of Doc's plan, Ferguson ordered the company under way. By redistributing the load, they cleared space for the injured man's litter in one of the wagons. Ferguson was asleep before the lead team took a step.

Ka-a-e-tano knelt to examine the tracks. Looking up, he grinned at Toh-Yah. "It seems Shadow has tired of flying. These are his prints."

"How far ahead is he? Half a day?" Toh-Yah guessed an answer to his own question.

"Less." Ka-a-e-tano stood and followed the clear trail with his eyes. "He is walking."

Toh-Yah wondered why Shadow traveled at a slow pace. Was he injured? He voiced the question to Ka-a-e-tano.

"I do not believe so," replied the tracker after another scrutiny of the tracks.

"He is a runner, more fleet than any of us," Toh-Yah mumbled. "Why wouldn't he run for the white settlements far to the south? We would not be able to catch him."

"Perhaps he does not know of the settlements," offered Akule, speaking for the first time.

It was possible, but Toh-Yah doubted it nonetheless. Shadow moved through the mountains with an ease that suggested knowledge of the country. Then why?

Reading his leader's thoughts, the tracker offered, "He may not think we could find his trail."

That was also possible, even likely; still Toh-Yah wavered. Shadow was shrewd. Was this another trick?

At a fast lope, the three warriors followed the tracks for a quarter mile. From atop a rise, the trail they followed suddenly angled southeast. The prints showed their quarry began to run.

"Shadow found what he wanted and is moving faster," said Toh-Yah. "We must hurry if we are to trap him."

Gunsi and Elu squatted in the shade of an overhang cut from the rock wall by Ocate Creek. Both warriors were tired though no longer thirsty, having satisfied their need for water. Gunsi, anxious to search the canyon, lingered because he knew Elu would complain at moving again so soon. Complaints meant nothing to Gunsi. Elu would not be thorough if forced to move now and, with only two searchers, they must be thorough.

"How do you know Shadow is in the canyon?"

"I don't," Gunsi replied.

Elu waited for an explanation of why they would search the hot, rugged canyon if Shadow wasn't there. Gunsi remained silent, arms folded around his knees as he stared into the canyon.

Elu grew tired of waiting and spoke. "Then why . . ."

"Because he might be there," Gunsi snapped.

Withdrawing into silence, Elu glowered at the warrior. Gunsi faced away from him so the act of defiance, though slight, was sufficient for the limited courage of Elu. The small Llanero took a moment's satisfaction in plotting against Gunsi. When they returned to the village, he would forbid his sister to marry Gunsi. Instead, he would pledge her to Toh-Yah. Nah-hi-mani was beautiful and Elu felt certain he could arrange a marriage. He was just as certain that Toh-Yah would pay any price he asked. Like Gunsi, Elu remained unaware that Nah-hi-mani already favored Toh-Yah. Her time with Gunsi came from Elu's insistence that she do so and not from any reason of her own.

The only large aspect of Elu was what he thought of himself. His father, Satl, achieved high rank and respect in all bands of the Jicarilla during a lifetime of bravery and wise council. The one failure of Satl was an inability to pass his traits on to his son. Even the idea of Nah-hi-mani marrying Gunsi or Toh-Yah came from Satl, whispered to his daughter just before his death. Apache society barred women from any outward appearance of authority, but Satl knew Nah-hi-mani, and not Elu, would be the salvation of his family. She could guide Elu, the oldest son, through innocent suggestions or comments, planning and leading the family from behind his back. Her beauty would allow her to marry a warrior capable of providing for her mother and her many younger brothers and sisters.

In spite of Elu's laziness, his father loved him. As with any father, Satl never lost hope that his firstborn son would mature to assume a respected place in the tribe. He trusted Nah-hi-mani to protect Elu from mistakes or ridicule until his son grew to manhood. It was a job she had performed too well; her shrewdness enlarged the wealth of her family with an ease that prevented Elu from recognizing his shortcomings. Once she married and moved her family into the lodge of her husband, Elu would finally be on his own. Then he would succeed or fail according to his own efforts.

"Let's move," ordered Gunsi.

The warriors stopped at the mouth of the canyon and gazed up at the sides. A steep boulder-covered slope of talus rose from the canyon floor to a height of one hundred feet. Above the talus towered a vertical wall of stone three hundred feet high. Looking up the canyon, Gunsi saw that the height of the vertical face remained constant and the talus slope tapered away as the floor of the canyon lifted toward the top of the mesa. Within a mile from the entrance, the talus disappeared altogether. They would need to search the slope for a short distance only; the remainder would be visible from the floor as they made their way up the canyon.

Somewhere within the stone-walled chasm, they would meet Toh-Yah. Gunsi hoped his rival was following the white man's trail. If not, they might never find him. Perhaps even now Toh-Yah drove the white man down the canyon toward him and Elu. Encouraged by the thought he spoke. "We will have to climb the slopes to search until we get farther into the canyon."

Renewed by his earlier plotting, Elu stepped forward with eagerness, pushing past Gunsi to lead the way into the canyon. The small warrior intentionally picked the steepest side and began to work his way upward. Gunsi watched as the small Apache scampered from boulder to boulder. With a perplexed shake of his head, the warrior crossed the canyon floor and started up the opposite slope.

✻　✻　✻

Where the creek began its gradual descent into the depths of the mesa, Doc hunkered down beside a boulder and studied the long narrow canyon. He couldn't see the mouth of the canyon as it was hidden by a bend a mile from where he sat. What he could see troubled him. Within the first half mile, the canyon dropped fifty feet between sheer walls of stone. If the walls were sheer all the way to the mouth, once he entered the canyon his only means of escape would be at the two ends. He needed a look at the rest of the canyon before he committed to its depths.

Doc stood to scan the plain behind him then trotted across the mesa at an angle to intersect the canyon beyond the bend. Cutting across the top of the mesa shortened the distance to three-quarters of a mile. If he could, he'd work his way down from the intersection point; if not, he would backtrack to the head of the canyon. In all, he figured he was risking no more than thirty minutes.

Slowing to a walk as he neared the canyon, he stopped on the lip. What he saw no longer troubled him; it scared him. Lying beneath him was a much longer and deeper chasm than he'd imagined. The canyon was walled by near-vertical rock for half its distance. Over the remaining mile-and-a-half to two-mile length to the mouth, the sheer walls gradually gave way to ever-widening slopes.

Scattered along several breaks in the walled portion were columns of very steep talus. At the base of the breaks, rubble from the collapsed sections of wall lay strewn across the canyon floor. Many of the fallen boulders were the size of wagons and one was so large it almost blocked the entire width. He could hear the rush of the water forced through the narrow opening as Ocate Creek poured down the canyon.

Large cracks in the mesa banded the canyon, signs of future collapses. Doc walked to the nearest one and peered down into the blackness. The crack, easily large enough to swallow a man, warned that the edge of the canyon was no place to wander at night. He pulled back from the fissure and sat down to think. Should he attempt to climb down here or return to the head of the canyon and travel through it to the distant plain? Once inside, he would be at risk if the Apaches hadn't fallen for his ruse. If they came hunting him, and found him in the canyon, he would likely die.

Looking east across the plateau, Doc tried to imagine what the edge of the mesa looked like as it fell away to the plain. Was it sloped or was it like the canyon with vertical rock faces with scattered fractures? If it had the same sheer walls, he would not be able to descend and would be trapped atop the mesa and cornered by the canyon. His chest tightened as he made the choice to take the only path he was certain allowed passage to Ocate crossing. He was going into the canyon.

Squatting beside the boulder at the head of the canyon, Doc watched the Apaches cross a high mound four miles away. They were headed straight for the creek and the spot where he'd found the rabbit. They had his trail. Waiting until the Indians disappeared into a low vale, Doc turned and ran into Ocate Canyon. He sprinted for a half mile, slowing amid the debris of a collapsed segment of the canyon wall. Most of the rubble was large, but the number of smaller pieces spread around was cause for worry. He had survived one sprained ankle, but a second might not turn out so well. Still, he moved faster than was sensible. He had to clear the bend and find a way past the rubble blocking Ocate Creek before the Apaches reached the head of the canyon.

The Indians were at least an hour behind and if they came straight into the canyon, his lead should be enough. But if they happened to follow his trail across the mesa to the point above the blocked creek, they might arrive in time to spot him working around the obstruction, and he'd have no chance at all.

An hour later, he stopped to rest in the shade of a giant boulder. He'd found a fairly easy way over the rubble dam and when the Apaches hadn't shown on the canyon rim, he knew they were coming down the gorge behind him. Doc could see the distant mouth of the canyon and the wide-open Canadian Plain beyond. With the Apaches behind him, his course was simple—clear the canyon as quickly as possible and then run for the Santa Fe Trail. He'd know which way to go upon reaching the Trail. If he found fresh wagon tracks, he'd go south; if not, he'd go north.

The three Indians behind were not as big a worry now that he believed them to be in the canyon. He was moving fast, and knowing they couldn't close the distance gave him some comfort. That there were only three was a problem. At least once before, the Apaches had split up to cover more ground, and twice they'd guessed his next move in time to lay traps for him. Doc was cautious enough to assume they might have done so again.

Craning his neck to peer up the canyon, Doc could see as far as the bend and he let his eyes slowly probe the walled confines. Satisfied the Apaches hadn't yet rounded the bend, he turned his attention downcanyon and watched for a full five minutes before moving out. He took three steps and dropped to the rocky ground, staring hard at a distant pile of rubble.

Something had flickered at the edge of his vision. Just a flash of movement, but enough to let him know he was in trouble. There was nothing in the bleak canyon to attract wildlife, so anything moving was going to be a man. Could it be Shep, he wondered? Sharp stones bit into his chest and legs and yet he remained motionless. The minutes dragged by while he watched. Not knowing who was down below and how many there might be forced Doc to ignore the pain and hold still—waiting.

CHAPTER SEVENTEEN

FAR BELOW, THE INDIAN STEPPED INTO VIEW. Doc watched as the Apache climbed a boulder and stared up the canyon. Doc's eyes were drawn to the opposite side when a second Indian appeared. Even from the distance that separated the hunters from the hunted, the huge Apache was easy to recognize. The Indians had done what he feared they would do. They had split up to trap him.

Moving slowly to avoid detection, Doc took five minutes to crawl backward into the shadowed recess of the boulder. The Apaches down-canyon were no longer in sight. He looked over his shoulder to see if the first group of three Indians had rounded the bend and was relieved to see they hadn't yet made it that far. Panic lingered at the edge of thought, in-truding on his plans for escape. Ideas began to form only to be wiped away, his mind distracted by some sound or sight, real or imagined.

Doc spoke aloud softly, obliging himself to focus. "All right, I can't go forward or back so that leaves one choice. I've got to hide."

The canyon was littered with remnants of fallen cliff sections, but the only boulder large enough to hide behind was where he now sat. He did a quick estimate of the time it would take for the two groups of Indians to meet. It was purely guesswork, but instinct told him they would meet within a hundred yards of his boulder. It would be impossible for him to let one group pass by and slip out behind them, and they wouldn't fail to look behind the only large boulder in sight.

He considered Shep's trick of hiding in the open and discarded it. That only worked if those you wanted to avoid weren't aware of your presence. These Indians were searching behind every stone and boulder and would not overlook Doc lying in plain view.

"Okay. I can't hide. What else?"

Panic seized him. He would have to fight. His frightened mind wildly considered every possibility, finally deciding his best chance was to use the bow. As one group passed, he could loose an arrow at the trailing man. There would be enough time to get an arrow into a second one before they realized they were under attack. He could then use the last ball from his rifle on a third.

Assuming he hit, and killed, two Apaches with the bow and one with the rifle, there would be two left. Chances were slim that he could get three; two were likely, but three was pushing hard on even Doc's remarkable streak of luck. Even if he killed three he would be trapped in a canyon with two or more Apaches and night approaching. Doc rolled his head back and stared up at the strip of sky between the walls.

Suddenly, he crawled around behind the boulder and studied the canyon cliff. The face went straight up but its surface was covered with cracks and small ledges. Reaching up he grasped on to a thin protruding edge and pulled. The edge held. Rising to a crouch, he looked across the top of the boulder for the Indians. The first group had not rounded the bend but they would at any moment. The two Apaches downcanyon were not in view.

To his right, a wide section of the cliff jutted five feet out from the face, and he scrambled over. He was more worried about the three following Apaches than the two searching below. When the three came around the bend, the first thing they would see was the wall he was attempting to climb, and him, if he was hanging there. The jutting face would allow him to climb out of sight of anyone coming behind until they were even with the protruding cliff. He would be at the edge of sight of the two Indians searching their way up the canyon—and the cleft was partly in shadow. Climbing in the darkened corner would also give him two faces of the cliff to work with.

Several handholds made for quick climbing and in a matter of minutes he was thirty feet up the wall. Grasping a thin edge with his right hand, he began to shift his weight when the edge crumbled, swinging him hard into the corner. The force of the blow knocked the breath from his lungs and he felt his left hand weakening. Fighting to stave off the enveloping dizziness, he concentrated on the tearing agony in his side, willing himself to feel every needle of pain.

When his breath returned, the huge intake of air made his side feel as if it had split apart. He dug at the cliff with his feet, feeling for resistance. Finally, his left foot found purchase and raised him, relieving the pressure on his left hand. The pain in his side subsided and he looked down to see that his ribs had been pressed against a sharp spine of rock. He twisted his torso to make certain that he'd not broken any ribs. "Shaken, but not broken," he mumbled and looked up.

The crumbled edge was gone and the next handhold was five feet overhead. Doc leaned his head back and twisted to look around his outstretched left arm at the adjoining wall. There was a ledge he might reach if he could switch his grip and use his left hand. He placed his right hand over the fingertips of his left hand and felt for the edge. It was too small; his left hand covered the entire width. He would have to let go in order to switch. Tentatively, he pressed down with his foot to carry more weight and lessen the importance of the handhold. His foot slipped from the notch and Doc scrambled until he regained the uncertain foothold.

He looked up again and studied the barren cliff face. Then he saw the crack. At first glance, he'd thought it was a shadow, a dark strip running up the corner. The bottom of the crack, less than two inches wide, was just out of reach of his right arm. It continued upward, widening gradually as it climbed from sight.

Doc took a deep breath and pushed into the notch with his foot while pulling hard with his left hand. His body rose up, and away from the wall. He would get only one chance. Swinging his right arm high overhead he jammed his hand into the narrow fissure, angled as if he were preparing to shake hands. The stiffened fingers and open palm slipped inside the crack and held. From somewhere up the canyon, he heard faint voices.

Pulling up on his right arm, he swung his left hand above the right and wedged it into the crack. Soon he was high enough to get his feet inside the widening fissure and he scrambled upward. As the voices drew nearer, he reached an arm up and felt—nothing. He looked up to find a wide lip. Swinging his leg up, he hooked it over the lip and rolled over the edge. A muffled roar, hammering to the beat of his heart, filled both ears as he lay panting on the rock shelf. Doc had come to rest on a wide ledge twenty feet below the canyon rim, and completely invisible from below.

He drew a deep breath of air, tantalized by the fresh taste after the stuffy air of the canyon. The scrambling climb loosened streams of dirt along with all sizes of small rocks. For the past hour he'd filled his lungs with the dusty, stagnant air. Doc clenched his hands then opened and closed them several times to ease their tired stiffness. He arched his back and stretched his body. Slowly, tension ebbed from muscles tightened by unrelenting strain.

When the voices sounded directly below, he rolled against the cliff face and scooted to the edge to peer over. The three Apaches had just passed underneath the jutting precipice and were continuing down the canyon. Careful not to lift his head, he raised his eyes to look down-canyon for the other two Indians, but found his vision blocked by the angled cliff face.

A loud call drew his attention back to the three Apaches and, a moment later, he was stunned to see the other two join them. He'd had no idea the two Indians coming up the canyon were so close. The angled wall had shielded him from their sight. A quick shock of fear whipped through as he realized he owed his life to the ledge. Had it not been there, he would now be on the cliff face in clear view of all five Apaches!

The conversation grew louder and several of the warriors added arm waving for emphasis. Although he left no tracks on the stone and rock floor of the canyon, his trail across the plateau left no doubt about his entrance. The two Indians were shouting at the three, and the three shouted back. Doc eased away from the edge and waited for the Indians to quiet down and move away.

Toh-Yah stood face to face with Gunsi. For once, he'd let his restraint slip and was enraged beyond even his vast self-control.

Hissing through clenched teeth he said, "I say again, for the *last* time: the white man did not slip past us. If you are not satisfied with my word . . . draw your knife!"

Gunsi glared at the Apache through eyes red with rage. Knowing the white man entered the canyon between the two groups and that they lost him was unbearable. The huge warrior's frustration at losing the white man yet again was beyond his patience. He wanted to smash the white man, to crush him with his hands. Since the white man wasn't within reach, his anger sought another target. And the old rivalry with Toh-Yah and his interfering with Nah-hi-mani made a prime target.

Slowly, Toh-Yah's last words sank beneath the seething of Gunsi's anger. "Draw your knife!" His hand dipped to the bone handle protruding from the wide belt. If Toh-Yah wanted to—a blast of cold air blew through his rage. Toh-Yah wanted to fight him! Looking into the face of his rival Gunsi felt the cold blast return. Toh-Yah was ready, eager to fight, and Toh-Yah was a dangerous man. The large Llanero didn't fear Toh-Yah, but he respected the skills and strength of his adversary. Enough so that he knew winning wouldn't keep him from a serious wound. More than settling the growing hatred for his former friend, he wanted the white man. To catch the white man he needed to be whole, and fighting Toh-Yah was a sure path to injury.

"Soon, Toh-Yah, we will settle our differences," Gunsi whispered. "After I have killed the white man!"

Gunsi stepped away from the angry warrior and stared up and down the canyon looking for any possible hideout. Without comment, Elu, Ka-a-e-tano, and Akule spread out and began searching. Toh-Yah, body rigid, followed Gunsi with a slight turn of his head. When he was able to bank the fire of his fury he too began to search, careful to keep one eye on the large Apache.

Thirty minutes later, Doc crawled to the edge and looked down. The loud arguing ended some time before and for the past twenty minutes there had been no sound at all. A careful scan of the canyon assured Doc the Indians had left, though he wasn't sure which direction, or if they'd all gone together. He slipped to the other end of the shelf and looked up the canyon, seeing no Apaches between the ledge and the bend. A look down from the front lip showed the area below the jutting precipice was empty. The Indians had all gone down the canyon.

Doc crawled across the ledge then stood at the canyon wall and looked up. The cliff face was not as weathered as the portion below and it had fewer handholds. Doc wondered at the difference as he stepped to the left side of the ledge and looked for the crack. It ended at the ledge. He backed away from the wall and looked up. Finally, he spotted a group of handholds that would get him started and reached up for the first notch.

The climb was difficult, much more so than the earlier ascent. The rock face was smooth and the thin edges he clung to were smaller and jagged. After ten minutes of exhausting effort, Doc found a good toehold and paused to rest. Panting and sweating, he pressed his face against the hot surface of the cliff, welcoming the brief rest and ignoring the searing heat on his cheek. He was still resting there when the stone above his head exploded in a spray of rock chips. He heard the boom of the rifle as his hands slipped from their holds. He fell, watching the cliff flash past.

As the rapid beating of his heart slowed, he began to hear their words of conversation. The words were a mystery to Doc, but the intent and the high-pitched, excited tone was clear. They had him and they knew it. He flinched as an arrow shattered against the cliff above him, snapping into several pieces before falling harmlessly to the ledge. A dozen more arrows followed the first, all without causing harm. The Apaches tried several tactics intended to drop an arrow onto the ledge but the canyon wasn't wide enough for the Indians to gain the proper angle.

Doc listened to the twang of the sinew as the bows loosed the arrows, discerning which were sent forth with a full pull from those with a partial pull of the string. In the end, all of the arrows hit the cliff wall, at least the ones that reached as high as the ledge. A final attempt, shooting an arrow straight up in the hope it would then drop straight back down on the ledge, failed miserably when the arrow missed the ledge and plunged back into the canyon. The scattering yelps of the Apaches ended the onslaught of arrows.

Doc now knew they couldn't get him from below, so they would try from above. Rolling to the cliff, he sat up and removed his weapons. Amazed that his fall hadn't caused any injury, he carefully wiped the dust from the rifle. The load had been in the rifle for days. Days filled with hard travel and rough treatment. He trusted the heavy Lancaster, but knew the odds of the weapon discharging were even at best. Still, it was his most powerful weapon and he increased his odds the only way he could, by emptying the pan and refilling it with the fine-grained powder.

He wiped the frizzen clean and lowered the pan cover before turning the rifle on its side and giving it a hard shake to seat the powder. He pulled the rod and dropped it down the barrel, listening for a tink and watching for a slight bounce of the rod. Satisfied by the proper sound and sight, he knew that the ball was seated tightly. Laying aside the rifle, he examined the bow and his supply of arrows.

Having heard no sound for some time, Doc chanced a peek over the front lip. The canyon appeared empty and he raised his head higher. He saw the Apache and pulled back just before the air split with the hiss of an arrow. Just one, he wondered? Quickly, he stuck his head over the lip and looked down, knowing he took a risk. If there were more than one, an arrow or rifle shot would be waiting for his move. His eyes found the Apache as the Indian fitted an arrow and released it toward him. Doc pulled back without concern and waited for the arrow to pass over.

He lay on the ledge thinking. The Apaches, believing that one man could keep Doc pinned on the ledge, had sent four men out of the canyon. "Well, they're pro'bly right," he muttered aloud. Still, he had his rifle and that gave him a chance. It would be hard to get the rifle over the lip and lined on the target while lying on the ledge. To aim it almost straight down the entire weapon would be over the edge and the Lancaster was too heavy to hold on target with so little leverage. He would have to stand and walk to the edge, acquire the target, and fire the weapon before the Apache saw him and reacted. The odds favored the Indian. Doc would have to guess where the Indian was and hope he guessed right. The Apache knew where Doc would be.

He poked his head over the lip and looked to see if the Indian was in the same place. He wasn't, and Doc spotted him as the sound of the bow reached his ears a hairbreadth before the arrow glanced off the lip. Shaken, Doc rolled all the way to the cliff and took several deep breaths. That had been too close. The Apache was clever and Doc was sure that he'd already moved again. Killing the warrior wasn't possible; there just wasn't time.

"There ain't much time for anything," he muttered. It would take at least two hours of fast travel for the four Apaches to clear the canyon and reach the cliff above his head, but two hours didn't seem that long. Briefly, Doc considered the possibility of jumping from the cliff. It was the only way down fast enough to avoid an arrow. If he lived and could move, he might kill the Apache. Surprise would certainly be on his side, he thought wryly. He remembered the height of the cliff and the rugged jumble of boulders littering the canyon floor and decided he'd rather take an arrow.

Resigning himself to the wait, Doc stacked his weapons at hand and stretched his legs. A small stone under his leg bit through the thin pants. He raised the leg and with the side of his foot scraped the stone toward the cliff face. He watched as it skittered across the ledge—and disappeared before reaching the wall!

He crawled over to investigate and found a six-inch-wide fissure between the ledge and wall. Looking down into the crevice, he could see daylight; and the oddity of the jutting precipice was revealed. The daylight visible through the fissure showed a wide space between the precipice and the cliff that extended all the way to the canyon floor. Doc was trapped atop a portion of the wall, more a column of stone, that had separated from the cliff but not fallen into the canyon. Well, he reasoned, hadn't fallen *yet*, at least not all of it. The jumble of boulders below had fallen from the top of the column, creating the ledge and explaining the smooth face of the wall above him. An idea formed as he gazed into the fissure. Doc crawled back to his weapons and thought out the idea.

Moments later he rolled to the lip and looked over, pulling back when he saw the Apache. For his plan to work the Indian had to move to the far side of the column, out of sight of the wide breach. From his position, the warrior could see the fissure, and Doc popped his head up two more times, the last showing his rifle, before he felt confident the Indian was as far as he would get from the fissure.

Doc shouldered the weapons and crawled to the ledge over the breach. Easing his head over the side in case he'd guessed wrong about the Apache, he looked down. The fissure was wide and deep enough for him to climb within its confines. It resembled a chimney missing one of its sides. A one-hundred-foot-tall chimney, Doc realized as he stared down the crack. The chimney also presented another problem: it had a cap on it. The fissure was only a few inches wide for the first three feet before it widened large enough for Doc to slip inside.

He would have to swing out over the ledge and climb down in plain sight until he could work into the fissure. He raised up further, inviting the warrior to shoot at him. When no arrow came, Doc rolled onto his stomach and slid his legs over the side. A brief moment of panic passed before his feet settled onto firm footing. Grasping the narrow fissure with his hand, he lowered his body over the edge.

Getting inside the breach was easier than he'd thought it would be. The chimney was lined with cracks and small protruding edges, testimony to the rough, and partial, separation between the column and the cliff. Doc scaled down as quickly as silence would allow, reaching the bottom of the fissure in minutes. Seen from above, Doc had thought the breach extended to the floor of the canyon, but upon reaching the bottom of the chimney, he found he was ten feet short.

Leaning out, he looked down to see the outside of the column was smooth. He would have to drop the remaining distance. He knelt and placed his hands on the edge of the fissure then slipped his legs down the column. Doc hung for a moment, preparing for a soft and quiet landing before dropping. He landed on the balls of his feet and let his knees collapse to absorb the weight.

Akule tried to guess the angle of the sun from the shadows high on the canyon wall. It would be a while before Gunsi and the others reached the top of the cliff, he decided. The young warrior looked up at the ledge and wondered what Shadow was doing. What must it feel like waiting to die? He wished Shadow would show his head again. Akule knew he had little chance of putting an arrow into the white man, but trying was great fun. Now that he'd seen Shadow duck and hide from his arrows, Akule had lost his fear. Shadow was a man after all.

The Apache refused to admit he was bored, hot, and tired. He had a job to do and he wanted to behave as a warrior, with great patience and cunning. The hide, shoot, and move game he'd played with Shadow was exciting, but the white man quit playing. At first, Akule felt important being selected as the one to prevent the white man from escaping the ledge. But he, and Shadow, soon learned there was no escape and the excitement of danger faded quickly.

The brashness of youth enticed the warrior to action. Perhaps if he moved or made some noise, Shadow might peek over the lip. Akule fitted an arrow and drew the string partway. Stepping to the top of his boulder, he extended a foot and toppled a pile of stones over the side, sending them clattering across the canyon floor. Quickly, he pulled the sinew taut and waited, his eyes locked onto the ledge. He lowered the bow a moment later, disappointed when Shadow didn't appear.

Akule switched his gaze to the lip of the canyon and looked along its length for the other warriors, who were not in sight. At a slight rustle of sound he turned to his right, brow furrowed; were the others returning? The thought vanished as Akule staggered from a blow to his chest. His agile feet held balance on the edge of the boulder as he looked down at his breast. The furrowed brow deepened and he stared openmouthed at the feather-tipped shaft. Whose arrow would be sticking in his chest?

His knees buckled and the warrior pitched forward onto his hands. His mind screamed at his clumsiness—to fall down would drive the arrow through his heart! He must be careful! Slowly, his head lifted, eyes straining to see through the dark. Wasn't it midday? As his sun set and the darkness deepened, he saw an odd thing—a shadow passed by. A shadow at night?

CHAPTER EIGHTEEN

Doc nocked another arrow and drew the string, ready to release if the first arrow failed to kill. His head cocked to one side with eyes lined along the shaft, Doc watched as the young warrior fell forward. Quickly, he scanned the canyon, unwilling to stake his life on his belief the Indian was alone. The canyon remained quiet and still. Easing forward the sinew, he removed the arrow and slipped it into the quiver. He slung the bow over his shoulder and removed the Lancaster.

He frowned as he looked back at the warrior and noticed how young the Indian was. His mind flashed back to the first day when he'd killed another boy. How many of the Apaches he'd killed were boys? Didn't any of their men fight? Doc didn't regret the death of an enemy, and knew the boy would have joyfully killed him. He was angry over the need to kill. He hadn't started the violence and after it did start, he'd tried to avoid the Apaches. He never looked for the fight. It was always the Indians and their relentless pursuit that forced him to kill. He pulled his eyes from the dying Apache, and dropped heavy and tired to his knees.

What drove them? Were all Apaches so hungry for blood? This was not the way of the Kaw or the Osage, or any of the other tribes he knew in the East. The Kaw and Osage were warriors and would fight with un-believable bravery if forced, but they were not of the same ilk as this band. Young men should not die as young men, their lives tossed aside in careless abandon. The warrior toppled to his side and lay still. Doc drew near, his anger building.

Maybe the boy hadn't cared about dying young, but Doc cared. He thought of his family and friends, of the new friends made on the Trail. He had a place in their lives, more in some than others, and to rip him from life would leave emptiness among those he knew. The death of so many Apaches reached far beyond their own lives. Even if Doc was an unwilling participant, he still played a part and so was partly account-able. Accountable for lives *they* had made him take. Doc was sick of the chase, the killing, yet he knew there would be more if he stayed in the mountains. And he intended to stay.

With instinct born of conflict and observation, Doc kenned the search was the fault of one man, the huge Apache wearing the wide black belt. The chase would continue until he or the Apache was dead. Maybe it was time to go after the cause of the trouble. Doc looked down at the rifle and questioned whether he could hunt a man as he'd hunted game. Staring down the gorge, he saw the Canadian Plain through the distant mouth of the canyon.

He could reach the wagons. The Apaches couldn't stop him now, but it would start again. When he returned to the mountains, they would find out and they would come. He was as tired of the running as he was the killing. How many more would die when he returned? How could he start the life he'd come west to build if he must always hide and run from the Apaches? It had to end.

As close to the canyon wall as possible, Doc ran for the head of the canyon. The other direction offered safety and his company of wagons, but Doc no longer ran from trouble, he ran toward it. The best hunting was in the mountains to the west where there was plenty of food, water, and cover. He ran with abandon, unconcerned with noise or signs of his passing. If they wanted him, he would be easy to find. And he'd left a sign no one could miss—or misunderstand.

Gunsi stared in disbelief. Toh-Yah recoiled, not from the sight but from the shadow that brushed his mind, more powerful and deadly than before. Elu and Ka-a-e-tano squatted and stared at the dirt between their feet. Both warriors wanted to go home. Far below, atop the boulder where he had died, Akule lay with his arms stretched above his head, hands clasped together, his feet spread apart. The arrow formed by his body pointed up the canyon.

"Is it a trick?" Gunsi could not hide the uncertainty in his voice.

"It is a challenge," Toh-Yah replied.

"A challenge? He would challenge us? No, it must be a trick!"

Angered by the waste of Akule, Toh-Yah roared, "It is no trick! He is taunting us! Daring us to follow"—his voice dropped to a whisper—"daring us to die."

"But—"

"He does not need to trick us now." Toh-Yah cut off Gunsi's reply. Lifting his arm to the east he continued, "The wagon road lies there and he knows this. We could not reach the road before him and he knows this also. His feet are fleeter than ours and he knows this."

Gunsi tore his eyes from Akule and looked east. Toh-Yah remained silent, letting his words speak again in Gunsi's mind.

"He has won and this he knows as well," Toh-Yah said finally.

Ka-a-e-tano raised his face to Toh-Yah. "What do we do?"

None was more shocked by his answer than Gunsi.

"We accept the challenge." Toh-Yah's eyes bored into Gunsi's. "Shadow will choose."

The large Apache nodded his agreement, understanding that the day of their shared vision had arrived. One would live to rule; the other would die. But Gunsi did not intend to let the white man determine his fate.

None of the four was related to Akule so there was no one to enforce the custom of an immediate burial.

"Forgive us, Akule," Toh-Yah said quietly, gazing into the canyon. "We will honor you when we return."

Doc drank and rested a short time on the spot where he'd killed the rabbit at Ocate Creek. The thought triggered his hunger. He squatted near the creek, listening to the soft splash of water flowing past. Inhaling deeply, he wrapped both arms around his knees and hugged them close; the temperature was dropping with the sun. He faced east, watching his back trail. Not anxiously as he had before, but oddly placid, almost curious. Would they come? Were the hunters willing to be hunted?

Over his shoulder, the last yellow arc of sun disappeared behind the mountain heights and the sky above burst into bands of orange, red, and violet. Nighthawks and swallows bobbed through the air, darting after insects drawn by the creek. When it became too dark to watch for pursuit, Doc took another long drink and stood. He splashed through the shallow water and paused on the opposite bank. Bending, he swept clean an area of sand.

"I've got to go have a look," Ferguson said. "I aim to know."

Shep Knorr eyed the bulky splint with obvious skepticism. But, he admitted, he'd had the same thought a dozen times through the morning hours. Doc had had a good lead on the Apaches when he and Shep parted over the grotto, and now Doc was a half day late. Later, really; Shep had expected the lost scout to come into camp during the night.

He'd advised Ferguson to caution the sentries to hold off shooting in the dark until they were certain they needed to.

"I can ride," Ferguson said, absently rubbing the broken leg.

"Know ya' can," Shep answered. "I also know it'll pain ya' somethin' awful."

"My choice."

"Yes sir, that it is."

Roland Ferguson demonstrated his anxious mood with a familiar emptying sling of his coffee cup. The effect was impressive since he had just filled the cup. Ferguson balanced on his good leg and bent at the waist to pick up the coffeepot. He refilled his cup and held it while glowering at the mountain man.

"You're gonna make me ask, ain't ya'," he snapped.

Shep grinned. "I reckon a man would have to be three kinds of a fool to volunteer, so yeah . . . you'll have to ask."

"Ask what?" Todd Bracken said as he strode over.

Shep tilted his head at the mouth of Ocate Canyon. "Your crippled boss wants I should take him up that canyon."

Ferguson remained silent, waiting for the argument his friend was sure to start. He also realized just what it was he'd badgered Shep into doing. The mountain man was risking his life, again, for people he barely knew.

"—because they all want to go."

"What?" The wagon master snapped out of his reverie to find Bracken staring at him.

"I said I'd saddle you a horse and asked which of the men you wanted along because they all want to go."

Relieved by Bracken's attitude, Ferguson pointed his cup at the mountain man. "Shep'll say. He's the boss out there."

"How many men ya' got? Eighteen or so?" Shep asked.

"On the button. We started with twenty, Doc you know about, and this"—he slapped his thigh—"is our second broke leg. That other feller went home."

"We'll take half, but make sure the ones stayin' keep loaded rifles close to hand. You got 'nuff stuff in them wagons to tempt a peaceful Indian to violence. They's plenty of Indians 'round here and very few are what you'd call peaceful."

Ferguson stared into the canyon while Bracken left to make the arrangements.

"I want to thank you proper for all you've done for us, Shep." As he spoke, he kept his gaze on the canyon, unable to bring himself to look at Shep. It wasn't easy for him to express gratitude, probably because it rarely happened. Roland Ferguson prided himself on handling his problems all by himself.

Continuing, he chose his words with care. Shep Knorr was a proud man as well and Ferguson didn't want to offend. "I couldn't help noticin' your rifle's a bit past its prime. I've no doubt that in your hands it's a good weapon, but . . ."

Finally, Ferguson cleared his throat and hobbled a slow turn to face the mountain man. "There's a crate of Sam Hawkins's new Plains rifles in the lead wagon. Pick one out, and all the powder and shot you can carry."

Shep stepped forward and opened his mouth to protest. Ferguson did an amazingly quick about-face for a man with a bound leg stuck straight out front, turning his back on Shep.

"Don't think of sayin' no," he barked. In a peculiar hobble-hop, Ferguson headed in the same direction as Bracken. In a voice audible only to his own ears, he added, "It's little enough for what you've done . . . and for what you're fixin' to do."

Shep hadn't guessed the half of it, Ferguson thought later, grimacing as the horse stumbled over another loose stone. "Blamed canyon must be where the Almighty keeps his rock supply."

"What's that, Boss?" Bracken asked.

"Nuthin'. Jus' thinkin' out loud."

Ferguson was pale and sweating heavily and Todd Bracken was worried. If they didn't find something soon he'd call a halt. Ferguson had to rest.

Ten minutes later, the band of men came to an abrupt halt. But not to rest; they stopped to stare openmouthed at an eerie figure lying atop a blood-soaked boulder—they had found Akule.

Shep scattered the armed men a hundred yards up and down the canyon and then spent a few minutes casting about the area reading the tracks. He, Ferguson, and Bracken gathered by the boulder and after a quick look the three men moved away, spurred by the ripening body in the stale, still air of the canyon.

Bracken picked a clear spot at the base of the stone column and helped Ferguson to sit down. The sun hung just above the mountains and most of the canyon was in deep shadow. Situated so that the sunlight hit the spot unfettered, the base of the column shone bright and pro-vided meager warmth. Ferguson was grateful for the heat, but the sun forced him to squint against the glare as he looked up at the two men.

The wagon master used both hands to shift his leg to a more com-fortable angle. "What do you think, Shep?"

"I think we'll let you rest up a mite and then get back to camp. Your wagons have some miles to travel."

Ferguson leaned forward. "I'm fine! And we ain't turnin' back with-out Doc!"

"You're a long ways from fine, Ferguson, and we are turnin' back. It'll be full dark in no time. 'Sides, Doc ain't here."

"How do you figure that?" Bracken asked.

"He took 'em to the mountains."

"He done what?"

Shep closed his eyes and took a deep breath. If these men couldn't see their wagon road any better than they could see Doc's sign, they would have gotten lost before leaving Independence. Maybe they figured all Indians lay down that way before dying. Or maybe it was just the ones with an arrow stuck in their chest.

"Your man's switched things around. He's doin' some chasin' of his own. There was sign in the lower canyon showin' two Apaches come in that way." Shep tipped his head toward the upper canyon. "Also got sign showin' three more come from up there.

"Doc was here too. Though I cain't figure where he was hidin'. For some reason the 'Paches left that one and the other four headed up-canyon."

"Chasin' Doc?" Ferguson asked.

"Nope. His tracks are on top of theirs, but he believed the 'Paches would come back here. That's why he left the sign."

Shep freed up another sigh at the baffled looks from Ferguson and Bracken before he continued. "After Doc kilt that 'Pache he laid him out a-pointin' the direction he took."

The two wagon men were still confused. "Don't ya' see? He *wants* them to follow him!" Shep couldn't take any more questions and stomped away to see if he could figure out what Doc did to elude the Indians. Not that it mattered; he was just curious.

Fifteen minutes later, still bewildered by Doc's movements, Shep walked over to Ferguson.

"If'n you can go, you better get to it. Doc'll know you won't wait at the crossing. Fact is, he's prob'ly countin' on it." Shep kept talking, knowing the wagon master would need the story explained. "Your man could've sashayed out of this canyon right down to your wagons, but he didn't do it. He's after them 'Paches and I don't know whether he cracked his head on a rock or just got so blamed mad that he don't care. Either way, I figure he's daft. The way he laid out that dead one must'a riled those 'Paches no end.

"When Doc's finished with whatever he's got planned he'll want to meet up with you. That means he'll take 'em south. Roll the wagons at your normal speed 'cause that's what he'll count on. You need to be where Doc expects you to be . . . whenever 'n wherever that is."

Ferguson stood up with Shep's help and told Bracken to bring the horse and gather the men from the upper canyon.

"You talk like you ain't going back with us."

"I ain't," Shep replied. He hefted the Plains rifle and grinned. "Thought I'd see how straight this fine gun of mine will shoot."

The wagon master knew where Shep was going and what he was likely to shoot. Extending his hand, Ferguson said, "I don't want no Indian shootin' at me with that gun. You watch yourself."

"Always do."

The two parties cleared the canyon under a black sky, Ferguson and his men at the mouth and Shep at the head.

Gunsi stepped across the patch of dirt and walked several paces ahead. He felt the anger and frustration that had become his companion since the death of his brother Sotli. Yet he could no longer deny the other feeling that grew stronger each day. A feeling of unease he couldn't quite define. It wasn't fear; he looked forward to meeting the white man. For a time, he believed the feeling was worry that the white man might escape. But now, the prey wasn't trying to escape; he was luring the warrior to follow.

Trying to distract the uncertainty and drive it from his mind, he faced Ka-a-e-tano and asked, "When?"

"Last night," replied the tracker as he stared at the sand.

Gunsi turned and trotted along the tracks of the white man's trail. A trail so plain a child could follow.

Toh-Yah fell in behind. Lingering a moment, Ka-a-e-tano and Elu shared a look and an unspoken wish. Finally, they trotted after their leaders. Elu's first step snapped a stem at the base of a water hemlock. The broken plant fell to the ground, scattering the small white flowers over the patch of sand. Bright morning sunlight glimmered in the tiny drops of poisonous fluid escaping the ruptured stem. A mild breeze nudged the flowers, pushing them in slow circles over the sand, trapping several in the two deep footprints left by Shadow. The prints, side by side, bracketed an arrow laid atop the ground, pointing south.

Sunrise found Doc sitting in thick foliage partway up a tree-covered hill. The hill overlooked a thin stream of cold water flowing slowly through a wide meadow of switchgrass and mountain brome. Sooner than he'd expected, the graze and water drew a doe. The mule deer hesitated at the meadow's edge, nose lifting to test the air for scent. Satisfied that all was as it should be, she stepped into the meadow and crossed to the stream. From the trees behind her came a second doe, then a third. The meadow held eight doe and a scattering of fawns before one of the mule deer grazed close enough that Doc risked a shot.

The arrow dropped the doe so abruptly the other deer failed to notice. Only when the hungry man walked from the trees did the meadow empty in a flurry of bounding leaps. The doe weighed one hundred and fifty pounds so Doc dressed her in the meadow. He used a portion of the hide to fashion a strap and crude sack, which he filled with meat. After rinsing his hands and arms in the stream, he drank his belly full of the cold water.

The heavy sack, bumping at the end of the strap hung across his shoulders, made it impossible for him to use the bow. He dropped the meat and removed the Lancaster, then slung the bow and sack into place. As he cradled the rifle and walked past the carcass, he noted he'd left plenty of meat for the scavengers and carrion. He was several hundred feet away when that thought gave rise to another and he turned back.

Over a small, smokeless fire, Doc broiled a sizable chunk of the venison. He was halfway through the meat when he cut another large piece to broil over the fire. He was hungrier than he'd thought. Later, after eating all he wanted, he lay back on the cushion of pine needles and closed his eyes. The depth of his comfort amazed him. Tranquil, but not careless. A man with four Apaches on his trail couldn't be careless, and Doc wasn't.

Beneath a copse of dark green pines, he'd found a high spot with a wide field of sight. His eyes were shut, but his ears were primed to the slightest sound. The copse was full of birds and after accepting Doc's quiet presence, they resumed their varied chorus of calls. The copse would fall silent again if anyone neared the trees.

He was content, even in the company of danger. The solid, massive presence of the mountains dwarfed a man and anything a man carried into their heights, even troubles such as Doc carried. In the lowlands men walked on the earth. They built cities and industry and carved into the soil with plows to reap a bounty of their own design. Men dammed rivers, built levees to control flooding, and canals to direct the course of water. Nature often arose to dash the labor, but afterward, she succumbed again to the whim of man, if only for a time. There, men stood on near-equal footing with the earth, neither holding dominion.

In the high country, men walked *around* the earth. The mountains were immovable, untamable. Here it was impossible to ignore the breadth of nature. The bounty was of the earth's choosing and man could do but little to influence the offering. Nothing in man or of man threatened the mountains. Rather than leave him feeling small or weak, the high country beckoned Doc to grow while providing all the room he'd need to do so. Shep Knorr had grown among the mountains. When he and Doc first met that morning north of Raton Pass, Doc sensed a wholeness in the mountain man.

It was easy for one to sense the Creator's power while amid the might of His creation. All life struggled and flourished, lived and died, yet the timeless foundation of His work remained. Doc thought of the Apaches; they too were a part of creation. Did he have the right to interfere? He recalled sermons by Brother Martin back home that told of battles and wars, many of which were ordered by the Almighty. Brother Martin said conflict and strife were man's own fault for sinning in the Garden. He said the Almighty gave every man and woman a will of their own, and the choices they made were up to them. Each was accountable for choices made, good or bad.

Had he made the wrong choice in coming here instead of going to the wagons? Men would die because of the decision he made. Perhaps he would die; the odds were against him. His eyes opened and he stared into the branches of the pines. He breathed in the rich smell and felt the light breeze move across his face. This is where he wanted to live. And there was room for all.

Until the Apaches cornered him in the canyon, he'd tried to avoid them. He knew now there couldn't be any peace until it was settled. If they came for him, he would fight. If they chose not to follow after, he would let them go. When he realized that the choice was theirs, the doubts faded. This was a struggle between men, as Brother Martin had said. It was something Doc could choose to face, or not. He could avoid the conflict by leaving. But there would be other struggles and fights to confront. Was the only right answer to hole up somewhere, reap nothing that anyone might want, and pray that no one ever bothered you? Somehow, Doc knew that wasn't what was expected of him.

Perhaps it was how a man handled the struggles that mattered. Leaving the signs in the canyon, beside the creek, and earlier today the sign left after killing the deer were things done in malice, not anger. The bitterness he embraced through constructing the signs was a different kind of danger than that posed by the Indians. In yielding to malice, Doc allowed himself to be encircled and held captive by vengeance, a desire to kill. Driven by spite, he was no different from the large Apache. The revulsion Doc felt as he watched the Indian boy die, a death caused by the spite of the boy's leader, was the very thing that had enflamed Doc to seek justice. It was a short step from righteous anger into malevolence, and Doc knew he'd put one foot too far.

He was still angry, but also felt he had a right to be. They *were* trying to kill him. It seemed like a natural response for a man to get angry in his situation. Doc wondered if the Apaches had found the sign he'd left in the meadow. Whether they had or not, it was the last time he'd taunt them, but he wasn't going to hide from them either. If they came, he would accept what it meant and defend himself. The choice was theirs.

CHAPTER NINETEEN

Shep squatted beside the footprints. He'd used a small twig to probe the sharp edges of the tracks and he now sat idly rolling it between his thumb and forefinger, lost in thought. Snapping the twig, he let the pieces fall to the dirt and rose from his haunches. His eyes never left the ground as he walked back to the creek along the trail left by Gunsi and his warriors. Judging from the tracks, he was a couple of hours behind the Indians. He had been right; Doc was leading the Apaches south. The arrow pointed straight into the heart of the Turkey Mountains.

Like a piece left over from building the Rockies, the secluded Turkeys, wild and lonesome, sat in the middle of the Canadian Plain twenty miles east of the Sangre de Cristo Range. The small cluster of mountains formed a circle eight or nine miles across. An outer loop of hills encircled a large double-peaked mountain, separated from the outer loop by a ring of lowland. The central peaks and one of the western hills in the outer ring reached heights of more than eighty-four hundred feet, a full thousand feet higher than the surrounding plain. Shep thought of the Turkeys as a massive granite castle, a moat, and an outer ring of high battlement walls.

He threw a last look at Doc's prints and the arrow, feeling a deeper chill than the weather permitted. Starting south, he whispered, "Let 'em go boy. It ain't worth it." A dozen steps later he broke into a lope; he needed to hurry.

Elu was first to see the carcass and point it out to the others. Cautious, the four knelt in the tall grass and stared at the pine tree and the remains of the doe hanging from its branches. The tree stood at the edge of the meadow and so near to the stream that its branches shaded the water. The doe hung out of the reach of ground scavengers and, between the doe and the stream, logs and kindling were laid out and waiting to be lit.

Gunsi signaled the warriors and motioned them into the nearby trees. In silence, the four Apaches withdrew into the forest.

Excited, Elu whispered, "We found his camp!"

"Yes." At last, Gunsi thought. Soon he would have the white man.

Ka-a-e-tano squatted facing toward the hanging doe. The others were all facing away so he was the only one to see the backside of the doe as the wind spun her partly around. Rising to his feet, he stepped past Gunsi and walked toward the tree. "It is not his camp."

When Gunsi, Elu, and Toh-Yah joined Ka-a-e-tano beside the hanging doe, he spun the carcass around to show them what he'd seen from the trees. Embedded into the deer's back were five arrows. The shaft of the top arrow was snapped below the feathers.

Eyes wide, Elu asked, "What does it mean?"

"It means . . . ," said the tracker, releasing the carcass to continue its slow pirouette, "that Shadow began hunting with Akule; his is the broken shaft." The doe rotated slowly, spinning the arrows from sight. "Ours are unbroken."

"For now," Toh-Yah added softly.

Elu was frightened. "We must leave this place! Now, before he kills us all!"

Gunsi ignored the wailing and ordered Ka-a-e-tano, "Find his tracks!"

The tracker left the group and began a slow searching circle around the tree.

The sharp click of flint striking flint pulled Elu's stare from the doe. Toh-Yah bent low over the wood and blew gently on the smoldering bits of twigs and dry leaves that Shadow left for kindling.

"What are you doing!" Elu cried out. "Shadow will see the smoke!"

"Good, maybe he will come," Gunsi said sharply. Then, leveling the frightened warrior with a glare of rancorous disgust, he said, "If you speak again of leaving . . . I will kill you."

Gunsi walked over to Ka-a-e-tano, leaving Elu openmouthed and trembling.

Toh-Yah arose from the growing flames and gazed at Elu. "When it is your time, Elu, death will find you whether you are afraid or brave. It is far better to live the life you are given in the respect of men. You are not a boy, Elu, yet you continue to act as one. Your father was a man of honor and courage"—Toh-Yah paused and a scant smile lifted the tight lines of his mouth—"and your sister, she is your father's daughter."

Toh-Yah unsheathed his knife and stepped forward. "When will you become your father's son?"

Alarmed, Elu stumbled quickly backward to fall beneath the doe. The hot shame of his cowardice blazed at the look of pity from Toh-Yah, who stepped over the prone Indian and lifted the blade to the carcass. Elu considered many things during the short time Toh-Yah worked on the deer.

The mustang tossed his head and blew, confused by the scents. One was familiar, but the others were frightening reminders of recent injuries and pain. He pawed the ground and trotted anxiously up and down the creek bank, stopping when he caught the familiar scent. The horse twisted his neck to look behind him, then swung his head forward to stare across the creek, ears cocked, nostrils flared. The powerful muscles in his chest quivered with nervous energy. Born wild, the four-year-old mustang had only been in the company of man for a short period, but it was long enough for the little horse to grow accustomed to the curry comb and the oats and corn. The familiar scent and an occasional lump of brown sugar shared the same memories in his mind.

Horses were not solitary creatures, and without a herd to join, the mustang was lonely, but still he hesitated. The fearsome scents overlaid the spoors of the familiar one. The mustang walked into the creek and dipped his head to drink, pausing twice to lift his dripping muzzle from the water while looking around. Thirst quenched, he cast another long look northward over his shoulder. After a long moment of indecision, he crossed to the opposite bank and continued south, blowing softly to clear his snout of the dreaded scent.

Shep ghosted into a dense thicket and watched the warriors from across the meadow. He had smelled smoke for the past ten minutes but it looked like the fire was dying out; it had been a big fire. Taking in the sight of the hanging doe, he wondered at the Apaches' use of time in hunting and preparing a meal. In particular, he wondered at their preparing a meal over such a large fire. Two of the four warriors lay prone upon the ground and none displayed an indication they would be moving soon.

If the Apaches were going to stay put, it was a good time to get around them. Slipping out of the thicket, Shep angled up the slope of the hill through the trees. When he'd put two hundred yards between himself and the meadow he sat down to figure which direction Doc might have taken. With the Apaches dozing in the middle of it, he couldn't follow Doc's trail anymore, not unless he circled around to pick it up on the far side.

The meadow, on the northern side of the Turkey Mountains, lay between two hills of the outer ring. Doc could have turned east or west, or continued south. If Shep guessed wrong, he'd have to double back, wait for the Indians to resume the trail, and then follow them. The circle of mountains covered more than forty square miles so, without a trail to follow, finding Doc would fall to luck. And Shep was a man who didn't leave much to luck.

Doubling back and following the Indians wasn't a solution he cared for. A man had to watch himself around Apaches even when they were in a good mood. Trailing a band of bruised, battered, and riled warriors would be one deadly bit of work. He'd have to lag far behind to avoid being spotted and that meant he wouldn't be close by when the Indians met up with Doc.

As it was, he would need to be careful in searching for Doc's trail. Shep wanted to keep his own presence hidden from the Indians and traipsing back and forth through the hills increased the chance the Apaches would cut his sign. Of Doc's three possible routes, south seemed the most likely as it would lead farther and higher into the Turkeys and to the thicker cover found there.

As he sat thinking, he kept his eyes and ears toward the meadow. He hadn't seen or heard any indication the Apaches had pulled out. That, Shep admitted glumly, meant they could be anywhere. Indians, Apaches in particular, were not famous for making a lot of noise. Stifling a yawn, it hit him that he was tired. The last couple of days were long ones. Lord! What must Doc be feeling?

Thirty minutes of soft-footed skulking by the mountain man turned up Doc's trail. Best of all, Shep saw Doc's trail from ten feet away, meaning he had kept his own tracks, light as they were, from crossing Doc's. The blatant swath of pressed-down grass was evidence the lost scout was still bent on luring the Apaches to follow him. Shep stepped to a large rock and then a broken limb to move closer to the trail. He was taking a small risk that one of the Apaches might glance aside and see some little disturbance he'd caused, but he had to get closer to sight along the path of pressed grass and get a fix on Doc's general bearing.

Moments later he was twenty feet from the trail, loping in the same direction. Twice more he stopped and crept nearer Doc's trail to be certain he hadn't strayed. Just as he thought of stopping a third time, he found Doc's camp. Again, the signs were clear. Doc wasn't trying to hide. No smoke rose from the ashes, nor was there any lingering smell of the fire. Doc had moved on. Shep made a slow, wide circle around the camp to the south side. Finding nothing, he continued around, thinking Doc had changed direction. After circling the entire area to find himself looking at the pressed-grass path of Doc's entrance into the camp, Shep Knorr knew he was in trouble.

Shep stood in silence beside the path and a tight-lipped concern that first appeared at not finding Doc's trail on the north side of the camp deepened into a worried scowl as he considered his next move. For some reason, Doc had decided to stop leaving the clear trail. Shep was sure he could have found it if he'd known to look for hints instead of the obvious. He was sure he could still find it, but he was no longer sure he wanted to. He had his own life to think about now. When the Apaches realized what Doc had done, they would spread out and try to cut sign. Shep, careful as he had been, knew that four sets of Apache eyes intent on finding tracks would soon learn there were two white men in the Turkeys. Suddenly desirous of being far from where he now stood, Shep Knorr turned and loped due east.

Doc entered the notch between the twin peaks of the large, single mountain that was the heart of the Turkey Range. To his right and left the tips of the peaks rose another three hundred feet. Ponderosa pine dominated the forest, but there was a mixture of other pines and spruce as well. The Mexican ox drivers who told him of this place also warned him against entering the Turkey Mountains, saying no man ever stayed for very long and those who did were never seen again.

To Doc's way of thinking, superstitions cropped up whenever grown men behaved as children, making made-up answers to riddles they couldn't explain. There was probably a basis for the superstition; a man went into the mountains and didn't return. A man experienced in the high country. A man who met with an accident that just happened to have occurred in the Turkeys, he thought wryly. If folks avoided every range of mountains wherein other folks had disappeared, there wouldn't be a two-legged creature above sea level.

If death overtook him in the Turkeys, would they add his demise to the legend? An addendum to the myth saying, "Doc outrun them 'Paches for more 'n a week and kilt a handful whilst doin' it. Then, just when his road was clear, he ups and goes into the Turkeys, never to be seen again . . ." Such a tale would have to ignore the four Apaches and their assistance in his "disappearance."

He would have laughed at the foolishness of it except that he *had* passed up safety to challenge the Indians. And now that he was thinking clearer, he knew the word *foolish* fit his action quite well. The Turkeys, though, had nothing to do with it.

The small cluster of mountains was beautiful, full of trees, shrubs, grass, and wildflowers. It occurred to Doc that aside from the herd of mule deer he'd seen at the stream, there was very little animal life. That fact was likely due to his not finding any other water supply. Birds were everywhere, but while getting to water wasn't a problem for birds, most other animals would choose to live around several sources of water instead of relying on a single stream. Now that he'd thought about water, Doc was thirsty.

An hour later, he cleared the notch and turned southeast, descending a slope thick with ponderosa pine. The Santa Fe Trail skirted the Turkey Mountains on the east, drawing nearest on the southeast side, and now that he'd abandoned his short-lived vendetta, Doc planned to meet the wagons as they rolled past. He picked his trail with care, stepping softly over the blanket of decaying needles to avoid the telltale signs of scuffs or crushed pinecones.

To reach the outer ring of hills overlooking the Trail he must cross the open band of grass that covered the inner ring, and the thought worried him. Doc suddenly regretted his decision to hide his trail leaving the last camp. The camp, located on the far side of the central mountain from where he now walked, was near the inner ring as it looped around the north side. Without intending to do so, he again placed the Apaches in a situation where they might split into two groups. With one group attempting to follow his faint trail over the mountain, the other group might use the easy passage offered by the inner ring to race around the mountain and cut him off.

The sudden interest in speed over stealth prompted Doc to pick up his pace. He had to assume, and act, as if the Indians were circling around. He had to cross the inner ring before they arrived. If he was caught in the open, he was dead.

The three warriors stood as Ka-a-e-tano walked up.

"Where did he come from?" Gunsi demanded, his tone curt with annoyance.

The tracker hesitated, scowling at the ground as if considering the question. In truth, he was allowing his hot reaction at Gunsi's tone to subside. Ka-a-e-tano knew the huge warrior was superior to him in strength and skill, but the harsh and arrogant attitude was unbearable.

"I went far enough to learn the new man traveled beside Shadow's path. He is very good; I saw but four dim prints in three hundred paces. It would take a half day or more to determine where he came from."

"I did not ask how long it would take!" Gunsi shouted. "I asked where he came from!"

As he finished speaking, Gunsi shot his hand forth to snatch the shirt of Ka-a-e-tano, yanking the tracker forward. White-hot fury took command of Ka-a-e-tano's reflexes and his reaction was instinctive. He didn't resist the pull; instead, he used his legs to push forward and let his body fly at Gunsi. The large Indian was braced for a pull and the quick move of the agile tracker caught him unprepared for the weight now hurtling toward him.

Ka-a-e-tano lifted his hands to grasp his leader and buried his head against Gunsi's chest. Staggered by the oncoming weight, Gunsi lifted a foot to step back and Ka-a-e-tano hooked a leg around the raised foot. His weight shifting backward and no foot to balance upon, Gunsi felt himself falling with no way to stop. The cushion of pine needles saved him from serious injury but the force of impact loosed his hold on the smaller warrior. Ka-a-e-tano tucked his head and rolled in a somersault as the two hit the ground. One tumble and he was on his feet, bent low to spin and face his adversary, knife in hand.

A savage roar burst from Gunsi and quicker than Ka-a-e-tano imagined possible the huge warrior sprang up and charged with a pantherlike lunge. Set for the oncoming shock and focused solely on each other, both men were swept from their feet by Toh-Yah's surprising tackle.

"Enough!" he shouted.

Gunsi and Ka-a-e-tano, astonished by the sudden intrusion, found themselves in a tangled heap beneath the weight and spitting fury of

Toh-Yah. In each hand, Toh-Yah held a blade of glistening steel pressed firmly against the throat of each combatant.

His rage evident, Toh-Yah's voice thundered, "I have heard and seen enough!"

Dropping to one knee at the edge of the trees, Shep listened to the forest behind him. Ahead lay the wide band of grass he must cross before he could enter the hills of the outer ring. He craned his neck to stare left into the open grass. Several moments passed before he switched his examination and searched the area to his right. The expanse of grass was empty, but because of the circular shape, he would be far into the crossing before he could see for any great distance around the curves.

Shep wasn't going to get to the far hills by sitting under the trees, so after a quick deep breath, he stood and walked into the open. After twenty paces, he turned and looked along his trail. He'd stepped as lightly as possible, working his feet carefully into the grass in a sliding gait meant to separate the stalks and not crush them. It took but a glance to see that his effort was futile. His trail was plain and would remain so for some time because the tender grass would be slow to stand upright. A brisk breeze would have helped brush the grass back into place, but it was an unusually windless day for the territory.

No sense in traveling slowly if they can follow, he decided, and set off in a lope toward the opposite hills. Each stride sent quivers along his exposed back and by the time he reached the middle of the mile-wide band of grass he was running flat out. Plunging into the sparse outer trees of the far hills, he kept running until the thickening forest demanded a more reasonable pace. Walking swiftly, he climbed five hundred feet to the top of the nearest hill, where he collapsed at the base of a shady pine and sucked in huge, rattling gasps of air.

When he could, he raised into a sitting position with his back propped hard against the pine. The tree-covered slope of the hill hid the close-in portion of the grass band, but the bulk of it lay open to view. It was empty of movement. As best as he could over the diminishing roar in his ears, Shep listened for sounds of someone moving up the slope. After a moment, he decided he'd made it across unseen and his mind turned to the problem of how, and where, to find Doc.

Ignorant of the movements of all who sought him, Doc, three miles south of Shep's resting place, stepped into the open and angled across the grass. Like Shep, after soon discovering a trail couldn't be hidden on the narrow grassy plain, Doc increased his speed. Every few steps his head twisted to look along the grass toward the north, the direction the Apaches would come if they chose to circle around the central mountain. Upon reaching the outer ring of hills and entering beneath the cool shade of the trees, a deep chill to his skin brought awareness that he was sweating heavily.

The hill above Doc was much higher than the one climbed by Shep and the thick cover of trees and brush looked impenetrable. Circling the base of the squat hill, he found a steep barren slope that promised to be a rough climb. Eager to leave the flat, open ground of the grassy band, he set a course for the top and climbed steadily. In order to see in all directions, and thus watch behind for the Apaches and ahead for the wagons, Doc didn't stop climbing until he'd reached the pinnacle. Shortly after Doc began his ascent, and hidden from sight by the shoulder of the hill, the four Indians trotted into the grass hard on his back trail.

Staying under the crest of the hill to avoid highlighting himself, Doc moved to a point where he could see the inner band. After a few minutes, he picked out what he thought was the point where he had left the trees of the large central mountain and entered the grassy band. From his height, the vast ring was open to view from north to south and the sight of miles of empty grass brought a welcome relief. The relief was short-lived, however, for almost as soon as he began to make his way around the hilltop to look out over the wagon road, the inner alarm of the hunted sounded a warning.

Abandoning his route, he reversed quickly and raced back to the top of the barren slope, where he settled in beside a dense thicket. Void of trees that would absorb sound, the empty hillside provided a channel for the clear mountain air to carry sounds from the valley floor, and Doc heard faint noises drifting up from below and off to his left. The Apaches had followed. They had made their choice, and their decision forced Doc to make a choice of his own.

Realizing the Indians had crossed the grass while he scrambled up the hidden slope, Doc wondered whether they would attempt to climb the exposed hillside or seek a way up through the trees. He crouched at the top and along one side of the barren slope. Doc studied the possible access of the forest, turning his head far enough to see down the forested hill, but not so far that the edge of his vision would miss movement at the base of the slope.

To his dismay, he saw instantly that the densest part of the forest and thicket lay within the lowest fifty feet of the hill. Beyond that point, a man could move with relative ease and stealth up the hill. As the sounds reaching up from below still came from his left, Doc bolted to his right across the open top of the slope, coming to a rest in the tree line on the far side. Dry mouthed and with his heart beating hammering blows against his ribs, he listened for the shout of discovery he feared would come.

When the stillness of the mountain continued undisturbed, he knew his sudden dash had passed unseen. Overjoyed and somewhat surprised, he moved a short distance farther into the trees before turning downhill.

Moving on feet that seemed to float above the ground, Doc worked his way through the forest, a shadow flickering from trunk to trunk.

Halfway down the slope he found what he wanted, a deep shaded thicket overhung by several large pines. The depths of the shadow made it impossible to spot him from any distance beyond five yards. He now had the empty slope between him and the Apaches. He might not see them if they worked their way up through the trees opposite, but if they wanted to get to him, they must cross open ground. From his hiding place, he could see the entire slope including its top and bottom. Depending on where the Indians chose to cross, if he didn't have a clear shot, he could either stay in hiding where he was or withdraw around the backside of the hill.

With somber determination, Doc checked and cleaned the Lancaster. He laid the bow on the ground at his knee and placed three of his remaining arrows nearby, arranged for quick retrieval and use. Keeping his eyes on the base of the slope where the sounds still seemed to originate, he let his hands move over the bow and arrows, locating them in his mind for later use without having to look or grope.

Satisfied that all was ready, Doc reached inside his pouch and gathered a handful of pinyon nuts he'd collected while on the plains. Chewing slowly, he watched the trees. The weight of the Lancaster was heavy and reassuring across his thighs; from below, the faint sounds of rustling underbrush drew closer.

CHAPTER TWENTY

NINETEEN APACHES BEGAN THE CHASE. Nine were dead, six had quit, and four remained. They'd hunted Doc day and night for six days, hounding him through the rugged mountains and across the wide expanse of the Canadian Plain. No time to rest or eat or even think. He'd been surprised at first, though surprise turned quickly into bewilderment as the relentless pursuit continued. When exhaustion had set in, he struggled to keep going.

For a brief time, he'd become motivated by revenge, a deep burning lust to hunt the hunters. The fervor, and the coupled self-destruction of that fervor, had quickly cooled and he again tried to evade his followers. All he wanted now was to live in peace. To explore and know the mountains he had loved even before he first saw them. A love born of the stories told by his uncle that long-ago night on his family farm in Missouri. Now he was tired—tired of running, tired of hiding, and tired of fighting. He was no longer vindictive, but he was committed to living and his anger was utterly, coldly, absolute.

Down the hill, the Indians stepped into view and Doc eyed the huge Apache leading the way. "You just won't quit, will you?" Doc whispered to the wind. There was no more time for thought of right or wrong. No more opportunity to weigh the moral import of man killing man.

A week ago, Doc would have blanched at the thought of killing a man from ambush, but the Apaches had proven themselves to be unmerciful hunters, to be men capable of killing without hesitation. Again, as if in prayer or penitence, Doc whispered in a soft, subdued voice, "I ain't partial to huntin' folks, but, in your case, I'm willin' to make an exception." The musket rose smoothly to his shoulder, then held steady as his finger wrapped around the trigger. He drew a breath and slowly exhaled as his eye lined the fore and rear sights of the heavy Lancaster rifle, holding them deathly still on the breast of the large, black-belted Apache.

Ka-a-e-tano halted suddenly and bent to examine the ground. His eyes found what he sought then lifted as they followed the scrambling trail up the hillside.

"Shadow has climbed the mountain."

All four faces lifted to study the barren slope. Toh-Yah felt the unmistakable rush of cold fear fill his chest. "He is waiting for us. We must find another way."

"No!" Gunsi growled. "His bravery lasted only a day. He is again hiding and running."

Turning uphill, the Apache said over his shoulder, "You women can find another way. I will not leave his trail."

Since leaving the camp Shadow prepared for his enemies, Elu had been contemplative and silent. Now he suddenly spoke and moved to intersect Gunsi.

"No. I will lead the way. I too will—"

As he stepped in front of Gunsi, his words were cut short by the wicked thump of the ball. The impact spun the young warrior half around to face his friends as the sharp crack of the Lancaster reached their ears.

Instantly, Elu stood on the slope alone. From the trees, Toh-Yah watched as Elu's legs buckled, dropping the warrior to his knees. A growing, bright red stain spread above his heart, sending small rivulets cascading toward the ground. Pale and shaken, Elu turned his head toward the nearby trees, locking eyes with Toh-Yah.

"Tell my sister . . ."

Elu squeezed his eyes shut against the pain then opened them. Toh-Yah saw clearly the agony he suffered. Toh-Yah wondered what kept the Llanero upright. He felt a jolt as Elu's eyes cleared and once again bored into his own.

Life continued its cruel, unhurried departure from its host and the young man teetered then pitched forward. But the words Elu spoke as he fell were forever entombed in Toh-Yah's memory, to rest there as long as he himself drew breath.

"I found my father's courage."

Up on the mountain, Doc stared at the prone Apache in disbelief. Somehow, he knew that killing the large Apache, the one Shep had called Gunsi, would put an end to the chase. Over the grotto, Shep had told him of Gunsi's oath. It was Gunsi Doc had wanted to kill. He had taken the shot with the same level of regard he would have shown a wolf preying on his goats back home.

But with his ball striking the wrong target, he was troubled nonetheless. That killing did feel as though it came from ambush. Like the other Apaches taken by Doc's hand, the dead warrior would have joyously claimed the life of Doc. Although that truth justified his action, it didn't seem to help much. The others had seen the face of their enemy before they died, and Doc believed that a man deserved to see what was coming, even a man hunting trouble. His belief didn't extend to Gunsi; Doc assumed the huge Apache was crazed.

Absently, his fingers searched his pouch while his mind worked over the problem of missing Gunsi. The emptiness of the pouch drew his attention like a spray of icy water. Of course! He'd shot his last ball. He stared at the rifle lying across his lap, the impact of his miss now fully upon him. From now on, he held no advantage. The Lancaster had always provided a measure of safety even though the Apaches had been, and still were, many. With the rifle, he had reach beyond their bows.

His eyes found the rifle lying on the rocks beside the dead warrior. Doc wanted that rifle. He didn't recognize the make of the gun and doubted it was much of a weapon, but it was loaded. Moreover, if it was of a larger bore he could shave the balls down with his knife for use in the Lancaster. That is, if he could get to it before the Apaches thought to pick it up. Doc had to draw the Indians away quickly, and in such a manner that they didn't think to pick up the rifle before they followed him.

Well out of bow range and confident the discarded rifle was the only one possessed by the Apaches, Doc broke from his cover and dashed across the slope for the far side, the same side the Apaches occupied. He ran into the trees and charged ahead, crashing through the underbrush. If one of the Indians had thought to start uphill under the cover of the trees, Doc was going to run smack into him. The thought added speed to his feet and he lifted the Lancaster to his chest for balance and use as a club. He made his way without care of noise. Soon a sound in the brush lower down and behind reached his ears. His plan was working; they were coming!

Doc began to angle up the slope as he ran. With the Indians following, he intended to circle the hill and return to the barren slope, and the dead warrior's rifle. Making his way ever higher up the side would shorten the circumference of the hill and quicken the time it would take him to reach the rifle. Nearer the base of the hill, the Apaches were in for a long run. Doc glanced back and down over his shoulder trying to hear or see the length of his lead. So intent on determining where the Apaches were, Doc forgot he was running all out through a forested hillside. Then abruptly, he wasn't running. Hanging his toe over a root, he cartwheeled wildly ahead.

Speed and gravity assumed control as up and down lost all meaning and Doc smashed into a tree trunk, losing his grip on the Lancaster. He hung momentarily as his brain fought against the spinning dizziness. He came to a rest head-down against the trunk, his feet splayed overhead. With sickening suddenness, the soft mat of needles under his head and shoulder began to slide and the wild tumble started anew, this time straight downhill.

Throwing out his hands, Doc clawed for control. He felt the hard ground against his body, the stinging of limbs and shrubs as they whipped and tore at him. Finally, his arm hooked a small tree and he jolted to a wrenching stop. Dazed and panting, he lay still and listened. At a click of sound from above, he twisted his head up just in time to take the full force of the sliding Lancaster's brass butt plate square on his forehead. Lights exploded across his eyes. They were so many and so brilliant that he wondered at how quickly they dimmed into absolute darkness.

Then the lights returned and there were vastly more of them, though much dimmer and unable to drive the blackness from his vision. His mind groped for a reason why a large area of blackness swept back and forth across the lights. Something struck his eye and his hand pawed in reflex, coming away with a pine needle. He couldn't see it in the strange blackness, but he knew it by touch.

A steady throbbing ache prompted the hand to return and feel the tender knot on his forehead. He felt a laceration and cold, sticky moisture. Lowering his arm, he saw the dim form of his hand pass before his eyes. He brought the hand back up and studied it as best he could.

Tiredly, he gave up and dropped his arm. He let his eyes close. Perhaps he could figure it all out in the morning.

Clarity returned with a jar so startling that it awakened pain all over his body. Morning! Night! It was night. Reaching up he grasped the low-hanging branch of a pine and saw that the sweeping blackness stopped. The dim lights were the stars. When he'd taken his fall there were three hours of daylight remaining, and now the depth of darkness and the cold touch of the air said it was far past dusk. How had they not found him?

A hundred yards away from where Doc lay, Gunsi squatted with his arms wrapped around his knees and stared into the night. Again, just out of his reach, the white man had vanished. Ka-a-e-tano and Toh-Yah were scattered far to his right and left around the curves of the hill, leaving each of the three warriors with more ground to watch than they could possibly guard in the daylight, much less a moonless night. Gunsi gave no thought to the warriors, or to where the white man might be.

He would find the white man, of that Gunsi was certain. It was the one clear thought in a mind whose madness was now complete. He had been untouchable in his rank among the warriors before the white man came into the mountains. He led a war party of nineteen Llanero braves and his leadership had seen the deaths of many whites in the days before. Now they were but three warriors and even the lifeless body of the white man dragged through his village would not regain his former rank.

Too many Llanero were dead. Too many warriors had faced the white man and found their own bravery lacking, returning in shame to their homes. His shame! The Llanero would not name the deserting warriors as cowards. They would blame *his* decisions—*his* inability to lead and attain victory. For a man so long used to absolute respect and the certainty of greatness, Gunsi had lost all he was and would be to the white man. An image of Nah-hi-mani flickered through the recesses of twisted thoughts and Gunsi squeezed his arms tightly about his knees and began rocking slowly. The fingers of his hands dug deep into his arms yet he felt no pain.

He didn't love the woman. In truth, he loathed her and her self-assuredness. His only desire for her was her beauty, which made her the choicest among the Llanero. As the greatest warrior, his privilege was to take the best. His plans of having her as his first wife only to keep her barren and as servant to his later wives brought a harsh, curl-lipped smile to his face. It was the greatest shame for a Llanero woman. Powerful fingers dug deeper into the hard muscles of his arms; he would break her, crush her into yielding to his power, and force her to a proper respect for him.

The ugly smile disappeared for he now knew that it would never be. The huge warrior continued his absent rocking in silence. Several minutes later, a low plaintive moan began an hours-long accompaniment of the endless rocking. So deep into emptiness was the mind of Gunsi that the faint rustle of movement through the underbrush nearby passed unnoticed.

Doc snapped to a sitting position, inhaling through clenched teeth against the sudden onslaught of pangs and spasms. Aching messages traveled from every part of his body to gather in the pit of his stomach where they raced in spinning circles. He felt a sudden drop in energy, as though the inner fluids and organs of his body passed directly into the earth. His brow broke into an icy cold sweat and he feared he would again lose consciousness.

The chill deepened and Doc had just enough time to fling himself over onto hands and knees before the retching started. Later, slumped against the thin trunk of pine that had stopped his wild plunge, Doc hung his head between upraised, shaky knees and breathed slow deep breaths. The riot in his stomach was over, and his brow, after losing the chill, felt hot. Besides the knot on his forehead and one over his ear, it seemed as though his other injuries were limited to scrapes and bruises.

The thick buckskin shirt had protected his torso, but his linsey-woolsey pants were in tatters and dried blood from a dozen shallow cuts had pasted the strips to his legs. Though he was stiff and sore, his flailing arms and legs had avoided contact with anything hard enough to cause a broken bone.

Standing, a sharp hiss escaped his lips as the pants ripped free of the dried blood. The warm tickle of blood on the hairs of his legs warned that the cuts had reopened. Surprised that his head remained clear, he held to the slim pine for moment and took in his surroundings. He thought of the dead warrior's rifle and decided against trying for it. To reach the weapon he would have to travel far through the dark forest with no idea where the Apaches were. Anyway, they had likely retrieved the rifle by this time.

Doc wanted to be off the hill. How he had avoided capture thus far was a mystery, and he did not intend to let the sunrise give the Apaches another chance of finding him. Like a baby's first step, Doc lifted a clumsy foot forward and placed his weight down. Letting go of the pine, he squatted to stretch out his arms and hands, feeling for the Lancaster in the vague shadows. His right hand brushed across cool brass and hard wood and he grasped the weapon, stood it on end, and pulled himself erect.

It took twenty minutes of blind movement to get to the bottom of the hill yet Doc was shocked upon reaching the bottom. His wild tumble had ended less than forty feet from the base of the hill; a slide of over three hundred feet down the forested hillside! At least it offered a reason for remaining undiscovered. The Apaches would never assume he could have traveled so far down the mountain so quickly. It was as if he had jumped from a cliff.

Stepping from tree to tree, merging his shadow with the trunks, Doc made his way over to the grassy band running along the base of the hill. For a short distance out from the hill, the trees grew sparse and scrawny. Beyond the last tree lay the open expanse of the mile-wide inner circle of grass. The light of the stars illuminated the plain for less than fifty feet. Past that point, the horizon was a mix of black and gray.

As he was unable to see more than a few feet in the forest, the grass band was the right choice for fast travel. But Doc remembered his earlier passage across the grass and was hesitant to expose himself in the open, even if under the partial cover of darkness. Finally, he walked out from the trees and into the grass. The rising moon had increased visibility to more than two hundred feet by the time Doc entered the protective covering of trees ringing the base of the large central mountain. Weary and weakened by the fall, he curled up in a ball beneath the trees and slept.

When he at last awoke, the sun had already cleared the low hills of the outer ring and its low angled rays of warmth and light penetrated beneath the canopy of trees where he lay. The haze of exhaustion fogged his mind, and overnight the scrapes and bruises had attained their full measure of soreness.

He couldn't suppress a groan as he rolled into a sitting position. His head and shoulders sagged with pain and fatigue. Shaking his head and rubbing his hands briskly over his face to clear his mind, he thought of the wagons. If Ferguson was on schedule, the wagons would roll past the southeast corner of the Turkeys sometime today. Recrossing the grass band in the dark of night had bought Doc temporary safety from the Apaches and an opportunity to rest, but it had also placed his hunters between him and the wagons.

If the wagon train cleared the Turkeys before he caught up to it, Doc would face endless miles of the wide-open Canadian Plain while chasing after the wagons. There would be no place to hide and no possibility of hiding his tracks. He felt the deep tiredness of his body and knew that missing the train today would prove fatal. The Apaches would find and catch him in the open country to the south. He must catch the wagons as they passed along the outer ring of hills, or be trapped.

Doc stood and stared across the grass toward the hill he'd fled in the dark. They were over there, somewhere, waiting for him. They knew as well as he what he must do. As his mind worked at the problem, Doc stretched his arms and legs, ignoring the pain as the muscles warmed. With a last look at the far hill, he picked a course that would keep him under the forest as long as possible and started walking.

Stiff muscles and joints relaxed as he walked, and the bright light of the sun, the morning songs of the birds, and the pine and wildflower scent of the air buoyed his spirit. A low outcrop of the mountain obliged a wide detour and as Doc stepped around the rocky shoulder, he stopped and stared openmouthed. Ten feet away, head up and eyes locked on Doc, stood a horse! When the animal nickered and took a step forward, Doc backed up and would have fallen if not for the hard support of the rocky outcrop.

"Lord Almighty . . . I thought they'd killed you."

Ten minutes later, riding bareback with a crude bridle made from cut strips of deer hide from his sack, Doc and the mustang rode out from the trees and galloped across the grassy band. He guided the mustang toward a notch in the outer ring of hills. Dropping the makeshift reins across the horse's shoulder to free his hands, he pulled the bow and adjusted the quiver of arrows before slinging the Lancaster over his back.

"All right boy, let's go find the wagons."

In moments, they were across the grass and Doc was slowing the pace to enter the narrower passage between the hills. They had three hundred yards to go before the notch opened onto the plain and where, at last, Doc could feel safe.

CHAPTER TWENTY-ONE

D OC'S EYES SWEPT THE HILLS AND TREES on both sides, his head constantly turning. Every few feet he threw a look over his shoulder. The mustang seemed to understand his concern for it stepped forward on high prancing hooves, eager to run. Like Doc, the horse was alert, ears forward, with its head turning and lifting to scent the air.

It was the mustang that sensed them first. Sidestepping quickly to a stop, he blew hard to clear the hated spoor from his nostrils. Doc dropped the reins and nocked an arrow, pulling the bow to half-draw.

As if on cue, the three Apaches rose from the short grass and stood in a silent line across his path, one hundred feet ahead. They had used Shep's trick of hiding in the open, though Doc couldn't believe that a man, let alone three men, could have hidden in the ankle-high grass. But there they were.

The four men, hunters and hunted, stared at each other across the short distance. To his left, a tall powerfully built Apache wearing a red sash waited. The muscles of his chest and arms seemed sculpted from stone. Bright eyes set above high cheekbones looked at Doc with a mixture of respect and curiosity.

On the right, a squat warrior, younger than the others, stood with a bow three-quarters drawn, the arrow pointing at the ground beneath his feet. The young warrior's eyes flitted constantly between Doc and the Apache standing in the middle of the line.

Based on Shep's description, that warrior was Gunsi. His face was square and full on a head too large for even his great size. As tall as, if not a little taller than, the first Apache, Gunsi was twenty pounds heavier and more thickly muscled. Great rounded mounds of corded muscle sloped away from the warrior's neck. His shoulders reminded Doc of the bargemen on the Missouri River who made their living using twenty-foot lengths of pole to push and pull cargo-laden barges along the river. It was his eyes that drew Doc's full attention. Vacant, yet burning with some unidentifiable emotion.

The air between the Apaches and white man crackled with energy, and they were so intent upon each other that none took notice of Shep until he cocked the hammer on his brand-new Hawkins. Not a head turned, but four sets of eyes rolled to the sound.

Shep began speaking to the tall Apache on Doc's left. A string of unintelligible sounds and grunts passed from the lips of the mountain man. The tall Apache replied briefly, never taking his eyes from Doc. The face of Gunsi began to color with rage. Shep spoke again; this time his voice was louder and threatening and the barrel of the Hawkins lifted higher.

Doc watched the tall Apache reply, then snapped his attention to Gunsi as the warrior faced about and bellowed at Shep. Spittle flew from his lips as he railed at the mountain man. Doc didn't have need of language; the warrior's tone and manner were evident. Shep had just bought into the game and Gunsi didn't like it.

Chancing a quick glance at his friend, Doc noted the mountain man's visage. The hard tight lines of his mouth and eyes showed he understood the danger of the moment, yet there was no trace of fear. Shep would stand. Reassured, Doc turned his attention back to the greatest danger, Gunsi.

A few quiet words passed between Shep and the tall Apache, and Doc was stunned to see the warrior walk over to stand calmly beside the mountain man. Gunsi spoke harsh and sharp at the two men, and then spun to face the smaller warrior. A moment under the withering glare of the huge Apache brought a wicked grin to the young Apache's face. He relaxed the drawstring of his bow and slipped the arrow over his shoulder to rest in the quiver. Then, with what could only be called a gesture of scornful contempt, the young man plopped down to sit cross-legged in the grass.

"Toh-Yah and Ka-a-e-tano are out of it," Shep said, speaking in English to Doc.

"Kinda figured that," Doc replied mildly.

"Guess you can also figure that Gunsi intends to kill you."

"Yeah."

"You want I should shoot 'im?"

Doc thought about it longer than Shep would have guessed before he said, "No. I reckon he's got himself all worked up over it, and to tell the truth, I'm right anxious myself to end this now. I plan on stayin' around here and if it ain't now, it might be sometime when I ain't so ready."

Shep nodded and Doc stared at Gunsi, who stared back, a triumphant gleam of malice sparkling in the black eyes.

"Say, Shep," Doc said. "Tell him somethin' for me. Tell Gunsi that my sorrow over the accidental death of his brother won't take any satisfaction away from my killin' him today."

At the use of his name by the hated white man, Gunsi walked forward. Shep's words had no impact until the end of his speech, when the huge Apache faltered a step. Then with a crazed howl, he lifted his bow and launched his arrow. Doc, prepared and hopeful of just such a reaction, easily ducked the arrow and slammed his heels into the mustang.

The horse bounded forward to hit full stride in three leaps, rushing down on the maddened warrior. Gunsi closed with power and agility, his coordination flawless as his hand blurred back to snatch an arrow from its quiver, drawing and raising the bow in one fluid movement. Doc loosed the reins and drew his bow full. At thirty paces' distance, Gunsi yelled in triumph and loosed his arrow.

Waiting for the movement, Doc slipped down the side of the running mustang, squeezing tightly with his knees in the manner of the Plains Indian, as taught him by his Osage boyhood friends. He felt the rip of Gunsi's arrow bite through the flesh of his shoulder as he loosed his own arrow. An instant fear that the hit might have altered his aim vanished as he saw his arrow bury deeply into the warrior's chest.

Gunsi staggered, then stumbled. But with catlike reflexes and the power of his huge strength, he managed to grasp Doc as the mustang thundered past and yank him from the horse. The two men rolled across the grass, both rising at once and separated by less than twenty feet. Doc was afraid, more so than he'd ever been. The Indian was mortally wounded. The flint point of Doc's arrow had penetrated so deeply that less than half the length of the long shaft protruded from Gunsi's chest. Yet there he stood.

As one the two men moved, hands flashing back for their quivers. Doc watched in horror as Gunsi smiled a cruel, knowing smile. Doc's quiver was gone! Ripped from his shoulder during the roll from the mustang. With cold deliberation, Gunsi fitted his arrow and widened his smile. It was a smile without joy, unless it be the joy of death, for his eyes were blacker and emptier than before.

The warrior hesitated, wanting to savor the moment he'd so long pursued. When his bow paused at the waist, Doc launched himself forward in a dive. Gunsi laughed at the feeble attempt. The white man was twenty feet away and could not possibly leap the distance. Just before he struck the ground, Doc ducked his head and landed on curled shoulders. His hands crossed over his stomach, reaching for his belt.

Continuing with the forward motion of the roll, he sprang to his feet, both hands raised shoulder high. Gunsi was startled into action by the glint of light in the white man's hands as they shot forward and down. Without raising the bow, Gunsi completed the draw and loosed the arrow from waist high. He howled with frustration as the arrow passed between the legs of the white man.

Still sure of the kill, he lifted his hand and pulled another arrow, but as he tried to draw the bow, something blocked the move. Again he roared; the white man had stopped rolling and now sat a mere few feet away looking at him with curiosity. Where was his fear! Is this how the white man would meet his death?

Gunsi looked down to see what hindered his bow. He stared in confusion at the two steel tomahawks buried in his ribs.

Toh-Yah watched Gunsi in wonder. His eyes sought Shadow's and found the white man staring back at him with a questioning look. Toh-Yah stretched out his arms, his hands palms-up in a gesture of peace. It was he, and not Gunsi, who was destined to lead the Llanero and so he could not fight the Shadow Warrior—to do so was to die.

In the still and dark hour that preceded the first gray hint of dawn, Doc rode quietly into the silent camp of slumbering men and oxen. Ferguson, as always at this hour, reclined by the fire holding a tin cup of coffee, his splinted leg thrust out before him. Doc slid from the back of the mustang and sagged against the animal's side. His mind and body, which for so many days had practiced the highest level of awareness, now responded to his thoughts with feeble numbness. It took several moments of repeated effort before he freed the horse of the crude bridle. No less a victim of repeated ordeals over the past week than Doc, the mustang merely lowered his head and slept.

Doc placed a grateful hand on the small horse's shoulder, and then shuffled to the fire to take the coffee Ferguson offered. The wagon master eyed the weary mustang while Doc drained the cup with the eagerness of a man bereft found suddenly in the midst of plenty. Doc poured a brimming refill and dropped to the ground to relax and savor the coffee. Taking a long sip, he looked across the top of the cup at Ferguson.

"When you rode that animal away from camp, he had a saddle on his back," the wagon master said, then grinned. "I reckon I'll have to dock your pay for it."

"I can live with that," Doc replied, too tired to return the grin.

Ferguson, pleased to have his friend back, wasn't above poking fun at the bedraggled scout.

"Game must be mighty scarce 'round here," he said. "First time I know'd you to come back from a hunt empty-handed."

Doc swallowed the last of the coffee and lay back, resting his head on the deer-hide sack and pile of weapons that sustained him through the past week. Closing his eyes he said softly, "I plan on takin' care of that tomorrow."

"Tomorrow?"

Doc loosed a long satisfied sigh and clasped his hands over his chest. "Yeah," he mumbled as the rhythmic rise and fall of his hands slowed perceptibly. "Figured I'd go out huntin'."

An exasperated snort of disbelief exploded from the wagon master and, mouth agape, he shook his head. Caught somewhere between rankle and amazement, he stared hard at the sleeping man. Slowly, the look softened and in spite of the recent difficulties, his mouth curved into a wide smile.